The Sighting

Moira Robinson

Published in 2011 by New Generation Publishing

Copyright © Moira Robinson 2011

First Edition

www.newgenerationpublishing.info

With her family grown up Moira Robinson gave up an established nursing career to go to Oxford Brookes University, where she gained a BA(Hons) and MA, and later a MLitt from Birmingham University. Her first book *Popular Fiction and Publishing 1960s-1990s* was published in 2008.

In 2010 she returned to Oxford Brookes to study for a MA in Creative Writing, and *The Sighting*, her first novel, is the result.

She lives in Kidlington, Oxfordshire, with her husband Brian, to whom this book is dedicated.

Chapter 1

'When I said 'stop' he did. Just like that. I just shouted 'stop' and immediately he...'

'Yes, yes we know all that. You've already told me,' said the policewoman. 'It's what happened before that that I want you to go over again'

'I've told you what happened before, and I've told you what happened afterwards, so why do you want me to spell it all out again?'

'I just want to be sure we have got the right sequence of events.'

'For goodness sake! You were taping the interview. Listen to that. I'm not repeating the story again.'

Claire was fed up. She felt as if she had been in the police station for hours, although in reality it wasn't that long. It just felt like it. It had been a trying day and she just wanted to go home. But the policewoman was persistent. Why, she didn't know. She hadn't been that keen to hear her story to begin with, but now it seemed she couldn't get enough of it.

The interview room was stuffy. It didn't look as if the window opened and the only movement of air was when someone swung the door open, and that had only happened twice. She presumed that the big mirrored window on the other side of the room had people behind it listening in, like she saw on television crime stories, otherwise why did another policeman come in and whisper something to the policewoman in front of her. She didn't catch what he said, but it was after that that she had had to go over her story again.

The second time the same policeman came in, he again whispered to the policewoman, and then she had to leave the room for a conversation with him outside. Claire didn't hear what they were saying but from the rising tones she guessed they were arguing, so it could

3

have been about another matter. There wasn't anything to argue about as far as she was concerned.

***

However it had all started with Claire and Tom Harrison having an argument in their car. This was an infrequent occurrence as Tom usually agreed with what Claire said. That was the way it was with them. She was saying that she did not think it was necessary for Tom to leave work in the middle of the day to visit his aunt in hospital. He disagreed. Although Tom usually let Claire make the decisions, today he decided, he would make a stand. It had been suggested that his beloved aunt may have had a heart attack. Claire had her own opinion on that too, not only because she was a nurse, but because she thought she was right as usual. Her interpretation of what the paramedics had said was that Aunt Lou appeared to have had a bad attack of indigestion. But, and it was a big but, to be on the safe side and in view of her age, they were going to take her to A&E to do another ECG in case it was a minor heart attack.

Thus, having made their respective points, their journey continued in companionable silence with Claire idly watching the world go by, as they trundled along behind slow moving traffic.

'Stop, Tom, stop! Tom stop', Claire suddenly shouted,' back up a bit...'

'For God's sake Claire', he shouted back as he performed a perfect emergency stop. 'What did you do that for? Can't you see there's traffic behind me?'

'I've just seen her. The girl who's missing. I saw her in that house. At that top bay window.'

'What girl?'

'You know - the one in the paper' said Claire, as she twisted around and scrabbled among the pile of things on the back seat, searching for the Guardian.

'Don't be daft. Of course you didn't.'

'I did, I did. That house we've just passed.'

The hooting behind them brought Tom's attention back to the road, and he released the brake and carried on.

'Tom, pull in somewhere. I did see her. I must check.'

'I can't here. Anyway I'm not going to. You're imagining things,' he grumbled, as he acknowledged the irate driver behind him with a wave of his hand, and carried on down the road the short distance to the local hospital.

After several minutes driving round and round the inadequate car park Tom eventually found a space, and they walked over to A&E as if they were strangers to each other. She was inwardly fuming but said nothing. Now she had to sort out Aunt Lou; afterwards she would think about the missing child.

Claire dealt with the officialdom of the hospital while Tom went to sit with Aunt Lou, who was very surprised to see him.

'Hello, Tom dear. What are you doing here? I told them it wasn't necessary for them to call you.'

'Of course it was necessary Aunt Lou', Tom replied, as he bent down and kissed her. 'You know I worry about you'.

'There's no need dear. I'm perfectly well. It was just a touch of indigestion, but that old biddy from next door just happened to be visiting when it came on and she called the ambulance without asking.'

'Well if the paramedics brought you in they must have thought it was necessary, whatever you say. And they don't wire you up to machines unless they need to', he said with finality. He looked up at the heart monitor by her trolley but couldn't make head nor tail of the squiggles it was making.

Minutes later Claire arrived with a doctor in tow. Her status as a sister obviously had some advantages. 'Hi, Aunt Lou. How are you feeling?'

'Very well, dear. It was a mistake bringing me in. I was just telling Tom. It was all because my neighbour ...'

'Better to be safe than sorry, Aunt Lou', Claire interrupted. ' I've brought Dr Lane with me. He wants to have another look at you before he decides what to do.'

Tom got up from his seat so that Dr Lane could get closer to Aunt Lou, and joined Claire outside the cubicle. 'What did he say?' he whispered.

'She's fine', she replied in a similar tone. 'But they want to keep her in and do a scan tomorrow to see why the so-called indigestion caused her so much pain. The heart monitor is showing nothing but they'll keep it on for a bit longer.'

'See you later, Miss Harrison, when you are settled upstairs', said Dr Lane as he emerged from the cubicle. Turning to Tom and Claire, he said: 'She's basically very fit for a lady of her age, but I'm not happy about the severity of the pain she said she had, so we'll keep an eye on her for a day or two. There's a bed waiting for her in Ward 7, so I'll see her there later today.' With that he rushed off before Claire could delay him again.

Within a couple of hours Aunt Lou was installed in a four bedded ward, a cup of tea in her hand. With the curious attention of the other three patients on her she recited her reasons for being there, adding embellishments where she saw fit. Claire felt that their presence was not appreciated, so with a wave to all four

ladies they left, telling the ward sister they'd be back tomorrow. Claire noted the ward sister's frown. Claire knew she was unpopular among the staff as she had a reputation; she was renowned for her insistence in having things done her way; her way, and only her way. True, the out-patients department was marvellously managed when she was on duty, which was great for the patients, but the medical staff didn't like it. They didn't appreciate
being 'managed', and the Ward 7 sister obviously didn't fancy it either. Claire hoped that Aunt Lou wouldn't be penalised because of her.

Tom and Claire were subdued as they walked back to the car. Both were wrapped up in their own trains of thought. They both loved Aunt Lou, but for Tom it was more emotional. Claire guessed that Tom was thinking of his Dad because the last time they had seen his Dad alive he too had been sitting up in a hospital bed. His Dad had been talking to his neighbour in the next bed, just like Aunt Lou, when they had left, and the next time they saw him he was dead. He had had a cardiac arrest during surgery – minor surgery too, for a lump on his foot, so Claire could see that Tom was looking quite tearful as they left the car park and turned into Callender Road again. Thus he appeared startled when Claire returned to the subject of the missing child.

'Look', she said, turning the front page of the Guardian towards him, 'that's her. That's Charlotte Alsopp.' He glanced sideways and briefly saw the picture of a pretty little girl. 'That's the child I saw.'

'I really think you were imagining it Claire, so just drop it', and as he spoke they passed the house called Atherstone again. They both glanced towards it but there was no sign of activity, no cars and definitely no people.

'I don't care what you say Tom, I did see her. I know I did.'

'How could you possible see anyone at that window? The trees are in the way.'

'They might be in this direction, but there was a gap between them going the other way.'

'Anyway, with a drive that long I don't think you could see anyone at a window from this road.'

'It's not that long and we were going very slowly, remember? The sun was out then and shining through the gap; and the window is huge. No curtains or anything. And the girl stood out because she was in a bright red top and waving.'

'So what are you going to do about it then? Join all the other loonies who think they've seen her, and tell the police.'

'What makes you think they are all loonies? I'm not a loony, and I'm sure I saw her. Just because you didn't see her too doesn't mean I didn't see her. And yes, I do think I should tell the police.'

'Well forget it for now because I want to go home, have something to eat, watch some mindless stuff on the telly and then go to bed, and forget about today.'

'I can't. I can't forget about it, and I'm not going to either.' And with that angry comment Claire mentally stamped her foot. It was particularly annoying because she couldn't prove her point. However she realised that going home now might be the best thing to do. She'd sleep on it.

It wasn't possible for either of them to forget about it as the abduction headed the news on all the television channels. Police said that they were inundated with reported sightings from as far apart as Bridport in the south to Newcastle in the north, and there was even one from Malaga, in Spain. Despite that the police were still asking the public to report anything they thought of as suspicious. They had no leads, they said, and so far no ransom demand had come to light. But the most poignant was the televised appeal made by Charlotte's father for information. He was shown sitting at a table loaded with microphones, flanked by a grim faced policeman and Charlotte's distraught mother. He spoke directly to the camera, but Claire's eyes were drawn to the mother, who sat hunched, with downcast eyes, indicating her misery so eloquently.

***

Claire had just finished clearing their supper dishes when Francesca, Tom's daughter, called in to find out how Great Aunt Lou was. She was also very fond of 'Gallou' because she had featured in her early life, taking over when her mother had died in an accident when she was eighteen months old. Now aged twenty-four, she lived in a flat on the other side of town, but she stayed in constant touch with Gallou, her champion. Today, however, she had finished work too late to visit the hospital.

It wasn't long before the subject of the missing child came up. Claire had left the paper on the end of the dining room table. 'Everyone at work is talking about her', said Fran. 'Must be awful for the poor mother.'

'Your mother thinks she saw her', said Tom. The second glass of wine had softened his antipathy to the subject of Claire's imagined sighting.

'I'm not surprised. She always wants to be in on things. She's just a nosy cow', said Fran with a dismissive swing of her hair.

'Francesca, that is no way to speak about your mother. Apologise.'

'She is *not* my mother, Dad. How many fucking times do I have to tell you?'

9

'She has been your mother for the last twenty years and I won't have you talking about her like that. How many times do I have to tell you? If you can't be civil and apologise go home and stay there until
you can', said Tom angrily. He got to his feet and held the door open for Fran to go. This scenario had been played out so often before.

Claire, as always, could hear what was going on. She could picture the scene. Tom fuming while holding the door, hating the poisoned atmosphere Fran so often created, and hating the feelings her destructive behaviour engendered in him.

The banging of the front door brought Claire back into the dining room. 'Oh, has she gone then?' she said brightly.

'Places to go. People to see', Tom quipped back, although they both knew she had heard every word while clearing up in the kitchen. Her eyes were suspiciously moist so he said nothing. She was always upset when Francesca behaved like that, and from long experience they knew that it just made matters worse if they attempted to discuss it. He moved towards, took the tea towel out of her hands, and put his arms round her and gave her a comforting hug. 'Forget that', he said as he flung the tea towel behind him in the direction of a chair. 'Let's go to bed.'

Later, just as Tom was drifting off into a satisfied sleep, she brought the subject up once more. 'Tom, I did see her. I'm sure I did', she murmured softly into his shoulder.

He shuffled round to face her. 'How can you be so sure you saw her? We were passed that house within seconds.'

'I just am' said Claire miserably. 'I wish I hadn't seen her, but I did.' Her eyes welled up with tears, and she turned away from him searching for a tissue.

'Well if you really feel that strongly about it, then perhaps you should go to the police. Then perhaps we can forget all about it.' He kissed her lightly before turning on his side again and settled himself for sleep. But it was a long time before Claire slept.

***

Twenty-four hours earlier.

Twin spots of colour decorated Darren Smith's normally pale cheekbones as he wrestled with the padlock key. His hands were shaking. He could hardly contain the exhilaration that was fizzing in his brain. They'd done it, they'd fucking done it!

When the padlock finally secured the old garage door, which was hiding the small red car, Darren crossed the yard to the back entry of a small nondescript cottage tucked behind some unused industrial buildings. Entering through the untidy kitchen he carefully turned the key in the recently oiled lock and pushed the top and bottom bolts home. Satisfied, he quietly approached the sitting room, not wanting to upset the child again. But she wasn't there. He twisted his skinny frame in one direction after another while exclaiming: 'Where is she Chell? What have you done with her?'

'Don't worry, Dazzer. Calm down. She was exhausted with all the crying, so I put her to bed.'

'Is the door locked?'

'Course it is. Do you think I'm daft or something.'

Darren flopped into the armchair, but was swiftly up again, pacing the small room.

'We've done it Chell. We've bleeding well gone and done it! At last, and I hope that fucking man is suffering in hell.' He stopped suddenly. 'Has she had anything to eat? We must feed her. Got to take care of her, haven't we?'

'She was too tired to eat, Daz, but I'll check in a bit and see how she is.'

'Did she like the room? What about the toys? Did she like them?' Darren was hopping from one foot to another as his questions came popping out of his mouth, in tune with the fizzing in his head. He was so pleased with himself. It had gone like clockwork. No one noticed them. Not one fucking person challenged them. It had been so easy.

He momentarily stopped his jigging about and dropped back into the chair, but his legs continued to jerk, and he couldn't decide what to do with his hands. Plucking at the pulled threads in the worn fabric covering the arms he anxiously looked at Michelle again. 'She'll be OK Chell, won't she?'

'Of course she will. It'll only be a few days then she can go home again. We'll just make sure he suffers as much as we did, then we'll let her go.'

'Not too soon though. He's got to fucking suffer big time.'

Darren aimed the remote at the large TV screen that was almost as wide as the wall, and flicked through the stations looking for local news.

'No point checking yet, Daz. They'll have hardly noticed she's missing. Wait for the later news. It might be on then.'

Michelle got up hurriedly and stood by the door with the staircase behind it listening. 'Shoosh, Daz. Turn it down. I think I heard her.' She opened the door and cocked her head to one side. 'No. All quiet.' She left the door slightly ajar and went towards the kitchen. 'Keep that down Daz, so that you can hear her while I get us something to eat.'

Darren had found a football match so he was happy to turn the sound off, while he listened to Chell opening packets and arranging frozen fish and chips on trays, followed by the irritating squeaky noise the oven door made as she opened and shut it. He waited for her to reappear before telling her that she ought to check on the girl again.

'She's called Charlotte, Daz. A real poncey name I know, but that's what she's called. So we must call her that too.'

'OK, OK. I will. But go and see if she's hungry yet.'

Michelle went up the cramped spiral staircase and listened outside the door of the smaller of the two bedrooms. Muffled hiccuppy sobs could be heard so Michelle unlocked the door and went in.

'I want my Mummy', Charlotte whispered. 'I want to go home. I want Mummy.'

'Soon, lovey, soon. You'll be home soon. But today you are staying with us.'

'I want to go home. Mummy will be worried. I want to see her.' She gulped, and clutched a dolly tightly to her chest. Her red puffy eyes looked beseechingly at Michelle. 'I can't stay her. I haven't got any things. So I must go home.' Large tears dropped down onto the brassy yellow hair of the doll and sat there. Charlotte pulled a piece of the sheet up and carefully dabbed at the dolly's head before wiping her own eyes. 'Please Mrs Smith, I want to go home.'

'You'll go tomorrow or the next day, but for now you are staying with us. And it's teatime. Are you hungry? Do you like fish and chips? And lots of ketchup? Dazzer likes ketchup. Lots and lots of it.

But I don't . I like my chips plain. What about you Charlotte? What do you like?' As she prattled on she approached Charlotte and took her hand, and gently pulled her up from where she had been sitting on the bed, and led her to the door.

'Do you want the loo before we go downstairs, lovey. It's just here. I'll wait outside. Wash your face too then you'll feel better. Shall I hold the dolly for you?'

Charlotte's arm tightened round the doll as she went into the bathroom and closed the door firmly. Michelle stood and listened intently. She heard Charlotte's hand slide over the latch as if looking for a key, but there wasn't one. Then it sounded as if she was trying to open the small opaque window, but that too had been dealt with. Michelle relaxed a bit as the tinkle of water was heard.

'There isn't a clean towel for me' Charlotte called, 'and I haven't got my toothbrush.'

'Use the towel on the rail. And the red toothbrush on the window sill is for you. It's a new one, I promise. I bought it specially for you. And the brush and comb. I hope you like them.'

Minutes later the door opened and Michelle was surprised and impressed at how composed the little girl now looked. She'd brushed her hair and the scrunchy holding her pony tail had been rearranged, and she'd made an attempt to wash the tears away. The dolly was still in place though, clutched under Charlotte's left arm. She ignored Michelle's outstretched hand and made her way downstairs, with Michelle following close behind.

***

The fish and chips hadn't been a great success. Charlotte had maintained her composure by not opening her mouth any more than she had too. She had sat on the sofa watching Darren and Michelle eat their tea, occasionally picking at a chip from the plate on her lap and sipping the milk from the fairy patterned tumbler left out for her.

Darren had tried to talk to her but soon decided that the football match was of more interest, and it was a relief when Michelle had taken her back upstairs. He got himself a lager and turned the sound up to hear the post match interviews and excuses, more relaxed now that he had been fed and the girl wasn't making as much fuss as she had done earlier.

In the meantime, while Charlotte was alone with Michelle, she had found her voice and had wanted to know why she wasn't allowed to go home; why had she been taken from her Mummy; where had the toys come from; whose room was she in, etc. and Michelle had been hard pushed to find answers for all her questions. She didn't want to tell her the real reason, but she sensed that Charlotte wasn't really listening to her replies; Charlotte was talking to keep Michelle in the room. Michelle played her part. She sat on the bed and she asked Charlotte questions about school and what she liked best, who her friends were, and where she was going on holiday. She heard about the swimming badge on her school track suit, how Mummy had had to get permission to sew it on because it wasn't a badge she got at school. Mummy couldn't swim so she was extra specially pleased that Charlotte could. But Mummy was going to learn when they went on holiday; she was going to help teach her.

The tears began to fall again as Charlotte talked about her Mummy. The dolly, who had been put down while she had got undressed ready for bed, was retrieved and again got its head wet. Michelle's eyes were suspiciously moist too as she hugged the small girl and promised her that she would go home soon. She'd left a pale pink star shaped night light on and reassured the weeping child that it wouldn't be long before she saw her Mummy again.

***

The following morning Charlotte appeared brighter and chattier, and had even eaten some cereal for breakfast. She had been persuaded to wear the rather un-Charlotte like clothes that Michelle had bought in readiness after Michelle had assured her that her own clothes should be washed and ironed ready to go home in. In fact Charlotte rather liked the patterned knickers Michelle had bought. They were more like the ones her friends wore. She had to wear plain white M&S ones as Mummy though them more suitable. But she hadn't allowed Michelle to take her track suit top and wash it because she didn't know if the badge would go funny in the wash, like her Brownie ones had when Mummy had used the wrong setting on the machine. They had turned all wrinkly. She wanted this badge to stay new looking for Mummy, and as they left the house Charlotte had put the track suit top on as she hadn't got a coat.

While Darren went off to collect the van Michelle explained to Charlotte what they were going to do that day. She managed to make it sound quite exciting although in reality clearing a house after all the good stuff had gone was just like clearing a waste tip. Sometimes they came across a small gem, missed by the specialists, but it was rare. But it did happen. Like last month. Last month they had found a tatty leather box hidden under old towels inside a scruffy cardboard carton that had been completely overlooked by the big boys. It was the 'under-the-counter' sale of those found jewels that allowed them to put into action their plan to steal Charlotte. The plan they had been dreaming about for the last twelve months, ever since they had heard about Shannon.

They arrived at the house again after the morning rush hour; after all the neighbours had gone off to their City jobs, or whatever else they went off to first thing in the mornings. They had taken the final clearance job of emptying Atherstone after checking out its surroundings, making sure they would not be easily noticed. The job had come to them from a mate of a mate in a dimly lit overcrowded noisy pub – not the sort of place that offered the police cooperation when questions were being asked as all the customers were instantly forgettable. The copied key had been handed over, and the original was going to be handed back to the estate agent the following evening, so they had to be out by the end of the day, or the following at the latest.

Michelle had been against them taking Charlotte with them on a job. She thought it unsafe. But then the Water Board had called round to say that they had to mend a leak that had sprung up outside one of the disused factory's main doors which meant that their water was going to be cut off for eight hours. So they decided that it was better to take

Charlotte with them. They didn't want people wandering around the yard with the possibility of seeing her.

In fact they thought the day had gone well. They had locked the doors and checked that all the window locks were secure before they felt it was safe to let Charlotte wander around out of their sight occasionally. Unfortunately for them they were excitedly clearing a large untouched cupboard on the landing, hoping to make another 'find', while Charlotte was waving to passing motorists from the big front bedroom.

That evening's supper of frozen pizza was more of a success than the fish and chips had been and, while eating, they all watched a Disney fairy tale video, and thus Charlotte was spared the anguished news pictures of her parents. While Michelle prepared her for bed again, Darren relished seeing a very distressed Giles Alsopp as he appealed for information about his missing daughter.

Chapter 2

Breakfast was a rushed affair the next morning so there wasn't time to discuss what was uppermost on Claire's mind. Tom's alarm had failed to go off, which was not a good start to any day but particularly today as a group of Chinese business men were coming to visit Tom's factory. As the boss, he had planned to be in early to make sure everything was just so. It needed to be just so because his company desperately needed outside investment, and the Chinese were reputed to have deep pockets. The factory was doing well, like most specialist electronic companies, but it had to do a whole lot better if it was to survive the downturn. So it was with a bit of toast in his left hand and car keys in the other, a kiss blown in Claire's direction that he shot out of the door to the car.

He phoned Claire while she was drinking her second cup of coffee to tell her that the Chinese delegation had been held up at Heathrow, something to do with visas, so all was well. It was a hurried call so there was no chance to say anything about what was worrying her. She looked at the paper spread out on the table in front of her. There was Charlotte's picture again, plus numerous incidences of sightings. Some were frankly ridiculous, she thought, no wonder they were referred to as loonies. How could she have possibly reached Spain in that short space of time? She might have been persuaded that some of the other sightings were feasible if she was prepared to dismiss her own sighting of the child, but she wasn't.

There were pictures of Charlotte's parents, Giles and Anne, as well as lots of different shots of Charlotte, plus their home and her school, and a long piece about child abductions in general. Not a piece I'd like to read if a child of mind had been abducted, thought Claire, with all that information about the murder rate in such cases. She inwardly shivered at the thought of Charlotte being part of those statistics. But she was alive yesterday, she reminded herself. And with that thought she stretched across the table to the radio and swivelled the dial for the local station to see if there was any more news. No, just the same, more mediums wanting to get involved, more sightings, and no ransom demand.

Claire's shift that day started at one with the diabetic clinic. So the decision she had to make was whether to go to the police before work or afterwards. What to do? If I check out the house for myself first, she reasoned, I might alert the kidnappers – but there again there might be nothing to see and I'll be wasting everybody's time if I say anything. *And* if the clinic runs late, it will be getting dark and I don't fancy going up that drive without any lights. She was mulling it over in her mind as she cleared up the breakfast things, and prepared the vegetables for dinner just in case Tom got back in time.

She had done all her household chores by mid-morning so she felt the decision was made for her about going to look at the house. But, uncharacteristically, she wasn't sure that it was a good idea. She knew she had seen Charlotte, and she knew that she ought to tell the police, but – and there were so many buts – she didn't want to look like just another so-called loony. After so many years of Francesca telling her that she was an interfering old so-and-so, she didn't want her proved right. That would be just too much to endure. But, sighed Claire, Charlotte had become real to her; not just some nameless child that has gone missing because she'd had a fight with her parents. Her Charlotte was real; a little blonde child that she had seen in the window waving; waving at her, she fantasized, waiting for someone to rescue her.

Claire mentally shook herself free of her fairy story thoughts and got ready to go to work early. She would look at the house and if it looked lifeless she'd say nothing.

She decided to park her car in the hospital staff car park and walk back. She'd only glanced briefly at Atherstone as she passed it but she thought she had seen a van in the drive, so that meant she had to go and investigate. She slipped a coat on to cover her uniform; the fewer clues to her identity the better. Why she thought this, she didn't know; she just felt that she had to be on her guard. It was a disturbing thought, and one she didn't want to examine. It might put her off. Having made the decision to do her own sleuthing she didn't want her conscience niggling away telling her to back out. Second thoughts were normally a stranger to her, but at this moment they added to the disquiet she was beginning to feel. Telling herself to stop being a ninny she locked the car and started to walk towards the exit, then stopped and turned and went back to the car to check the locks again.

Atherstone was about two hundred metres back up the road. At Claire's usual brisk pace she should have been there in minutes, but this time it took considerably longer. Her mind was in a mess. Tom had agreed that she should go to the police but he didn't know that she was planning to visit the house. That, she knew, he would disapprove of. Her staunch belief that she was always right was beginning to falter. Perhaps that was why she was dawdling. Tom would probably think she was taking an unnecessary risk. Perhaps she was, but by now she had reached Atherstone's drive.

Decision time.

She marched up the drive keeping her eyes on the first floor bay window, clearly visible from the road, hoping to get another chance to see Charlotte. Her second thoughts had gone, her mind focused, and as she stared at the window the surrounding scenery faded into the background like it does when eyes are fixed on one point. The drive ran alongside a high hedge on the left and a short brick wall on the right, behind which were shrubs and bushes of some sort. Some ten metres or so in length it ended in front of a garage, with its doors wide open. Partially blocking these doors was an old dilapidated white van. To the right was unkempt lawn with a flagged path leading to the front door, which was wide open.

A youngish looking woman was putting large cardboard boxes into the scruffy van and as Claire approached the woman yelled to someone inside 'there's a woman on the drive' before she went inside herself and called to someone.

Claire's focus dropped from the window, where she had seen nothing this time. She blinked her eyes a few times and made her way to the door. As she reached it the young woman reappeared and stood in the doorway with her arms out either side, with her hands holding the door jamb, as if to bar her way.

'What the hell do you want? This place isn't ready yet.'

'I, err…'

'We haven't finished clearing it. You'll have to wait.'

'I only want…'

'The agent said no one was going to look till we'd finished.'

'No, it's not about …'

'The agent said no viewers. Not till we're finished.'

'It's about the child', Claire said with a rush, before she could be cut off again. 'The little girl I saw in the top room when I passed yesterday.'

The young woman stiffened and her face reddened. 'There's no child here. Just me and Darren.' As she said that Claire saw a very het up young man come hurriedly down the stairs into the hallway. He immediately fired questions at her; about who she was and why she was there, and Claire repeated her question about the child.

'There ain't no child here. Just her and me.'

By now Claire was feeling very uncomfortable. Something wasn't right. Why were they so angry? Why didn't they ask who the child was she was asking about? Why didn't they say anything about why they were there? She was beginning to feel frightened. This young couple, with their red faces, looked as if they could make mincemeat of her if they had wanted to. She decided that she ought to leave but just as she was thinking about what to say Darren unexpectedly said in a sneering tone, 'Do you want to look then?' He turned as if to go up the stairs again, suggesting that she should follow him. She declined, and with muttered apologies about disturbing them, she turned and made her way off the property. As she did so she noticed a For Sale sign tangled in the bushes. She was so anxious to get away that that was about the only thing she really did notice. Everything else was a bit of a blur but the uneasy feelings remained with her as she supervised the clinic, visited Aunt Lou, and then made her way to the police station on the way home.

***

'What I don't understand' said the policewoman, 'is why you waited so long before telling us.'

'Well, my husband kept telling me that I had imagined it. Then during the night, thinking about it, it was all so real, I decided that I had to do my duty and tell you. But', said Claire, getting to her feet, 'I'm beginning to wish I hadn't now, because you'll class me as yet another time waster. And another thing,' she said as she reached the door, 'it's hardly the right way to do things for the officer at the front desk to shout facetiously into the inner office 'here's another one. Who wants to take her story?' *Her story* – as if it were a fairy story I'd come to tell. He didn't even have the manners to call it a statement. You can't expect to get cooperation from the public if that is the way you are going to treat them.' In full steam now Claire picked up her handbag, her copy of her statement, and pulled the door open.

Claire noted that the WPC had the grace to blush. She'd hit home she was pleased to see.

'I'll just check with the sergeant that your statement is all in order. If you'd just wait a few minutes longer, then you're free to go' and the WPC made a hurried exit.

Claire heard the sergeant say that the house had been checked and that there was no sign of activity, so to let Mrs Harrison go. 'Of course there's no activity now', muttered Claire to the empty room. 'The couple looked as if they were packing up when I was there!' As she said that her mind was given a nasty jolt. If she had gone to the police immediately they might have seen the couple she saw. They might have found the child.

As Claire drove home she pondered over what had gone on at the police station and mentally castigated herself for being so indecisive. It was unlike her. She was disappointed with herself and her statement. She realized that she had not really noticed many details;

details that might have made all the different. She couldn't even remember much about the van. It was scruffy, originally white, she had told them, but she hadn't noted the number plate, or any writing on it, or anything distinctive about it at all. Saying it was 'scruffy' could be the description of half the white vans in the country. It was unlike her to be so lax. Even her description of the couple was valueless. It could be fitted to almost everyone she saw out and about most days. However, on one aspect she was absolutely confident; she was very sure of her description of the child. If she shut her eyes the image appeared like a photograph – and it was with her eyes shut she had described the image to the WPC, so she didn't notice the WPC's surprise when she mentioned the badge on the child's red track suit. This was the point when Claire's sighting became *the* sighting. This was the one detail the police had not released to the press.

***

Earlier that day

Although Darren and Michelle had cleared a considerable amount the previous day there was still much to do. In fact they were surprised at how much had been left behind by the official house clearers. Perhaps they had only been interested in the furniture and things of obvious value. But they were quite happy about the extra work as they knew there was a market for much of the stuff that had been left behind and they were already planning what and where they would make the sales.

Charlotte hadn't been quite so cooperative that morning. She had insisted on putting on all her own clothes when she got up, because, she said, 'Mrs Smith, you said I was going home today'. Rather than risk further upsetting her, and putting them behind schedule, they let her believe that. However Michelle was worried about what would happen later when she realised that she wasn't going home that day. She and Darren didn't think Giles Alsopp had suffered enough yet. Michelle just shut her mind to Anne Alsopp's pain, even though she found it very difficult.

All was going to plan until the arrival of their visitor.

Panic.

Michelle was petrified, and shouted to Darren that there was a woman on the drive. Luckily Charlotte was upstairs helping seal some boxes with parcel tape. Darren had let her roll the tape along the box openings while he held them together. When they had tried it the other way round Charlotte hadn't been strong enough to bring the edges together. She was enjoying herself, doing an important job, and Darren was being nice to her and not shouting at her like he had done yesterday when she had cried. She hadn't cried today because today she was going home to Mummy.

Charlotte had heard Michelle's shout to Darren before she started to talk to someone downstairs, so she dropped the roll of tape and moved towards the door as if to investigate the visitor.

In the meantime Michelle was barring the door to their visitor, hoping and praying that Darren had caught on to the danger she posed and had done something about Charlotte.

Thus she was surprised and a bit wary when Darren, looking unusually red in the face, bounded down the stairs and suggested that the woman search the house if she was so sure they had a child there. The woman appeared equally flabbergasted by Darren's suggestion and with muttered apologies for disturbing them almost ran down the driveway to the road, much to Michelle's relief.

'God, Dazzer, what were you thinking about? That nosey cow might have gone upstairs. What have you done with her? What ...'

'Stop fussing, Chell. I hid her. She wouldn't have fucking found her. I made sure of that as soon as you started shouting. Gave me an awful bleeding fright though, you shouting like that. Had to get her hid quick. She'll be OK for a bit so let's clear the rest of these fucking boxes and get out of here.'

So the two of them spent the next twenty minutes or so hauling boxes and black bin bags across the beautiful parquet floor of the hall and loading them into the van.

'Let's hide Charlotte in one of the boxes. Don't want anyone else thinking they've seen her, eh Dazzer?', and she laughed as she pushed the last poly bag alongside a bulging box.

'OK. Is everything else done? Kitchen clear?'

Darren tipped out the debris from the bottom of the remaining box into the back of the van, before taking the stairs two at a time, in a rush to get the job done and them out of there.

A stream of obscenities came down the stairs, each one a tone higher as panic set in, which brought Michelle running up the stairs to find out what was going on. She stopped dead in the doorway when she saw Darren pumping the chest of the very dead looking child.

'Dazzer, what you done? What's happened? Why's she like that? What have you done, Dazzer? Speak to me Dazzer. What have you done?'

'I ain't done fucking anything. I hid her in that cupboard there. That one with the tank. I just hid her in there when you shouted about that fucking cow.'

'But she's dead Dazzer. She's dead. You've killed her Dazzer.'

'I didn't fucking kill her. I just shoved her in the cupboard.

'But she's dead, Dazzer, she's dead.'

'I fucking know that! I can fucking see with my own fucking eyes that she's dead! I'm not fucking stupid!

He collapsed back against the wall, pulled his knees up and wrapped his arms tightly around them, and in a small voice asked 'What are we going to do, Chell?'

She slid down the wall beside him and looked at the crumpled little body, and even in her dazed state was able to recognise the reason for her death. Tape had been haphazardly wrapped around her mouth, but not only her mouth, it covered her nose too. And around her wrists, And around her ankles. She hadn't had a hope.

Silently, each in their own way, they contemplated their predicament.

'What we going to do now Chell?'

' I dunno, Daz. But we can't leave her here.' She moved over to Charlotte, brushing away the tears that were threatening to blind her. With infinite tenderness she carefully eased away the tape from the small nose and mouth exposing the ragged lips, bitten roughly in her panic, trying to bite through the tape, before the lack of air had finally overcome her. Strand by strand she loosened the long blonde hair stuck to the tape and tucked it behind Charlotte's ears.

' 'Spose someone had done this to our Shannon, Dazzer. What would we have done? Eh, Dazzer, what would we have done?'

She continued to gently unwrap the tape holding the feet together, and then the hands before bringing them round to the front of the child. She then lifted her on to her lap, holding her close, softly zipping up the little red top so that the collar stood up round her face, hiding from view the evidence of her last frantic struggle.

'Why did you do it, Dazzer? Why, Dazzer?'

'You shouted, babe, and I panicked. I had to hide her quick.'

'I know Dazzer, but you didn't need to kill her.'

'I didn't mean to kill her, babe, I just wanted her to shut up.'

Michelle gathered the child in her arms and got awkwardly to her feet. 'Come on Dazzer, we can't stay here. She might come back.' And with that she made for the door.

'Bring the box Dazzer, we'll have to use it 'til we decide what to do. Bring a poly bag too.'

She waited for Darren to get up and join her and slowly they descended the stairs. She took the poly bag from Darren and clumsily got the body into it before putting it in the last of the boxes. She looked around for some of the sticky tape. Darren had it in his pocket, and she sealed the box.

'Put that in the van, Dazzer, while I go and check the cupboard. Don't want anything left there. They know we've been here. She's seen us. She might go to the police.'

She could see nothing in the cupboard but to make sure she sat in it and squirmed around, hoping to confuse the scene should the police come calling.

Chapter 3

Claire got into the routine of starting her day with a phone call to the hospital to check on Aunt Lou, before scanning the paper for the latest news on Charlotte. Then she would turn to the local radio for a more immediate update. Tom noticed what she was doing but made no comment. As long as her new obsession with news gathering didn't interfere with what he wanted to watch on TV then he let her get on with it.

Little by little it became known at the hospital that Claire had told the police that she had seen the child. Claire had said nothing, except to Aunt Lou. But she knew from experience that once you told one person something in a four-bedded ward it soon became common knowledge. At Tom's workplace they knew too, but how they found out there Claire had not been able to work out, and the tittle-tattle was uncomplimentary as far as Claire was concerned. Her loyalty to Tom was unquestioned, and she was respected by his colleagues for the support she gave him and his work through lean times as well as the good ones, but she was unpopular with their wives. Claire didn't really like socializing, and she made this plain; only turning up at works functions when not doing so would reflect badly on Tom. She was basically a shy person, and having misjudged the mood of a gathering on one occasion and said things that could be misconstrued, she felt that she had let Tom down. He, needless to say, said she hadn't. But the wives thought she was stuck up and considered herself too grand to mix with them, which was unfortunate because she would have liked to have been asked to join in their activities occasionally. Thus, as time had gone on, Claire no longer visited the works. Tom had got used to offering lame excuses as to why she wasn't at any particular function but he was very quick to point out all she did behind the scene.

Francesca, on the other hand, continued to attend functions with her Dad, as she had done from a very young age. Then, as she grew up she could be found gossiping with the women, always ready with a snide remark about Claire. She had been a popular child, and still was as a young woman, but there was a lot of ongoing speculation as to why she had turned against Claire in her teenage years, but not enough for any of them to offer an overture of friendship to Claire.

The hospital gossip wasn't quite so malicious. It was mostly believed that if Claire said she had seen the child then she probably had, but anyone approaching her about the subject got short shrift. Not that many were likely to. Her reputation as a very efficient manager of the Out-Patients department, a job not to everyone's taste, kept her somewhat aloof from the rest of the staff. They had to admit though she did a great job. When she was on duty clinics ran on time, doctors filled in their paperwork correctly, patients dispatched to X-ray and blood tests in the right order, and staff knew exactly what was expected of them. But this competency came at a cost; Claire had no friends at work. Lots of acquaintances, but no friends.

***

The national paper Claire had spread out on the kitchen table had relegated Charlotte's story to an inside page. A bad sign, thought Claire. People are losing interest. She leafed through the others pages while finishing her coffee, and decided to get on with the housework before looking at the free local paper that she'd just heard drop through her letterbox. It was full of adverts for local businesses, and such like, but very little actual news so it tended to be used for wrapping rubbish, rather than read, but she always skimmed through it.

However, Claire had a shock when she picked it up from the doormat. Her preconceptions were wrong. This week the freebie had large headlines on the front page and there was a special pullout section devoted to Charlotte, and to missing children in general. Claire wondered who in the paper's editorial team had a special interest. It was so unlike them to publish a feature like this. She took it through to the kitchen. She scanned the headings to see if there was anything new and as her eyes skimmed down the page her heart missed a beat as she saw the word 'Harrison'. A fairly common name perhaps, but *not* when it had 'Claire' in front of it. The page blurred under her intense scrutiny. She blinked rapidly, almost as fast as her pulse, to make sure she had seen what she thought she had seen. There it was 'Claire Harrison'. Under a heading THE PEOPLE WTH SECOND SIGHT!!! There she was listed as one of the oddballs who said they had seen Charlotte, along with sections of what looked like their statements to the police.

Claire slumped into a chair. She shivered. She was angry; very angry. Apprehensive too, and possibly a bit frightened. This wasn't right. Her statement to the police should be private. It was never meant to be a public document. How had the paper got it? Who had leaked it? She looked at the article again. There was nothing there to suggest answers. No explanations; no nothing. Scouring the page she noted that some of the reported sightings were totally outlandish – the descriptions of Charlotte were nothing like her, despite all the pictures in the press and on TV. But the section of her statement that was printed, and this was the most worrying aspect, was the description of the two people at the house. There it was – in print, for everyone to see. The name of the house, the people, everything – and her name attached to it. They could trace her.

Claire got up and went to her so-called 'to do' file lying on the sideboard and flicked through it to find her copy of her statement. She took it back to the table to compare it with the printed sections. Yes, parts of hers had been definitely copied. She read the statement that had the name Lily Jenkins under it:

I was waiting outside the main gates of the Sacred Heart Primary School on the High Street at approximately 2.50pm on Monday the 10th June. I was with a group of five parents and three of us had small children in push chairs. The weather was dry and sunny and I could see the road clearly. At 3pm the children started coming out and I saw Charlotte Alsopp coming towards the gate with a group of friends. As she reached the gate a young man with a white peaked hat and sunglasses approached her. He was about five foot nine, very thin, and wearing a plain white T-shirt and baggy jeans. I didn't hear what he said to her but he pointed to a silver BMW car about 25 yards up the road that I recognized as her mother's car. There was a young man with Anne Alsopp in what looked like RAC uniform, and there was a RAC van parked behind the BMW so my view of the car was partially blocked, and they looked as if they were looking at the front nearside tyre of the car. As I was watching Anne waved at Charlotte and then she went round the other side of the car and the RAC van blocked my view so I don't know what happened then. When I turned back I saw Charlotte walk down the High Street about 10 yards with the young man who had been talking to her, and she got into a car with him. It was a small, very dirty, red car; a bit bigger than a Mini, and quite old looking. I didn't look at the number because I didn't realize that I would need to know it. I looked back to see where Anne was but I didn't see her again. My son came out then so I went home.

Claire remembered Lily being interviewed on the television and her statement looked very much like what she had said to the reporter, though not in such a formal tone. What was so worrying for Claire was that Lily's description of the young man could almost match hers. During the TV interview she hadn't noticed the similarity. Now it was much more obvious. And there it was again in the bit of Anne Alsopp's statement:

I parked my car outside Haddon's, the butcher's shop on the High Street at approximately 2.20pm on Monday the 10th of June. I went into the butcher's and bought some meat and as I came out a young man approached me and said that it looked as if my front nearside tyre was flat. He was wearing a white peaked hat and sunglasses, a plain white T-shirt and jeans that looked too big for him, and he spoke with a local accent. He asked if I needed help changing it. I thanked him and said no, and said that I'd call the RAC, which I did. While waiting I was watching the school gate because it was nearly time for Charlotte to come out. The RAC man came within a few minutes. He said he had been in the vicinity when I rang. By now it was almost three o'clock so I told the man that I had to go to the school and fetch my daughter. I was just about to go when I saw Charlotte so I waved to attract her attention and she waved back. So when the RAC man wanted me to look at the offside tyre, I went, thinking that Charlotte would walk down the road to join me. She knows about the RAC since I've called them out before. The RAC man said that it looked as if both of my front tyres had been slashed, and we discussed what to do. We talked for only a few minutes and then I started to walk to the school because I couldn't see Charlotte. I got to the main gate just as some of Charlotte's friends were being collected and I asked them where Charlotte was. They all said they didn't know, but Agnes, one of the mother's, said that she had seen Charlotte get into a car with a young man. She said that she hadn't been concerned because she had seen me wave at Charlotte and Charlotte wave back, and assumed that as I was with the RAC I had made arrangements for Charlotte to get home. It was then that I decided to call the police.

Claire shivered again. It looked as if they had all seen the same young man, but she was the one who had placed him at a particular house. She did a quick scan of all the columns of newsprint again and sure enough Atherstone was mentioned once more, and it looked as if the reporter had been to the house to do some investigation of his own. He gave a description of the house – with a lot more detail than I gave, thought Claire, and he went on to describe the tall dense hedges either side of Atherstone, suggesting that the neighbours wouldn't have been able to see, or possibly hear, anything. However, one neighbour had been ready to gossip and had told him that she knew house clearers were coming because she had quizzed the estate agent. But she didn't know when they were coming, and she proved the reporter right when she said that she saw and heard nothing. The agent, also visited, said the house clearers were nothing to do with him – it was the lawyers acting for the owners who organized them. The lawyers, in their turn, also denied all knowledge of them too – it was a friend of a friend of the owners who supposedly had booked them – and so it went on. The reporter ended by saying that the new owners of the house lived in Australia, and that they had inherited the house from an aged unknown relative. Then he had added – as if with a flourish, a gratuitous final damning phrase: 'they were being far from helpful about whom they had asked to clear the house prior to selling it – not surprising really as they had left the UK under a cloud.'

As Claire read that she knew that this particular reporter had absolutely no scruples about who he maligned or endangered. In a state she decided to do something she had promised herself she'd never do; she rang Tom. His secretary answered. He was busy. She'd get him to ring back.

Claire had just put the phone down when it rang. 'I'm sorry, darling. She shouldn't have done that. What's the matter? What's happened? Are you ill? Shall I come...?'

Claire interrupted his anxious questioning. 'I'm fine, Tom. I'm just in a bit of a panic.'

'Why? What's happened? Tell me.'

'It's the Advertiser. It's got my name in it and part of my police statement about Charlotte.'

'So? What's so awful about that?'

'Oh, Tom. Think. It's got my name and the name of the house where I saw her, *and* the description of the people I saw! They'll find out where I live!'

'Hmm.'

'What shall I do about it?'

'Well, there's not much you can do. It's out there now. But I'll get onto Josh and ask him how his reporter got the information. Whose name is on the article?'

'Who's Josh?

'The chap who owns the paper. What's the name?'

'Hang on a moment I'll look.' Claire dragged the paper closer to the phone, 'It's Gareth Jones. Does that name mean anything to you?'

There was a pause. 'Yes, it does.'

Claire waited. Seconds passed. 'Well, who is it?'

'I met him a while back. At the Red Lion. When Jim had his retirement do. He was with Francesca.'

This time it was Claire's turn to pause. She had to be very careful.

'Just a coincidence, Claire. I'm sure that's all it is,' but the tone of Tom's voice belied that statement. The fraught relationship Claire had with Francesca was something they had discussed ad nauseam. However, he was convinced, as he had told Claire so often; she wouldn't do anything to harm her. But Claire wasn't so sure.

'Shall I come home? Would you like me to come and have lunch with you? I haven't got anything important on this afternoon.'

'No, I'm fine. Now I've told you I can see it's not really anything to worry about. Anyway I've got that extra clinic to do this afternoon. Jane's off sick again, and I said I'd do it for her. I'll be fine. Really I will. I'll see you about six, as usual.'

Claire had trouble replacing the phone in its socket. Her hand was shaking. She was *not* fine, and she *was* worried.

***

Tom went to see Aunt Lou on his way home and found her so much better. On closer examination of the ECG it had been found that she had had a minor heart attack - which had been a major shock to Claire's diagnostic abilities - and no reason had been found for what was thought to be the indigestion pain, so she was being discharged once the doctor gave her the all clear. He had left work early to get his visit in and to get home before Claire that evening. He had made sure he was because he wanted to have time to look at the paper on his own. He didn't doubt what she said, but he wanted to read it without her being there. His interpretation may be different.

He looked at the double page spread that Claire had left open on the table, and 'yes' Claire's name did tend to jump out at him. But then any name they knew would do that. He looked at the other sections: a profile of the Alsopps'; what mediums had to say; what the police were saying; ransom notes or no ransom notes; similar cases and their outcomes, and so on. He went back to the sightings list and scanned the other names. He didn't recognize any of them. In fact the only name on the whole spread, apart from Claire's, that he did recognize, was Gareth's.

Tom had left a message for Josh at the paper, and another on his home phone, but neither had produced a result as yet. Francesca wasn't answering her phone either so he hadn't been able to ask her about Gareth. He had had the police on his list to be phoned as well because there was no doubt there had been a leak there, but he had decided to wait and discuss it with Claire before calling them.

Claire was surprised to see him when she got in from the hospital, and thankfully accepted the glass of wine he handed her. The fact that she didn't immediately rush to change out of her uniform was an indication of the turmoil her mind was in.

'Well' she said, as she sank into the chair, 'what do you think?'

'Quite honestly I don't know.' He paused, and took a sip of his drink, playing for time. 'Several names besides yours are mentioned, so perhaps no one will notice. And it is very unusual for the Advertiser to print stuff like this – maybe very few will read it. Anyway, what made you look at it?'

Claire sighed. 'Did you look at the front page?'

'No, why?'

'Just look at it, while I go and change.'

Tom folded over the open paper. In heavy type across the top of the front page it had three lines, SPECIAL EDITION/ CHARLOTTE/ INSIDER INFORMATION. He called up the stairs: 'I see what you mean. Wonder what her poor parents think of it?'

Claire too wondered what her poor parents thought. She vaguely knew Anne Alsopp because she was a volunteer at the League of Friends coffee shop in the hospital. That's where Claire knew her from, but others knew her from her work at the local hospice charity shop and her general availability to help a good cause. Her husband, on the other hand, had a very different reputation, so Claire had heard. He was not well-liked as he was the head of the county's social services, and as such had arbitrarily introduced unpopular changes in the way children's services were organized, and there was some, probably unfounded, gossip about how he had got to the head of the queue to adopt Charlotte. The press was always having a go at him about something. But that had all changed since Charlotte's abduction.

Claire had overheard gossip while collecting coffee the other day, about Anne, who had obviously not appeared since the abduction. They were saying that the police had told her that none of the sightings were relevant, and that they were looking at all the cases Giles Alsopp had dealt with to see if anyone had a grudge against him. Possible, she thought. So many children were taken into care these days there was bound to be some who weren't happy about it. But, so the gossip went, the police thought that there would soon be a ransom note. Claire was surprised by that. She thought ransom notes were sent almost immediately after the abduction, not several days later like an afterthought. She folded her uniform and put her sensible work shoes together under the chair, before slipping on a pair of comfy jeans and a rich red sweatshirt. She smiled to herself at the thought of what her staff would say if they could see her now, but the smile soon faded when she thought of the conversation she and Tom would be having later.

He was still at the bottom of the stairs, waiting for her, and as she reached him he pulled her into his arms and gave her a greatly appreciated hug. 'We'll sort it out darling. Somehow,' and with a comforting arm still round her they went into the kitchen to prepare dinner.

The phone rang while they were eating, and Tom let it ring. No one was allowed to interrupt their dinner, but he was eager to see if it was Josh as soon as he had finished. It wasn't. It was Francesca. She'd left a message, asking him if he had seen the Advertiser, which he erased. He didn't like her gleeful tone.

'Who was it?' Claire called from the kitchen.

'Wrong number' he called back. Putting his coffee down, he picked up the Advertiser and looked again at the various articles about Charlotte. He was looking at what one medium had to say when Claire came into the sitting room, having finished the washing up.

'I hope this woman is wrong', he said, without looking up. 'She thinks Charlotte is dead and in a watery grave because she can see fish swimming around her.'

'On balance I think she is probably right about her being dead. If you look at the others they talk about, they nearly all were dead by this time. Only one, they say, was found and she died later of her injuries.'

'But what about the kidnapped ones? The three cases here were all OK after the ransom was paid, and they got the kidnapper, plus the money back, of that boy in Manchester.'

'But there hasn't been a ransom note according to the police, or that lot there' said Claire, indicating the paper he was reading.

'I wonder why it was Charlotte that was taken. Why her? I don't suppose her Dad is particularly wealthy. Though maybe she has rich grandparents. It could, of course, be something to do with her adoption. Perhaps her birth parents have taken her.'

'I would have thought they were the first people the police checked, wouldn't you? I just hope it's not a paedophile ring, or something like that. Thinking about what they do to children, makes me feel sick.' She shuddered as she said it. She shifted a cushion out of the way and sat down beside Tom. 'So what are we going to do? Is there anything we *can* do? Do we complain to the police, or what?' She looked enquiringly at Tom, but she guessed that he had no more idea about what to do than she did.

'I think we should ask the police how details of your statement got out, and I'm waiting for Josh to ring back and tell me how he came to print it. I'm sure it must be illegal to do that. But apart from that I think we will just have to forget about it, and hope that the people who have Charlotte don't read the Advertiser.'

'Do you think the couple I saw did have her? That Darren could be the chap who was seen taking Charlotte to the car outside the school. I wonder if I'd recognize him again if I saw him. I'm not sure I would. The only person I am absolutely sure about is Charlotte. I only have to shut my eyes and I see her. The picture is still so sharp in my mind.' Her flow of words stopped abruptly as the shrill noise of the phone broke in.

Tom picked it up. 'Hello. Oh, it's you.' His face was grim. 'Yes, we did see it.'

If Tom had had the phone in his right hand Claire would have heard enough to know who it was calling, but he had switched it to his left as soon as he was aware of the caller. That meant it was Francesca. She got up and collected their coffee cups and took them through to the kitchen. She shut the door.

***

When Claire was upset she cleaned. It didn't matter whether whatever it was needed it or not she just scrubbed and polished until she was worn out. It didn't happen that often these days as she had a beautiful house, impeccably decorated and furnished, with just enough items out of alignment to make it feel like a home. But there were still occasions when circumstances evolved around her that took her straight back to her childhood; to the period of her life she had tried to obliterate from her mind.

This was one such occasion.

She put the coffee cups in the sink and then just stood and stared at them. But she was not seeing her delicate bone china cups. She was seeing a sink full of dirty, chipped, mismatched crockery heaped together in a bowl of scummy cold water. This was the sight that had greeted her every day when she had come home from school. At age five it hadn't bothered her too much but by the time she was eight or nine she had realized that washing up the used dishes was something that should be done routinely throughout the day. However her mother didn't agree. So at the end of every school day it became Claire's first job to clean up the kitchen.

How she hated it. The smell, mingling with the odour coming from the farmyard, seemed to seep into her clothes and even her skin. It didn't help that her mother was often found in the chair by the Aga bottle feeding a runty looking piglet; one too small and weak to fight for a place along the row of teats on the sow's belly. It was no wonder she was nicknamed 'Piggy' at school.

The name followed her to her secondary school and it was after one particularly vicious bullying episode that she ended up in hospital. The clean crisp uniform of the nurses persuaded her that that was going to be her way out. She would get away and never go back.

As Claire rinsed the cups before putting them in the dishwasher she let her mind wander back to those days, knowing that she was safe from ever experiencing them again. Her father had wanted a boy. A boy to help him on the farm, although she came to realize that it wasn't really a farm, just a small holding with pigs and a few chickens, just big enough to allow them a very meagre income. Certainly not enough to provide her with a new school uniform, always it was second hand, and what books she had were given to her by thoughtful teachers who had encouraged her.

There had been a rough number of years but finally her chosen hospital had offered her a place and she had packed her single bag and left. Never to return. She had no idea if her parents were alive or dead, and she didn't care. Tom had tried to persuade her to go and make her peace with them before they got married, but she had remained faithful to her aim of never going back. She was sure that they had cared as little about her as she had them.

Chapter 4

Claire had arranged with Tom that he would take the following morning off to go and collect Aunt Lou from the hospital and take her home. She felt that he would be better at deflecting questions about Charlotte, and any other items of gossip that Aunt Lou had stored up ready for them. And she had been full of beans, so Tom told her later.

Mrs Donaldson, Aunt Lou's cleaner had been waiting for her, along with the shopping Claire had asked her to get, so he had thankfully handed her over. Claire guessed that any cleaning done that day would amount to the washing up of two coffee mugs. Much as she liked Mrs Donaldson, and she was extremely grateful for all the extra care she gave Aunt Lou, there were times when she found her continual chatter just a little bit wearing. But, in the course of the two ladies nattering, Tom had said that he had been very pleased to over hear them talk about how attentive Francesca had been, and that she had promised to call in with lunch for Aunt Lou later on. Make that three coffee mugs to wash up then.

But the joy of getting Aunt Lou home had soon subsided. Neither Claire nor Tom had slept well the night before. Their morning routine had been subdued despite the fact that they were relieved that Aunt Lou was well again, so much so that Claire hadn't even bothered to look at the daily paper before she left for work. It was still folded on the worktop.

However it was the Advertiser that had occupied much of Tom's afternoon. He was still frustrated when he got home about his inability to find out who had been responsible for its unusual centre-fold. He told Claire that he had got Tracey to try a variety of numbers for him but none of them were of any use, so in the end he had phoned the police because he was sure the statements should never have been printed. And, he admitted ruefully to Claire, he took out his frustration on the hapless civilian telephonist at the police station because every time she tried to put him through 'to someone in charge' the line was engaged.

Claire hoped that Tracey, his private secretary, had heeded the code of private secretaries and not blabbed to all and sundry about Tom's business. But she doubted it. She guessed that there were already stories going around the works about how Tom's awful wife had let him down again. Tracey, she knew from past experience, never missed an opportunity to instigate malicious rumours about her – not perhaps because Claire was Claire, but because Claire was the wife of her precious boss.

However, Tom's ear-battered police telephonist must have finally got through to someone as that evening they got a surprise visitor. A senior police officer had come to apologise about the leakage of information. Regrettably, by the time he had reached Claire's name on the list of those who had to be visited because their statement was quoted in the paper, he had got over the embarrassment of his force's failure and was now on the defensive. This attitude was not one he should have presented, to Claire in particular. She had not forgotten the dismissive stance of some of his fellow officers when she had given her statement, so she was not prepared to accept any excuses, and questioned him at length about their deplorable security lapse. He was not able to answer most of her questions because he didn't really know himself what had happened. At first it was thought that someone had hacked into the force's computer, but this was found not to be the case. Now, he told them, they were looking at all those who had access to the paper copies of the statements. Since there was a large team of police and civilians involved with the search for Charlotte it was going to take time to find out where the leak occurred.

When Claire interrupted and suggested to him that it must be illegal to publish statements made in good faith to the police, he became very evasive and wouldn't give her a straight answer. It depends, he told her, on how the reporter came by the statements. When Claire pressed for a straight answer he prevaricated even more before insisting that they were still trying to get hold of Gareth Jones. But, he said with finality, if past experience is anything to go by, he'll refuse to reveal his source. By this time Claire could have hit him, she was so frustrated by the whole thing.

Josh, Tom had told her earlier, didn't know how Gareth had got the information, and he didn't really care. Despite Tom's prodding Josh said he hadn't questioned why *his* paper was offered the information. If it was legit why wasn't it offered to one of the dailies? Tom had persisted. Why wasn't it offered to the local newspaper, instead of a small circulation advertising rag, like his? But Josh could not be riled. His paper had a scoop as far as he was concerned, and he wasn't going to turn down the chance of boosting his advertising revenue. As Gareth had assured him that he had come by the statements legally he felt justified in printing them. He couldn't help it if the police couldn't look after their paperwork securely, and he was blithely unconcerned about the ramifications of his actions.

Tom was still livid with Josh some hours after speaking to him. He felt particularly let down, so he told Claire, that his friend had dropped her in it, and even more so by the fact he hadn't warned Tom that he was going to do it. He couldn't believe that any right thinking person would not realize the danger Claire was now in.

The beleaguered police officer was also foolish enough to suggest to Tom that he was making a mountain out of a molehill because Claire had probably imagined the sighting of Charlotte. He waded even further into the mire by saying that all the newspaper and television coverage had obviously persuaded her that she had seen something when really she hadn't. 'We get a lot of ladies coming to us with tales of sightings after a case like this,' were his parting words.

**

That senior policeman's parting words stung Tom almost as much as Claire, so when Tom suggested that they take off to their favourite seaside hotel for the weekend, to get away from it all, Claire was only too happy to agree.

They had found the 'Sea View' hotel by accident when travelling along the south coast years before. They had noticed its beautiful position, on a cliff top overlooking a sandy bay, and had decided on the spur of the moment to see if it had any vacancies. It did, and they had been back several times despite its increase in size and new management.

They arrived just as the sun was setting, but it was still warm, so after dumping their bags they decided to renew their acquaintance with the beach. Tom was all for attempting the precipitous path from the hotel garden down the cliff face, but Claire wasn't having any of it. She knew that path of old and she wasn't going to risk it, especially as the ground underfoot was wet.

'You can go that way if you want to. I'm going down the road way,' she announced and set off in that direction. Tom caught up with her and took her hand.

'I was only joking! Even I'm not daft enough to take that path at this time of day.'

The tide was out when they got there and they were the only people on the wide, clean expanse of sand. Only the odd shell or pebble marred the flat surface, while the last of the sunlight reflected off the small, rippling waves. It was calm and peaceful – the perfect antidote to the pressures of the last few days.

'Race you to that rock.'

'Which one?' But Tom was talking to himself. She was off, sprinting away from him. He raced to catch up with her but, he soon discovered, office work was not conducive to sudden spurts of activity. He was puffing and panting by the time he reached her, and slumped down beside her to recover.

'I'm too old to do that', he groaned.

'No you're not. You're just out of condition. Come on,' Claire said, as she pulled him to his feet, 'I'll race you back.'

'No, I can't. Let's just walk back and enjoy this glorious place and think about what we'll have for dinner.'

'You're getting soft Thomas Harrison, but I love you anyway,' and with a swift kiss Claire took his hand. 'We'll have a swim in the new pool before eating and *then* you can decide what you are going to have for your dinner.'

'No, I won't. You can if you like. I'm going to have a sleep first. I'm knackered.'

'You poor old thing! And you were the one that wanted to come down the cliff path. Come on then. Let's make for home.'

They ambled quietly along the darkening lane, enjoying the feeling of being alone, just the two of them, before the lights of the hotel welcomed them back to reality.

Leaving Tom to have his sleep Claire headed for the pool and found an elderly couple appreciating its warmth, slowly swimming from side to side, but they changed direction when they saw that Claire meant business. She didn't want to interrupt their stately progress but they appeared to be quite happy to stop and watch her perform a very powerful crawl as she swam up and down the twenty-five metre length. Stopping after a swift ten lengths she swam over to the couple to thank them for letting her interrupt their tranquillity.

'Oh no, you didn't. We like to watch you young people. It reminds us of our youth when we could swim like you.' Claire coloured slightly at the praise, momentarily speechless, as the old man continued, 'We were very good in our day,' he laughed.

'Are you staying here, dear?' his partner butted in, and as Claire nodded she carried on, 'it's lovely isn't it? This pool is much better than the old one. Much cleaner looking, and children aren't allowed in in the evening, so we usually get it to ourselves, don't we Jim?'

Jim looked as if he was going to say something but she didn't pause. 'We swim every evening before dinner. Usually just the two of us. But it's nice to see new people, isn't it Jim? So don't mind us. You carry on, dear.'

Not sure of whether she was being dismissed or invited to chat, Claire smiled at them both again, having decided it was dismissal, and started off on another series of lengths.

The same couple were seated at a table near them in the dining room later, but maybe she looked different in clothes as there was no spark of recognition when Claire wished them a good evening in passing.

***

The weather the following morning looked promising. The sun was shining out of a clear blue sky, positively encouraging them to take off on a long walk. Debating the pros and cons of a hotel packed lunch versus a pub meal, they came down in favour of the pub, before setting out to walk from 'their' bay to the next one, just visible in the distance.

Claire reluctantly agreed to the hazardous cliff path to the sea, since Tom was so keen to try it again, but she very much regretted it by the time they were only a quarter of the way down. It was still muddy and there seemed to be more scree and less vegetation to hang on to than last time. The notice at the top had said that the path was maintained but she was damned if she could see any maintenance. Tom appeared to relish the slipping and sliding, and his tiredness of the previous evening was long gone. He was enjoying himself almost as much as she was hating it. By the time she reached the base she was hot and sweaty and in no mood to be teased by Tom about being a less than 'young person', as the elderly swimmer had called her. She made it very clear that she wasn't going back that way as she stomped off down to the water's edge to wash the grit and mud off her hands.

The water appeared to be warm enough to paddle so she stripped off her mucky shoes and mud spattered socks allowing the small waves to cool her overheated feet, and her bad temper. 'I'm sorry, Tom. I shouldn't have let it get to me, should I?

'You can't be perfect at everything, you know,' he replied with a grin as he struggled to pull off his own sweaty socks. He leant against her to get the second one off, and she was very tempted to move, to get even with him for that last remark. But she didn't. Today was going to be a good day.

Although the tide was coming in there was enough beach above the high tide line for them to take their time walking along the water's edge, dodging the odd bigger wave, before they rounded the end of their bay and into the next one. Here lots of people had had the same idea as them and there were several family groups with beach mats and wind breaks set out like small encampments all over the sand. Commerce had arrived too; huts selling buckets and spades, ice creams, drinks, etc. – all the things necessary to make a good day out by the sea. And beyond them, above the car park, could be seen a pub sign.

'Saved' said Tom, as he indicated the sign. 'Let's go and see what they have to offer.' They sat on a low sea wall and unsuccessfully attempted to brush the salt and sand off their sticky feet before putting their shoes and socks back on. Arriving at the aptly named Salty Seadog they realized that their efforts had been unnecessary as several couples sitting out on the pub's wide wooden deck were bare foot. After catching the eye of a waiter they sat themselves down at a table with a view holiday makers pay a fortune for, and removed their footwear too.

Fish and chips always taste better when eaten by the sea they decided, as they sat back and contemplated their empty plates. But by now the deck was packed and a queue for seats was forming, which persuaded them that it was time to move on, via the loos where the hot air dryers did a great job on their feet.

With more comfortable feet they decided to explore the cliff path that meandered up gently from the car park until they were high above the beach, and followed it along to the grounds of their hotel. But the path they were on seemed to bypass the hotel and following it they found themselves in a wooded area they hadn't seen before. They could hear the rumble of traffic on their left but the trees hid the road, and on the right they just caught glimpses of the sea as the trees thinned in places. This path was maintained and after a few hundred metres they came out of the trees into a wide meadow that gradually sloped down towards another bay.

'This is the way we should have come, instead of that disastrous so-called path you insisted we take' said Claire, as they started down the slope.

'But it's a different bay. Not the one the hotel advertises as theirs.' And as Tom spoke he moved off to the right, towards the edge of the field, then stopped suddenly.

'Hey Claire, come and look at this'

'Why? What have you found?' she called back, as she walked over to join him. She gasped when she saw what he was looking at. Beyond their feet, with no fence or any sort of barricade to impede them, was a vertical drop down to a boulder strewn cove. It looked dark, dank and dangerous, with the high cliffs on the three sides. The sunlight seemed to have detoured around it and the sound of the sea being sucked in and out over the large pebbles made it even more frightening.

'No wonder the hotel doesn't mention this route. Come away Tom. I don't like it.' She tugged his arm to pull him back and away from the cliff edge.

'I wonder why they don't have a fence here, or even a warning notice' he said, peering over. 'I can't see any sign of one.'

'Tom, come away,' and she tugged his arm again. She was becoming seriously rattled and anxious to get away. She turned away and looked at the tranquil scene in front of her to allay her fears. The thick, lush grass underfoot and the low hedge protecting it from the road were comforting, and at the bottom of the slope she could see another sandy bay, just like the one they had walked along earlier. Without waiting to see if Tom was following her she marched to the middle of the field before slowing down and turning to wait for him.

'What a place! Imagine going over the cliff there. No one would ever find you,' he said. 'I wonder why it isn't fenced. Health and safety people would have a fit.' He grinned as he said that, and she responded, as they each thought about all the times they had complained about health and safety issues at work.

'Shall we look at this bay, or go back to our room with its lovely big bed and think of something more interesting to do?' he suggested.

Chapter 5

It was during the Diabetic clinic the following week that Claire noticed an unusual buzz among the patients waiting to be seen. It was generally a fairly sociable clinic because the same patients attended month after month, year after year. They had got to know each other well enough to discuss their various ailments and what the doctors said about them. Many of the doctors they considered old friends, and woe betide a new one that tried to change their treatment.

Today was different though. There was an air of suppressed excitement, so much so that Claire asked a receptionist what was going on. 'Haven't you heard' she said, 'they've found a body. It was on the local radio about ten past two. They broke into Dan's programme and said that a child's body has been found but they can't say whether or not it is Charlotte...' As the receptionist prattled on about who had said what, Claire clutched the reception desk with both hands. Her head was spinning and her body broke out into a sweat. She fought to keep upright. 'Excuse me' she murmured as she moved away.

The receptionist was still talking as Claire made off in the direction of the staff toilets, one hand on the wall, and as she watched her slow progress she commented to her colleague that Sister Harrison didn't look well.

'I'm not surprised, you idiot. Don't you know she saw Charlotte? Soon after she went missing. It was all over the papers. No wonder she looked ill, after you blurting that out like that.'

'Oh God, I didn't think. She just asked me what was going on, and I told her. Shall I go and see if she's OK?'

'No, leave it for a bit. If she's not back in a few minutes I'll go and check.'

Claire leant against the locked loo door, and gulped air, willing herself not to be sick. Gradually the feeling passed and she felt stable enough to venture out and splash cold water on her face. She hardly recognized the bleak white face staring at her in the mirror. Even her pale lipstick stood out as a stark streak of colour. She rubbed her face roughly with a hand towel and managed to bring a hint of pinkness to her cheeks. She tidied her hair, straightened her uniform, and told herself to go back to work.

She might have managed to ignore the chatter if old Mr Evans hadn't made a point of stopping her and asking what she thought about the news. She tried to pretend she didn't know about the find, which just made matters worse, because Mr Evans deafness meant that he had to explain it all to her in a very loud voice. By the time he had vanished into cubicle 3 the whole waiting room was quiet.

Claire momentarily stood by the closed cubicle door before briskly going to the nurses' station for the clinic list, and announcing the name of the next patient to be seen. All eyes were on her but as the named patient stood and muttered apologies to those he had to disturb to get out, the waiting room recommenced its chattering. This appeared to be the signal to all and sundry to ask her what she thought about the find and during the course of that long, long afternoon Claire had to put up with numerous questions which she ignored or answered with the briefest of terse phrases.

For the first time in her working life Claire hated her job.

***

Tom found her sunk in an armchair, still in her uniform; her face streaked with tears, staring at BBC

News 24 which was showing endless pictures of the grieving Alsopps'. He turned the television off and sat himself down in the chair next to her. 'How did you find out?'

Claire turned to him, her reddened eyes expressionless. 'Sorry. What was that?'

'I asked how you found out.'

'They were discussing it in the clinic.'

'But they've only just announced that it's Charlotte.'

'They heard that a body had been found, so I suppose they took it for granted that it was Charlotte. They kept on and on about it. All afternoon.' The memory of that afternoon brought on the tears again.

Tom reached for her hand, took the soggy tissue out of it and replaced it with his own clean white cotton handkerchief. She scrubbed at her eyes. 'I don't know how I got through it. Everyone asking me questions. As if I knew anything about it. All I did was get a brief glimpse of her, yet they behaved as if I was an expert on the subject. Mr Evans - you know, that old deaf chap we met in Sainsbury's, with the booming voice. The one who said he was looking for sugar that didn't have sugar in it' Tom nodded, the memory causing him to smile. 'He was there today' Claire continued, 'and he went on at great length about the finding of a body. He must have memorised every news bulletin before he came in, he went on so long. With everyone listening. I didn't know what to do with myself.' She started to rub her eyes again, but Tom took the hankie from her. 'That's enough, love. You'll make them sore.'

She gave a long unladylike sniff as she shuffled through her pockets for another tissue to wipe her nose, until Tom took pity on her and handed back the hankie.

'Come on', he said. 'It's time you got changed. I'm hungry.'

'I'm sorry Tom. I forgot the time. I won't be a moment.' She got up and took her coat off and went to hang it in the hall. Tom's ploy of claiming hunger made her climb the stairs two at a time, and change in double quick time. It was a long time since she had wallowed in self pity.

She apologized again when she came down into the kitchen, to find Tom going through the file of take-away outlets. 'I thought we'd order a take-away to save cooking. What do you think?'

'No. It will do me good to do something. Anyway we are only going to have left-over's so it won't take long. But you could get me a drink, if you want something to do', she said with the suggestion of a smile. The warmth of his amused grin made her feel better.

But the feeling didn't last long. Whatever TV channel they turned to, after they had eaten, seemed to be showing something about Charlotte, or something related to her. After more fruitless channel hopping Claire took the remote from Tom saying, 'It's no good Tom. We both have to face people at work so we might as well watch the news, and then if anyone says anything we'll know what they are on about.'

Tom agreed, but he soon wished he hadn't. It was heart breaking to see Giles and Anne Alsopp leaving the police station in such a distressed state. Despite their police escort's best efforts, they were having to elbow their way through hordes of reporters pushing microphones into their faces, with flashes from the cameramen's equipment making them blink repeatedly, and then there was the ceaseless noise as questions were shouted at them. It was absolute mayhem. Over the din coming from the TV, Claire commented, 'I can understand now why we get those awful interviews with grieving relatives after some disaster or other after watching this. In the long run it must be easier to sit at a table and say what you have to say, then leave by the back door in peace.'

'I expect there are people by the back door too if we .....' Tom was about to go on but Claire lifted her hand to indicate he should listen. A senior police officer was about to make a statement about the discovery of the body. His statement didn't amount to much apart from saying in formal police language that a child's body had been found in a spinney on private land, and the child had since been identified as that of Charlotte Alsopp.

As that picture faded it was replaced by the scene of the discovery. It looked far too beautiful to be the scene of a crime: a small dense wooded area at the side of a field. Sunlight was flickering through the leaves, turning the image into a patchwork of light and dark, while the herd of black and white serene looking cows in the background added their own variegated colour scheme. Though the cows were passively chewing the cud their big dark eyes were all turned in the direction of the commotion on their patch but making no move towards the humans erecting a tent among the trees. Deep in a hollow, what they were covering was a roughly made tepee. Quite small, like something children make during long hot summer holidays, when they were pretending to be cowboys and Indians. But it looked as if the scenes of crime people were having considerable trouble trying to get the scene covered because the overhanging branches kept catching the canvas and twisting it.

The reporter was on the edge of the field watching the activity but Claire noticed that he kept turning a wary eye on the cows in case they got nosey and moved towards him. He was accompanied by a tall thickset man who was introduced as the owner of the land, and the finder of Charlotte's body. He was being asked about how he came to find her.

The landowner talked in a high-pitched drawl which momentarily surprised Claire. The sound and vision didn't go together, but this odd combination soon became irrelevant as she listened to the words not the sound. He was saying that his cowman had told him that one of the cows hadn't followed the others when it was time for milking. This was such an unusual situation the cowman had crossed the field to see why this particular cow wasn't behaving normally. He found her near the spinney gazing at what he thought was children's hidden play area. Thinking nothing of it the cowman had persuaded the cow to follow the others, and he got on with the milking. Later, remembering the little camp, he told the boss about it.

The following morning the landowner, who was now being referred to as Sir John, said he went to investigate. He wasn't going to have children making camps on his land, he told the reporter, especially near that field as sometimes his bull had the run of it.

It was the smell he noticed first. It was so bad, he said, he had to put his handkerchief to his nose just to get anywhere near the little tepee construction. As he clambered down into the hollow the sticks sagged to one side and he could see a sleeping bag on the ground.

'What colour was it?' the reporter cut in.

Sir John turned to him with a startled expression on his face. Claire decided that Sir

John wasn't the sort of person who was accustomed to being questioned.

'Reddish, brown – I don't know. It was dirty.'

'So what did you do then?' the reporter said encouragingly, thrusting the microphone nearer Sir John.

'If you'd stop interrupting I'll tell you', he said

'Yes' said Claire to the television 'Stop interrupting.' And thankfully he did, letting Sir John carry on with his account of finding the sleeping bag. As he had got nearer, he continued, he could see that there was someone, or something, very small in the bag. Thinking that maybe it was toys left behind by children because, he said, he also thought it was a children's den, he pulled back the top of the bag.

Sir John stopped. Claire watched him swallow. Then he noisily cleared his throat. He was visibly moved. Claire guessed what he was going to say next and sure enough he did. It was a child, he said. A little girl. With long blonde hair.

There was a pause in the interview, and Claire willed the reporter to shut up, but of course he didn't.

'So what did you do then?' he said for the second time.

'I put the top of the bag back where I had found it, went home and called the police.' With that hurried last sentence he nodded to the reporter and strode of in the direction of his gentle speechless cows.

Claire had tears in her eyes as she turned to Tom and made very disparaging remarks about insensitive, ignorant upstarts who asked silly questions!

'Par for the course these days, I'm afraid. They all seem to do it.' Tom's statement was verified almost immediately when the cowman was interviewed about his perceptive cow. He was actually asked what he thought the cow was thinking about when she was looking in the direction of the so-called camp! The poor cowman looked flummoxed.

'See' he said, pointing at the television, 'there he goes again. I don't suppose that poor chap has ever considered what his cows thought about before.'

Claire reached across him to get the remote and turned the television off. As she did so she turned to

Tom and said, 'Did you notice how quickly that reporter got to the scene? The SOCO team looked as if they had only just arrived because they were still putting that tent up. How did the press get onto it so soon? I reckon someone is listening into the police radio.'

'Quite likely, I suppose. Must be a problem for them too if the public get to a crime scene before them; trampling all over the evidence. I wouldn't be at all surprised if that Gareth Jones doesn't have some sort of monitor rigged up to the police waveband.'

'We'd better keep an eye on the Advertiser to see what he comes up with next then. Incidentally, have you got any more information on him? Have the police let you know anything? I'd really like to know how he got my statement. Has Francesca said anything? It's about time we had some answers. The police seem to be dragging their feet. Still, with this, any enquiries they were making will be put on the back burner now.'

'No – to all three questions. I rang the police and they said they were still making enquiries and they'd let us know when they find anything. But they don't seem unduly bothered. At least the 'spokesperson' I was put through didn't.'

'Does anyone care about anything these days I wonder,' Claire said with a yawn. 'Anyway now we know about Charlotte' she continued quietly. 'No more waiting.'

***

Sometime earlier

With the box holding Charlotte safely in the back of the van Darren and Michelle made their way home, carefully sticking to the Highway Code, so as not to attract attention.

Darren momentarily parked the van as close to the back door of the cottage as possible so that Michelle could get the box inside quickly, before he took it the garage to unload. He took his time sorting the boxes. He didn't want to go home and face Michelle again. Not yet anyway. Give her time to make a plan. Give her time to sort things out. He knew she would. She just needed a bit of time. He would do the sorting. He was good at that. She was good at thinking, so he made sure he gave her plenty of time to think.

Meanwhile Michelle had got Charlotte out of the box and the poly bag and had put her on the sofa. She gazed at the small face but in her mind's eye she was seeing her own child. Tears slid noiselessly down her cheeks. She slumped onto the sofa and picked up Charlotte and held her tightly against her as if trying to put some warmth into the cold little body, but she soon became aware that Charlotte was wet so she took her upstairs to her room to change her out of her wet knickers and tracksuit trousers.

As she slid Charlotte's shoes and socks off her mind was beginning to formulate a plan. She lifted Charlotte off the bed and held her with one arm, while with the other she pulled all the bedclothes off the bed until all that was left was the waterproof mattress cover. She put the child back down onto the chilly plastic and proceeded to strip her as well. She opened the window to let the cold air blow in before bundling up the clothes and the bedding. She took the pile downstairs and put them all into the washing machine, and, as she turned the dials, she remembered Charlotte's words about the wrinkly Brownie badges, and set the temperature lower.

With her mind in neutral Michelle ran a cold bath, because in the back of her mind was something she'd seen on the telly about having to keep a body cold, and laid Charlotte in it. She didn't want her smelling of urine when she went back to her mother, and, as she brushed her fingernails, she acknowledged to herself that she didn't want the police to find any connection to her. But as Charlotte's hair floated around her head Michelle's neutrality disappeared as she gently ran her fingers through it to release any tangles, just as she had done with her own child. She washed the little body and carefully dried her with a cold towel, although she ached to wrap her in something warm.

Michelle laid Charlotte across the bed so that her damp hair was lying over the edge, and with her hair dryer set on the lowest level, Michelle sat on the floor by the child's head and let the tepid air take its time drying the silky hair. Alternating the hands holding the dryer and the hairbrush Michelle stroked the hair until it hung like a golden curtain along the bed frame.

With a sigh, Michelle lifted the hair to put it back into a ponytail, just like it had been when they had first seen her; not so easy without the child's cooperation.

As she was putting away the hairdryer she heard Darren come through the bad door.

'That you, Dazzer?', she called down the stairs, realizing almost immediately how silly that sounded. Of course it was Dazzer. Who else could it be? Nevertheless she was relieved when it was him that replied.

'What are we going to do, Chell? Have you decided on a plan yet?'

She came down the stairs, and headed to the kitchen. Darren trailing along behind her.

'Have you thought yet, Chell? Chell, have you got a plan?'

'Stop hassling me, Dazzer. I'm thinking. I'll let you know in a bit. Get yourself a sandwich or something , or watch the telly. I'm busy at the moment.'

The washing machine's final beep sounded quite loud to Michelle's overstretched nerves in the silent kitchen as Darren stopped his chatter and went through to the sitting room. She sorted out Charlotte's clothes and put them into the tumble dryer, again, being mindful of the swimming badge, setting it on low. She heard the TV go on but she was too uptight to sit and watch it, so she pottered around moving things from one place to another, wiping surfaces, and cleaning the sink; anything to take her mind off their predicament.

Knowing that there would be no warm body to help get rid of the creases in the little cotton vest and t-shirt Michelle got the ironing board out and ironed all of Charlotte's clothes, taking particular care to see that the badge looked as good as new. She hadn't made it wrinkly, a point that gave her a brief moment of satisfaction.

While re-dressing Charlotte in her own clean clothes Michelle debated with herself about the next step. She could take her straight round to the police station. That idea rather appealed to her conscience, but it would be unfair on Darren. So what else to do? Hide her, so that she was never found, or hide her long enough for them to get away? Michelle looked down on the small damaged face. Bruises from

Darren's rough handling when he had taped her were beginning to show, and her ragged bottom lip was looking messier. Michelle lightly ran her thumb over the lip, hoping to improve things, but it didn't work.

Downstairs Darren was also thinking. He knew it was his fault that the child was dead, but he had panicked. When he had seen Charlotte move towards the door, he had grabbed her without thinking and clamped his hand across her mouth. She had struggled violently, desperate to get his hand off her mouth. Her big eyes, wide with fear, frightened him, so much so he had thought of putting the tape over them too but by the time he had wrapped her mouth in tape, and held her down to tape her wrists and ankles, she was limp and the fear in her eyes was fading. Within minutes he had her secreted in the airing cupboard, and was able to safely join Michelle, knowing that no one would find her there.

He would give anything for it not to have happened. But it had.

He went upstairs to find Michelle. He didn't want to be on his own.

He found her looking at the child with an expression of absolute misery on her face. He stood beside her, not daring to touch her for fear of being rebuffed. 'I'm so sorry, Chell. I really am. I didn't mean to do it. You know that don't you?' he murmured, as he leant slightly more towards her. She shifted away.

'I know you didn't mean it Dazzer but that makes no difference now. Now we've got to decide what we are going to do with her.'

'What do you think we should do Chell?'

Michelle turned to him as a thought came to her. 'What did you do with that red sleeping bag we found in that other house? Have we still got it? That one wrapped in a dry cleaner's bag. The one we found in the spare room cupboard.'

'It's in a box in the garage. Why?'

'I want to put Charlotte in it.'

'But it's a good one. It'll sell well. You can't use that one.'

'Think Dazzer, think. It's been cleaned. It won't have any clues for the police on it. And I think we should leave Charlotte somewhere where she will be found. I want her to be found. I don't want her to rot away somewhere on her own. I want her Mum to have her back, even if she is dead. And her Dad will have suffered enough then.'

Darren headed back down the stairs. He wasn't happy about losing a potential sale. But Chell did have a point - if the sleeping bag had been cleaned then no one would know it was them. He cheered up a bit then, pleased with Michelle's cleverness, and with a lighter heart went out to the garage to find which box he had put it in.

He wasn't long and came back with the bag still in its wrapper.

'We mustn't touch the bag too much should we Chell? Don't want the cops finding hairs or anything, do we?'

Darren broke the piece of sticky tape holding the bag in a roll and laid it out on the bed next to the body, eased away the plastic wrapping and then unzipped it. Between them they got the small body in the bag and zipped it up again, and replaced the plastic covering.

'What now Chell?'

'Get the van and park by the door again, and when it is getting dark we'll go out and leave her somewhere to be found.'

'Where have you got in mind, Chell?'

'Remember that wood we used to play in as kids? Where we used to make a camp, and things? I thought we'd take her there.'

'But it's been sold. That old man that owns Laurel Farm bought it. We won't be able to leave her there.'

'But that's good Dazzer. Someone is more likely to find her. I want her found Dazzer. I don't want the maggots to get her, and they will if we leave her somewhere where she won't be found.'

'You're right Chell. We must let someone find her.' As he spoke he made for the door and went off to get the van as Michelle had asked.

She listened to the silence settle around her before pulling back the top of the sleeping bag and looking at the small face one last time. She didn't see the pale damaged face but the bright shiny-eyed look that Charlotte had had while they had been emptying the house. The look she had had when she thought she was going home to her Mummy.

As the reality swam into view Michelle's face crumbled and the tears slid down her cheeks, and she ached to pick up the child again. Without thinking she turned from the child and let her eyes roam the room until they settled on the chair holding the dolly; the dolly that had seemed to comfort the child in her initial distress. She moved to the chair, picked it up, straightened its clothes and smoothed its hair before tucking it into the crook of Charlotte's left arm, seemingly oblivious to the fact that she had just undone all their careful work of avoiding clues for the police.

Chapter 6

Claire's obsession with news gathering would have had a tremendous boost the following morning if she still wanted it. Page after page of the local paper was given over to Charlotte. Even the nationals gave her a full page spread, and BBC News 24 were going excitedly from one minor point to another trying to put a spin on even the most humdrum of details. But it was Tom who was paying attention to it this morning - they'd never had the television on at that time before. He was the one following the headlines, in between mouthfuls of toast. The nitty-gritty details of the finding seemed to stimulate his previous lack of interest. Pausing his viewing to fill his coffee cup, his animated chatter on the subject though, fell on deaf ears. Claire thought it all a bit tactless and insensitive, and was surprised that Tom had reacted the way he had. She just felt flat. She didn't need any more details. The finding of Charlotte's body was the end as far as she was concerned; the end of hope.

Seeing Tom off to work was a relief; relief too that she didn't have to go in that day. She wanted quiet. Time to think. Her peace however was disturbed by the insistent ringing of the phone. Hoping that whoever it was would give up eventually, she ignored it – or tried to. But her instinct to answer it was automatic, and she was relieved to hear the quiet voice of Aunt Lou at the other end.

'Are you busy today, dear?'

'Hadn't really thought about it, Aunt Lou. Why? Do you need anything?'

'No, I don't need anything. I just thought you might like some company. A quiet chat about everything that is going on, perhaps.'

'That's kind of you.' She stopped momentarily. How to say no without hurting her feelings. But it would hurt her feelings if she said no. 'How about coffee later?'

'That's a lovely idea. I'll be round about ten thirty. Give Mrs Donaldson a chance to get some work done!'

'That's fine. I'll see you then.'

Claire put the phone down. Aunt Lou obviously had something to say; but she wished she hadn't needed to say it today. She didn't want to talk about 'what's going on'. She didn't really know herself 'what's going on'. What *is* going on, she asked herself. I saw a missing child. I told the police. That's it. But why has it got to me so badly?

Claire plonked her elbows on the table and rested her chin in her hands, and stared into space. She had no children of her own so she couldn't be relating her reaction to the possible abduction and loss of her own child, she decided. She had got over her sadness about her childlessness many years ago. But she didn't feel that her lack of children was the reason why she felt the loss of Charlotte so acutely. Was it the fact that her sighting hadn't helped find her? Was she at fault? She had tried. She'd told the police. They were the ones that should have done the finding, not her. But – and it was this but that really niggled – if she had gone to the police on the day she saw Charlotte, would that have saved her? She'd let herself be talked out of it. Is that what was troubling her? Her giving into Tom, instead of sticking to her guns. But she couldn't blame Tom. He was worried sick about Aunt Lou, that's why he hadn't taken her sighting seriously. And at that time, she remembered, he was inclined to believe she was imagining things. Listening to him now though, especially his unexpected knowledgeable chatter this morning, he very much believed her now.

Claire's introspection was interrupted by the post clattering through the letter box. She glanced at her watch and got up hurriedly and started clearing the clutter left from breakfast. But in the back of her mind her shameful feelings were pricking away at her conscience, spiteful little prods accentuating her feelings of failure.

***

Aunt Lou's arrival was a relief from her brooding, and she needn't have been concerned about what she had to say. She had come to 'say it with flowers'- to say thank you to them both for their care and concern while she was in hospital. The flowers were a wonderful display of blooms from Aunt Lou's garden and as Claire exclaimed over them, placing them in a tall vase on the dining room table, Aunt Lou was able to note Claire's pallor and loss of weight.

'Are you well, dear? You look a little peaky?'

'I'm fine Aunt Lou', she replied without much conviction. 'I am, really. Just a little low thinking about Charlotte.'

'Well dear, you did your best. You told the police where you had seen her. It was up to them to go and find her.'

'That's what I keep telling myself. But it doesn't help. If only I had gone to the police on the day I saw her, perhaps she'd be alive today.'

'Perhaps. But whoever took her may have killed her soon after she was taken. We just don't know, so there's no point blaming yourself. And there's no point speculating about who took her because we don't know that either.'

'I know you're right Aunt Lou, but it doesn't feel right.'

'You're being too hard on yourself Claire. You'll make yourself ill if you keep moping like this. Let's think of something cheerful to talk about. Did you know that Viv and I are going on a coach trip to Cornwall? We are going with an Age Concern group, which is a bit of a hoot. Can you imagine us with a bunch of old folk?'

Claire could imagine it quite easily. They would fit in well, but of course she didn't say so.

'When are you going? Tom and I are going to Venice for a few days next month, the fifteenth to the nineteenth. Did he tell you? He thought we could do with a change of scenery.'

'No, he didn't tell me, Fran did. She must have seen her Dad recently. It's a good idea. I went to Venice for a month or so when I was young. I loved the place. Nearly came home with a handsome Italian but unfortunately I saw sense at the last minute. My life might have been very different.'

'I hope it wasn't Jocelyn's death that ruined your plans.'

'Definitely not. That all happened long before the accident. I'd decided that I liked my freedom far too much then to be shackled to some man for the rest of my days.'

'Aunt Lou! Surely you don't see marriage like that, do you?'

'I did then, and I don't regret it. I've seen and done a lot more than most people.'

Aunt Lou's almost defiant tone of voice made Claire wonder if she did regret it now. The repetition of the word 'then' seemed significant - but that was something Claire didn't feel she should ask her about. Not directly anyway. She changed tack.

73

'It must have been hard for you taking on Francesca when Jocelyn died. But you never showed it. I thought you were remarkable. Still do as a matter of fact.'

'There was no one else. Tom's mother had died before his marriage, and his father couldn't do it, so I had to. Tom wasn't able to look after her on his own, and he'd just got the works up and running. Just as well he had that job though because it helped with the grieving process. Then he met you!'

'Yes, he did.' Claire smiled at the memory. Two busy people rushing round Sainsbury's after work. Him to find a bottle of something to celebrate a birthday, and her to get in several bottles for a party. Him bumping into someone, breaking a bottle and cutting his hand, and her doing her Florence act. 'It was your birthday Tom was getting the wine for when we met, wasn't it?'

'Yes, and he came home with a grin from ear to ear, saying that he was going to a party. And I ended up drinking the wine on my own!'

'When he told me that it was your birthday I tried to encourage him to go home, but he wouldn't!'

'And in the morning I had to tell Fran why her Daddy hadn't come home!'

Claire blushed. She could still remember the embarrassment of Francesca's questions when Tom took her home with him later that morning. Aunt Lou had found it very funny and had made no attempt to help her out.

'Did you ever resent me coming into Tom's life, because I really upset yours?'

'No, absolutely not.' Aunt Lou answered immediately and with conviction. 'I was quite happy to hand Tom and Fran over to you. Three years, or whatever it was, of Fran was quite enough for me to be more than convinced that I didn't want a family. Or even family life. Much as I loved them both, I needed my own space. Once I knew that you and Tom were serious about each other I started planning my future.'

'Yes, you made that very plain to Tom and me at the time. But I've often wondered if you really meant it because there was gossip at the time about us upsetting you and that's why you went off to Canada so soon after our wedding. Some people got quite nasty.'

'That was sad, I grant you, but we can't be responsible for what other people think. Anyway I don't think anyone could possibly still think that now. We have a good relationship, don't we?'

'Oh Aunt Lou, you know we do. I love you to bits. I don't think I could have coped with Francesca if it weren't for you.'

'She has had her moments, hasn't she?'

Aunt Lou leaned across the kitchen table and covered Claire's hand with her own. 'You do know Claire, don't you, how much I admire the way you cope with Fran. However abominable her behaviour has been towards you, you've never told anyone why, never complained, or anything. I've told her more times than I care to remember how much she owes you, but she won't listen.'

Claire looked at her with surprise. 'I didn't know you knew.'

'I knew alright.'

'Well I'm glad she told you. I suppose deep down I knew she had because you never questioned Tom or me about the change in her, which I would have expected if you hadn't known.'

'I've never mentioned it to Tom, but I remember at the time how ill he looked.'

'Yes, it was a terrible shock to him. He wanted the police involved but Francesca threatened to kill herself if he did, so he didn't. Much against his, and my, better judgment though.'

Claire paused to consider whether or not to say any more about those dark days but Aunt Lou forestalled her.

'On a happier note, has Tom met the new man in her life? I don't know anything about him apart from the fact she is besotted with him.'

'I think he may have done. Tom saw her with a chap called Gareth Jones in a pub recently. He's the one who is responsible for the piece in the Advertiser about Charlotte. The piece about me.'

'Is he, by Jove.' Aunt Lou looked at Claire as she spoke, and Claire felt that she was debating in her mind about what to say next. Could Aunt Lou bring herself to suggest that maybe Francesca was deliberately targeting her through Gareth? Could she think Francesca was that spiteful? But they were saved from any further revelations not by the bell but by the gloved hand of a parcel courier as he thumped on the front door, bringing another book from Amazon.

'Well' announced Aunt Lou, 'time, I think, to go and see what Mrs Donaldson has been up to. What are you going to do with the rest of your day, dear? Anything exciting?'

'If going to Sainsbury's is considered exciting, then I am.'

'Good. Can you drop me off on your way? I've got to pick up a prescription. Dr Morrow has put me on some new heart stuff.'

That sounds ominous Claire thought. The hospital was supposed to have sorted things out for her. Why the change? But she knew better than to ask. To Claire, Aunt Lou always said that she was fine, and that there was no need to fuss, so Claire was very careful not to fuss – in front of her. But in front of Tom she would.

Chapter 7

It was the baby doll that was found with Charlotte that upset Claire more than any of the other details about her death. The killer had gone to the trouble of finding a dolly for her. Claire knew that at aged eight Charlotte was probably past dolls but she thought it was a reassuring gesture; a thoughtful gesture. She hadn't just been dumped. But to Claire it also hinted that a woman might have been involved. Would a man abducting a girl of eight think she might like a doll? Claire didn't want to go down the path of why a paedophile might want to give a child a doll, but the police seemed to think that no sexual perversion was involved. Charlotte had not been molested. It was reported that her clothes hadn't been disturbed at all.

So why was she killed? Was it an accident? When was she killed? How much did she suffer? These were the questions being asked at the press conferences and in Claire's home too.

Much was made of the doll in the press; lots of pictures, with and without its clothes because it was an old fashioned type, the sort that had moveable arms and legs because they were hooked onto elastic bands within the body cavity. Perhaps it belonged to the killers. It had obviously belonged to someone who cared as the clothes were hand knitted, by a granny, or a mother perhaps. Or perhaps it had been bought in a charity shop already dressed. The police were appealing to the public for information about it, but the public's prurient instincts were more interested in the state of Charlotte's body rather than that of the dolly – or so the press would have them believe. Claire listened to the press conferences and then read a reporter's interpretation of the conferences and she wondered where they got their information from.

The television reporter who had announced the discovery of Charlotte's body presented many more interviews from the spinney site. The senior police officer gave his version of events, as much as he knew, and then it appeared that every Tom, Dick and Harry who had cause to use the road nearest to the spinney was asked his or her opinion. Claire was surprised that the road hadn't been closed. Surely the scenes of crime people would have wanted to go over every inch of it to see how Charlotte ended up there. Perhaps they had, and Claire had missed that sequence. Perhaps she had just had an overdose of the public venting their feelings about various nefarious individuals and had tuned out.

By the time Tom was due home from work Claire had had enough. Charlotte was dead, and there was nothing she could do about that. Speculation about her part in the proceedings was pointless. As she prepared dinner she put her favourite Mozart concerto on the CD player and let the soothing sound waft over her disturbed thoughts as she mindlessly chopped and stirred ingredients for the lasagne. The satisfaction of shutting the oven door on her *pièce de résistance* stayed with her as she uncorked a bottle of good red wine, or so Sainsbury's had informed her as she had trawled up and down the booze aisles wondering which to buy.

She was glad it was a 'good' wine when Tom got in as they didn't have any champagne to celebrate Tom's news: the Chinese delegation had been impressed with his expertise and his workforce and a formal letter had arrived saying that they were prepared to invest a vast sum. Tom was on cloud nine and only too happy to collude with Claire's contrived mood that everything in the garden was lovely. Dinner was a cheerful affair as they discussed what the investment would mean for the business and their employees – although, for them, it meant that they would have to cancel their planned short trip to Venice as the Chinese wanted to come back that particular week. Claire was disappointed. She had been looking forward to getting away with just Tom for company. However newspapers and television were ignored that evening, and life appeared to settle momentarily into its old routine.

***

Perhaps it was that extra glass of wine, or was it glasses, Claire couldn't remember, that wouldn't let her drift off to sleep. Tom was lying facing her; little puffs of air fanning her face as he quietly snored beside her. She extricated herself carefully from his encircling arm and rolled him over, hoping the snoring would stop. It didn't normally bother her; she was sure she snored too at times, but tonight it did bother her. It looked as if Tom was sleeping the sleep of the just, or whatever that old saying was, but she wasn't or couldn't. The excess of wine had lubricated her conscience, rather than jamming it and it was skidding about all over the place.

She settled herself on her back and gave in to the thoughts about Charlotte that she had managed to hold at bay for the last few hours. She mentally reviewed what she knew, or what she had been told by the papers and television that day. So, Charlotte had been found, fully clothed, in a relatively new, but dirty, sleeping bag, with a dolly tucked under one arm, and with no signs of trauma. That was good. Perhaps she hadn't been hurt. Perhaps she'd died by accident. But a child just doesn't die. She hadn't been ill, and her Mum had said that she didn't have any pre-existing conditions that could have caused her sudden death. So she had to have been killed. How? The police were not saying anything useful. They just said that there had to be a post mortem and then perhaps they'd know more. She was surprised by the implication that the post mortem hadn't yet been done; she was sure it must have been, so why weren't they releasing the details? After all they had announced the funeral date so they must know the cause of death. What were they hiding?

Claire's recent dealings with the police had left her with a very poor opinion of them, which in clearer moments she knew was a bit unfair, but she did wish she knew more. No doubt they could trace the sleeping bag, and the dolly too if they got any help from the public. Someone must know something. The police thought that more than one person was involved but they didn't say why they thought that. They also believed that someone might have seen Charlotte's body being taken to the spinney, or at least a car parked in that area. The road wasn't used much but cyclists were known to use it as a short cut, and the local running club often used it for practice runs. So they were all to be interviewed despite the club secretary saying no one knew anything. That wasn't really very helpful as no one yet had said when they thought Charlotte had died, or when she had been put in her tepee. The police were crawling all over Sir John's farm, scaring his cows he said, and the cow man had had to put up with endless questions about why he hadn't noticed the tepee before considering the smell that came from it, which, someone said, meant Charlotte had been dead for some time. The cow man was upset by the tone of the questions; he thought they were blaming him for not finding her before. He got his own back on one reporter by shovelling a spadeful of cow manure under her nose and said that if she had to live with that smell morning noon and night she might not have noticed the smell from a spinney across the other side of the field. Claire had felt like saying Hurray – one up to common sense, but then the cow man admitted that he had previously said that he had gone across the field to get the reluctant cow, so why hadn't he smelt the smell then he was asked. He didn't have an answer for that, poor chap, and the reporter had smirked as if she had won the argument. The reporter, however, failed to point out that the cowman had told Sir John about the tepee on the day he noticed it and Charlotte was found the following day so he couldn't be blamed for anything. The inanity of the questioning led Claire to wonder how soon it would be before they blamed the cow for not standing her ground until the tepee was investigated.

If Charlotte had been dead for some time what did that mean? Days, a week, or what? Claire was used to dead bodies, but someone dying in a hospital was not quite the same as someone dying and being left out in the open. Only once had she seen a body that had started to putrefy and that was when she had had cause to go to the mortuary for something. Why, she couldn't remember. But it wasn't a pleasant sight, or smell – although she remembered that fans were blasting cold air around the room, which had helped. The thought of Charlotte's little body with maggots crawling all over it made her feel sick. What it must have done to her father when he had to identify her; what a ghastly thing to have to do. She hoped Anne hadn't gone in with him. She hoped she had resisted the chance to see her child one last time, but from her distraught state shown on the television Claire felt she might have done.

So, what had she learned? Nothing really. Except that someone had cared enough to find a dolly to put in the sleeping bag with her. Or perhaps they had used a doll to lure her into the car, but that came back to the idea that an eight year old didn't play with dolls. And the doll would have had to have been one of hers, or one she recognized for that to work. Perhaps the killers, as Claire now thought of them – not a him or a her, but them, didn't know enough about children to know at what age dolls were playthings.

Round and round her thoughts skid until she finally dropped into an intermittent restless sleep, more the fault of her troubling thoughts than the wine. She dreamt about a dolly she had given Francesca soon after she had met her. It had had a lovely set of pink clothes, even down to matching pants and vest. And Francesca had immediately pulled off the pants to see if the dolly would do a wee in the potty for her, and was most indignant when it didn't. It must have been round about the time that Aunt Lou had been attempting to potty train Francesca. Those were the days when Francesca thought the world of Claire. She had been such a lovely child, and it had made her childlessness almost bearable.

Then it all changed.

Claire gave up on her efforts to sleep and allowed the memory of that awful period in their lives to surface yet again, and like every other time she wondered whether she should or could have handled things differently. Could she have prevented Francesca from changing from a happy-go-lucky youngster into a sullen, monosyllabic monster? Claire shifted uncomfortably as the details reappeared but, she had to admit, she had been pretty awful at that age too, so perhaps it was a period all teenagers went through. Maybe Jocelyn would have handled things better. Is there a difference between mothers and step-mothers when it comes to teenage angst, she wondered? Of course there is, she told herself sharply, remembering the verbal battering she got from Francesca at the time. Step-mothers were wicked; dead mothers were saints. But Jocelyn was no saint according to Tom.

Claire wondered sometimes whether Tom deliberately down played his relationship with his first wife just to make Claire feel good. The way he explained it, and she had not verified his side of the story with anyone else, he had been tricked into marriage. They had been students together, and Jocelyn had had a reputation of sleeping around, yet she managed to convince Tom that the child she was carrying was his. The dates seem to match so he had done the honourable thing and offered to marry her, hoping against hope that she'd say no. Unfortunately she very happily said yes. He was later to find out, after the registry office wedding, and her so-called miscarriage, that her intention all along was to get Tom. She had been facing the prospect of failing her degree whilst he was on line for a first, and she didn't like the idea of having to find a job. Snaring Tom was therefore a better alternative. Even though at that time Tom's plans for his subsequent business were embryonic, Jocelyn had noted the affluent lifestyle Tom's father had, and had hoped that he would fund them. He didn't. He strongly disapproved of Tom's decision and had turned his back on the pair of them.

Jocelyn went on to have Francesca in the second year of their marriage, and, as far as Tom was concerned, that was the only decent thing she did. And when she was killed driving home from a drunken night out with friends he wasn't that unhappy. Having already spent a lot of time caring for Francesca, doing it full time he didn't consider much of a problem. Also his father came back into his life and Aunt Lou was always there ready to help, so life was fairly stable – until he met me.

Claire's thoughts happily remembered that period of their lives. She had had one or two boyfriends but had never seriously thought about marriage. She was essentially a loner, quite happy with her own company after work. Tom was something of a loner too because his college friends had fallen by the wayside after his abrupt marriage, and with a small child in tow, he lacked the time and the inclination to socialize like other young men. However they had clicked immediately. The party they had gone to that night was the start of their long and happy relationship.

***

About the same time

Dazzer rarely looked at the TV news and even more rarely looked at a newspaper, unless it was for the racing results, so it was just by chance that he saw a picture of a doll on the TV that looked vaguely familiar.

'Hey, Chell' he yelled, loud enough for Michelle to hear him in the kitchen, 'where's Shannon's doll?'

'What?' she said, as she came into the living room, wiping her hands on the dish cloth.

'Where's Shannon's doll?'

'I don't know, why?' she replied, backing out of the room again.

'Come back here. I fucking asked you a question. Where is it?' As he spoke he got up and followed Michelle into the kitchen. He grabbed her arm and swung her away from the sink, causing her to lose her balance and fall. He bent towards her with his arm outstretched as if he was going to slap her, but she managed to scrabble away from him on all fours, just before he raised his arm again to have another try.

'Where the fucking hell is the doll?' he yelled again.

By now Michelle had got her back to the wall and her knees drawn up tightly in front. She replied quietly from behind her hands, which were up protecting her face, 'You know perfectly well where Shannon's doll is.'

Darren looked down at her, his hands now loosely by his side, and his reddened face slowing returning to its usual pasty colour.

'You bloody fool Chell. Now the cops have got it. What were you thinking?'

'She needed it, Dazzer. She looked so lonely, and she did like the dolly so much.'

'But the cops have got it. 'S'posing they find it's our Shannon's? They'll be after us.'

'How can they know that? Lots of kiddies have dolls like that.'

'But Ma made the clothes, didn't she. 'S'posing she sees the picture on the telly? She'll know it's us, and s'posing she tells the coppers?'

'Course she won't. She doesn't know we're out.' Michelle scrambled to her feet and took a menacing step towards Darren. 'She doesn't, does she?'

Darren backed away, frightened now that Michelle had got the upper hand. 'No, no. Not really.'

'What do you mean 'not really'? She either does or she doesn't.'

'Well, I saw her coming out of the hospital, with Aunt Winnie, but I don't think she saw me.'

'Did she see you, Dazzer?'

'I don't think so.' He shuffled his feet and flapped his hands uselessly, looking embarrassed.

'Dazzer, tell me. I have to know. If she knows we have to make a plan.'

'Aunt Winnie saw me and waved, but I dodged behind a car.'

'What happened then?'

'I dunno.' Michelle gave him a look. The sort of look she often gave him when she was mad. He edged further away from her, feeling for the door frame behind him. 'I ran Chell, so I don't know what happened', and with that he escaped and a few moments later Michelle heard the front door slam shut.

Michelle knew they were in trouble. She had known from the moment she put the dolly in the sleeping bag with Charlotte. She just knew at the time that it was the right thing to do. But what now? She had watched all the news items about Charlotte but hadn't discussed them with Darren, and when they made such a big thing about the doll she guessed the police had found something significant about it. It couldn't be the clothes. Lots of grannies made clothes for dolls. It had had home knitted things on when she'd got it from a charity shop. Shannon had loved that doll; maybe because she didn't really have any other toys. There was never money for toys. There was never enough money for anything much.

As Michelle stood there, once more at the sink, she wondered whether Ma would split on them or not. Would she guess they had something to do with Charlotte? She suspected that she might - there were no flies on Ma, and she had loved Shannon. Ma didn't like her though, she thought she was a bad influence on her precious son, but it was Darren that was the bad influence; he was the one who had got her into trouble. She hadn't got a Mum or Dad to worry about her, like Ma worried about Darren, and no matter what Darren said she was sure he would have been to see her, especially since he'd seen her come out of the hospital. He'd want to know why she was there. Probably something to do with the ulcers on Aunt Winnie's leg, but Darren wouldn't think of that. He'd think there was something wrong with his Ma.

'Legs' Michelle suddenly exclaimed at her reflection in the kitchen window. 'That's what it is. It's the doll's legs! I bet it is.' She thumped the edge of the sink repeatedly as she talked to herself. How many dolls have their legs mended with Post Office red elastic bands? That's why the cops made such a thing about what sort of doll it was. They'd specifically said the arms and legs were hooked onto elastic inside the body. And Ma would remember the red elastic bands.

On one of her good days Michelle had taken Shannon to see Ma. Ma had sent a message to say that she had something for Shannon, she hadn't said what, and Michelle was hoping it was something useful like new shoes. But it wasn't. It was a new set of clothes for the doll, so Michelle was the only one disappointed. Then in her haste to strip one lot of clothes off and to put the new ones on Shannon had wrenched a leg out of its socket and the old elastic had snapped. There had been a moment of shocked silence as Shannon had looked in disbelief at the leg in one hand and her dolly in the other, before she had let rip. She had been almost hysterical – and many times in the last few years Michelle had been able bring to mind those screams, and remember how useless she had felt.

While Ma had tried to comfort Shannon Michelle had looked around for something to mend the leg with, and it was several of the dropped red rubber bands, that Ma had collected from the pavement on her walk to the shops, that Michelle had used. It had been very fiddly trying to get the bands onto the hook fixed inside the doll's body, but eventually she'd done it and the leg looked as good as knew.

Chapter 8

Thinking about it later Claire couldn't decide when it came to her that she was definitely the last person to see Charlotte alive, and that as a result of her delay in going to the police she could be accused of being responsible for her death. The first intimation that anyone else had made that unexpected connection was on the day of Charlotte's funeral.

Watching an extended version of the local news on television Claire saw that it was a huge affair. Flowers galore. Hordes of people getting in on the act, wanting to be seen on the television. Giles and Anne Alsopp almost swamped by the crowds. It was all so undignified. The church was small and somehow the vicar had managed to keep the television and press cameras out, so for a short time the family could grieve in peace. It looked, from where Claire was sitting, as if the vicar was also vetting those that got admitted to the church. He knew his congregation, and those that were there just for show. Local dignitaries were let in, plus what looked like senior police officers, and Claire noticed several other ranks mingling with the crowd. She wondered whether they would see or hear anything useful. When the service started the faltering hymn singing within the church was swallowed up by the robust sound of the people outside the church joining in. The service was relayed to the crowds but the eulogy by the vicar was interrupted by people clapping when he made any reference to finding Charlotte's killer, and with hisses and boos from some when he asked God's forgiveness on the killer. Claire was ashamed of her fellow human beings.

After the service she briefly saw the white faces of Giles and Anne as they were bundled into the lead car, followed by the hearse, strewn with flowers thrown at it as it moved away from the church. The television camera panned round the crowd before settling on the hearse again as it made its way to the crematorium for a private ceremony. The voice over told the viewers that a short service had been arranged in Charlotte's school for her friends so that they could say their goodbyes privately. Someone had made a good decision there, thought Claire. A pity the Alsopps hadn't been offered that same privacy.

That had all happened in the morning before Claire went to work. She only had the one clinic that day. She had swept up a pile of mail from the hall floor and just dumped it on the kitchen table, meaning to look at it later, but it was only when she got home that she remembered it. Tom had got home ahead of her and he was sifting through the pile when she joined him in the kitchen.

'Anything of interest, Tom?'

'Doesn't appear to be. That's your pile there.' She smiled as she realized that in her pile was all the advertising stuff the postmen had to deliver these days. Why couldn't Tom put it in the recycling bin like she did instead of putting it with her mail – she was no more likely to look at it than him. About to sweep the lot into the bin she noticed a white envelope amongst the free offers. It wasn't the usual special insurance or solar power offer, although the envelopes did have similarities, it just had her name written in capitals, no address, no return address, no postmark and no stamp.

'This looks odd', she said as she waved the envelope to get Tom's attention.

'Why?' He briefly looked up from a trade journal as he replied, but it was obvious his attention was elsewhere.

'This doesn't look as if it came with the post.'

'So? Just open it,' said Tom as his eyes and interest went back to his reading.

Claire pushed her thumb under the flap and tore the envelope open. Pulling out the enclosed sheet of paper and flicking it open there was an odd sound. Odd enough for Tom to notice. He looked up. Dropping his journal he moved quickly towards Claire and caught her just before she sank to the floor, the letter fluttering after her. He swung a chair away from the table and propped her on it.

'What is it? What's happened? Are you ill? Claire talk to me.' He took her cold hands in his and anxiously rubbed them. 'Claire, what is it?'

Her large frightened eyes stared vacantly at him for her for a few moments, then she shook her head slowly and blinked. 'The letter' she said, 'the letter.'

Tom let go one hand and bent down and picked up the letter. The words YOU KILLED CHARLOTTE YOU BITCH were stuck haphazardly across the page; the letters cut from a newspaper. Tom's first unbidden muttered words, for which he was later ashamed, were 'how trite.'

Tom flicked the letter onto the table and picked up Claire's hand again. He twisted an ankle around another chair leg and manoeuvred the chair into position so that he could sit opposite Claire. They sat looking at each other. Claire slowly withdrew her hands and made a move towards the letter.

'Don't' Tom yelped. 'Don't touch it. Leave it for the police.' He got up hurriedly and started shuffling cutlery around in a drawer.

'What are you looking for Tom?

'I'm looking for those prong things you using for turning things when you're cooking.'

'Well, you won't find them there. Anyway what do you want them for?'

'I need a clean poly bag too to put the letter in for the police. We've got to preserve fingerprints.'

'Don't be daft Tom. There must be hundreds of prints on it. Another lot of ours is not going to make any difference.'

'Maybe not but we must try.' As he talked he pulled other drawers open trying to find what he wanted, until Claire joined him and found the prong things, as he called them. She got a clean poly bag from a roll and Tom picked up the letter gingerly with the prongs, trying not to squeeze the ends together too tightly, and dropped the letter into the bag.

The movement had brought a little colour back into Claire's face, although she still looked very shaken. Although Tom's knowledge of the whereabouts of kitchen cutlery was limited he did know where the brandy bottle was, so it wasn't long before a large glass of it was placed in Claire's hand. 'Drink that, darling. It may help.' He snapped the cap back on the bottle after pouring himself a generous measure to match Claire's.

'If we are going to the police should we be drinking' she asked with a wry smile.

'They can come to us. I'm not going out and leaving you, and you're not in a fit state to go anywhere. Drink up while I phone them.'

Tom sat down and pulled the phone towards him. 'We should dial 999, shouldn't we? It is an emergency don't you think?' But without waiting for an answer Claire watched him dial 999.

After going through the rigmarole of 'which service' Tom was put through to a human voice. A human voice that was totally unimpressed with what Tom counted as an emergency and without further argument he found himself shifted to an answer phone service that dealt with mundane complaints. He slammed the phone down, to cut the connection, and immediately picked it up again and redialled. Getting through to the police again he started to tell them what he thought about their emergency classifications, his voice getting higher and faster after each response that Claire couldn't hear. As the phone was slammed down for the second time Claire put her hand over Tom's to stop him possibly dialling for a third time.

'Stop it Tom. Calm down. You have to accept that to them it isn't an emergency. They must get lots of people complaining about abusive mail. What's one more bit to them? Leave it for now. Tomorrow we'll see if we can find someone that is dealing with Charlotte's case and ask them what we should do about it.'

'How can you be so calm about it? I'm livid! It is an emergency for any normal person!'

'I'm not calm Tom. I feel sick. I'm...' She got no further. Tom had put his arms around in a hug so fierce she could hardly breathe let alone talk. 'I'm sorry, I'm sorry, I'm sorry' he kept repeating, 'I'm so angry, and I don't know what to do.' He loosened his grip enough for Claire to bring her hands up and cup his face. 'I love you, darling Tom. I love you for caring so much. But there's nothing we can do now. So let's forget it.' She brushed her lips against his before resting her head on his chest. He sighed, kissed the top of her head and released her.

'Dinner time then?'

'Good idea.'

***

After they had picked at what would normally be considered an excellent dinner Claire brought up the subject of the letter again.

'Tom', she asked quietly, 'what did you mean when you said 'how trite'? When you first saw the letter.'

Tom reddened slightly. 'I'm sorry. That was really thoughtless.' He paused. 'I don't know why I said it, except my first instinct was that it was trite. It's hard to explain. Why did I notice how it was written before seeing what was written? I don't know. It all seemed a little theatrical, as if it couldn't really be happening to us. Like it was a joke, somehow. The hackneyed way of doing it, like they do in old films. Just for a second I couldn't believe it was for real.' Too embarrassed to look at Claire while speaking, he now turned to her and apologized again.

'I agree about the theatricality of it,' she began, 'but nonetheless it is true. Maybe I am not in actual fact a bitch, but I did kill her.' She made a shushing sound towards Tom as he tried to interrupt. 'I saw her, I told the police, but too late. I should have told them that same day. I know we don't know officially that she died the day I saw her but the press are saying that she died soon after being taken.'

'No Claire, you can't believe that. Lots of people said they saw her, both before and after you. You are not responsible.'

'I think I am Tom. I do really think I am. And now someone else does too.'

'A nutter, Claire. Just a nutter.'

'Regardless of whether he or she is a nutter, if they think that, how long before others do?'

'Oh Claire, you mustn't think like that. You're not responsible. You're not.' Tom was pleading with her to agree with him, but she couldn't. Later they got onto the subject of who had possibly composed it. Who did they know who would take the trouble to cut out the letters? Who hated her enough to do it? Why? They even studied the letters to see if they could work out which newspaper they came from. A daft idea, but it led them to lightening the atmosphere a bit by joking that they were definitely from a tabloid. No one who read a broadsheet would bother cutting out letters. They would write it and probably sign it!

As Claire was trying to sleep that night the same questions were still going round and round in her mind. She was trying very, very hard not to let the name Francesca come to the fore.

Chapter 9

As Claire expected the police were not interested in her poison pen letter. She was relieved in a way because she didn't want to draw attention to herself. They thought it was a prank. Someone out to upset her; it isn't threatening you, they said. Tom was far from happy about their reaction, and by the time Claire felt his 'what do I pay my taxes for' speech coming on she was guiding him out the door of the police station. But Tom wasn't to be dissuaded and insisted on speaking to the senior policeman that had come to the house to apologize about the statements being printed. The desk sergeant said that that particular officer worked from another police station so he suggested that they went there to find him, and as he said this he came out from behind the counter and politely held the door open for them to leave.

Claire was embarrassed by Tom's insistence, but in her heart of hearts she knew that she would have done the same if it had been Tom who had received the letter. He was just so angry because she was hurting and he couldn't make it better. She took his hand as they went back to the car.

'Let's not bother going to the other police station. Can we just forget it?'

'I'm sorry Claire. I feel I'm letting you down.'

'You're not Tom. You're not letting me down at all. Look, you take the car and go on to work, and I'll go and see that Aunt Lou is OK before going to work.'

Claire watched the car pull out of the car park, and instead of going to see Aunt Lou, she went straight back home to check the morning mail. Nothing. Well, nothing sinister. She dropped the mail on the kitchen table, put the kettle on, and then pulled the phone towards her. She decided that she'd better have a quick word with Aunt Lou in case Tom asked about her, but surprisingly there was no answer. Claire thought that odd. Aunt Lou should have been there waiting for Mrs Donaldson to arrive. She never went out before Mrs D was there. Worried, Claire made her coffee. She checked the time – in twenty minutes Mrs D would be there, so she'd try the phone again then.

It was a very long twenty minutes, and the phone rang for a very long time before a breathless Aunt Lou answered it.

'Hello dear. What's up? You don't usually phone me at this time.'

'Nothing's up Aunt Lou,' Claire snapped back, her relief making her tetchy. 'I just wanted to see how you were,' she continued in a calmer tone, 'you sound breathless.'

'So would you be if you had to race to open the door and get to the phone before it stopped ringing!'

'I'm sorry, Aunt Lou. Where have you been so bright and early then?'

'It's a long story,' she sighed, 'but what it boils down to is that new boyfriend of Fran's has dropped her in favour of someone else. It seems she is no use to him anymore.'

'That's an odd phrase – 'no use to him anymore'. What was he using her for?'

'I don't know dear. That's just what she said. But I must admit I thought it odd too, but she was in such a state I forgot to ask her what she meant.'

'So you were at her flat, were you?'

'Yes. She rang in tears, having been up half the night, so I thought I ought to go and see her.'

'That's kind of you Aunt Lou. Has she gone to work now?'

'No. Much against my better judgment she called in sick. So I came home. I disagree with people doing that. There was no reason for her not to go to work. She'd probably be better off going, take her mind off him.'

Claire was about to say something else but she heard the door bell ring at Aunt Lou's so she knew that once Mrs Donaldson arrived Aunt Lou would probably want to gossip to her about the way young people behave today!

'Oh, there's Mrs D, so I'll have to go dear.' And the phone went down with a clatter.

***

The phrase 'no use to him' continued to haunt Claire for the rest of the day, and it made her a bit absent minded at work. Having sent someone off for a blood test instead of an x-ray she realized that she'd better pull herself together otherwise her reputation for efficiency would go down the drain.

The young clinic receptionists noticed her pre-occupation and gossiped among themselves about the possible reason, and if Claire had been on the ball she might have noticed that the clinic atmosphere was not as it usually was. As most patients were frequent visitors to the clinic there was usually a buzz of light hearted chatter about symptoms and waiting times and such like, but today, on the whole, there wasn't any. The rustling of the local paper, as it was handed around was the predominant sound with muttered asides as it went from patient to patient.

Surprisingly Claire didn't notice – to begin with anyway. It was only when old Mrs Barnard shook off her helping hand as she went to help her rise off her seat that she realized that something was wrong. Mrs Barnard was normally a delightful old lady, chatty and cheerful despite her medical condition, and Claire had always had the impression that her visit to the clinic was an important social occasion. So much so that Claire, as the boss, always made a point of being available personally to take her in to see the doctor; and Mrs Barnard played her part to the hilt. She would let Claire help her collect up her belongings and find her stick, and then as they processed from the waiting room to the doctor's office she would tell Claire all about what had been going on in her life since the last visit. But today was different. She ignored Claire and asked another patient very pointedly for help. Claire was puzzled and, she had to admit, a bit hurt, but she stepped back and let Mrs Barnard do her own thing.

Straightening a few chairs and collecting up some stray magazines gave Claire the opportunity to do something while she considered the reason for the snub. She didn't notice the newspaper that had been doing the rounds of the patients. As she stacked the magazines tidily on a nearby table she covertly glanced around at the dwindling number of patients and was aware of a smirk on the faces of the two men who had been either side of Mrs Barnard. She knew both of them of old; one in particular. She and Gerald Pontin had never got on because he saw no reason to give up eating junk food. She had spent more time than she cared to remember trying to persuade him that a healthy diet would do more to help his condition than anything they did in the clinic, but he wasn't convinced. According to him the NHS was there to cure him, not dictate what he ate. The other chap, as far as Claire was concerned, was a malingerer; the type of patient she had no time for.

For the rest of her working day Claire was aware of an atmosphere. She couldn't put her finger on it. She just knew something wasn't right - a bit like Francesca's comment.

***

Tom was later than usual so Claire was well into the dinner preparation by the time he got home. She poured him a glass of wine as she asked how his day had gone.

'I called in on Fran on the way home.'

Claire couldn't quite describe it as a deathly hush the moment's silence that followed Tom's remark but she did experience a slight feeling of apprehension.

'Is she OK now?' Claire asked, as she brought her second hand up to steady her wine glass. 'Aunt Lou was out at her flat when I called this morning.' Claire was conscious of having left out the 'in' after 'called' but hoped that Tom wouldn't notice. 'I phoned Aunt Lou when I got home and she told me about the boyfriend trouble.'

'Well she's as OK as any girl is likely to be after she has found that her boyfriend has been two-timing her.'

'Aunt Lou didn't say anything about that. She just said he'd ditched her.'

'Well that's what she told me. She rang me at work and went on and on about this other woman. Ally, I think her name is, and apparently she's all Fran isn't, according to Gareth.'

'Did Francesca say anything about Gareth using her?'

'No. Why? What do you mean?'

'Aunt Lou said that Francesca had said that she was 'no use to him' anymore. I thought it seemed an odd thing to say.'

'Why? Sounds to me like an offhand way of saying it was all over.'

'Perhaps.'

'Perhaps what Claire? You're surely not imagining what I think you're imagining.'

'What do you think I'm imagining?'

Tom gave her a look. The sort of look she'd often had in the past when they were about to argue about Francesca. 'Let's not go there Claire. Fran's been ditched by a worm. End of story.'

Claire raised her glass to Tom and with a fake smile said, 'Cheers!'

***

Dinner was a quiet affair but by the time they had got to their coffee it appeared that both had forgotten the earlier almost disagreement. This veneer of peace and harmony though didn't last long. Claire finally found the reason for the unpleasant atmosphere at work.

The local weekly paper could usually be depended on to fill in all the gaps in local knowledge - from the numerous court cases where the town's toe rags were given a pat on the head and told to behave, to the listings for all the flower shows, concerts, cinema etc. It was amazing what some of her neighbours, and patients, got up to in their other lives. The letters page was always good value as the so-called great and the good ranted and raved about various local authority plans, and anything else that had caught their eye that week. The same names occurred time and time again so Claire could almost predict the subject of the letter just by looking at the name and address at the end. She was sure some of them were being deliberately provocative just to cause a reaction. The current *bête noire* was the long running saga about the proposed incinerator for the county's waste. The nimbys were having a field day.

As she flicked the letter pages over she saw a name that certainly provoked a reaction in her. It jumped out at her so unexpectedly that it felt as if she had been physically hit. Her hands shook as she straightened the page to see what Gareth Jones had to say. It was quite a long article, densely typed, no pictures, headed with the title:

WHO ARE THESE PEOPLE?

Who are these people who report sightings of missing children? Why do they imagine they have seen them? What's missing in their lives that they have to draw attention to themselves? Do they get a thrill from visiting a police station? Does it make them feel important? Do they tell their friends?

Several years ago some of you may remember the two little girls who went missing in the Midlands. Before they were found lots of people told the police that they had seen them, giving the parents false hope that they were alive and well. As we all know these were imagined sightings. Now, here in our town, we have had a similar occurrence. One of our children went missing and true to form a stream of misguided people contacted the police with their versions of reality, wasting their time, which could have been better spent searching for Charlotte ...

Claire didn't need to know any more of his unhelpful prejudiced views so she ran her eye down the rest of the article to find the inevitable – yes, there it was, her name.

... Claire Harrison, a nursing sister at our own hospital. A person we would expect to know right from wrong. The sort of person we would expect to do the right thing, but no, she had more important things to do than save the life of a small girl. She didn't think it necessary to go to the police when she saw Charlotte. She waited 24 hours, and in that 24 hours Charlotte was killed...

Claire's trembling hands dropped the paper. As it slithered to the floor she slumped back into the chair and closed her eyes. She felt faint, nauseous, and angry – very, very angry. There was no doubt in her mind about how this Gareth Jones had got his information, and having got his information he had dumped his informant – or, at least, one of his informants. There was also the small matter of the leaked statements. Perhaps he had a pet policewoman who had provided those.

She remained in the chair until she felt in control again; until she could think rationally about her situation. She couldn't have got up even if she had wanted to. Her legs wouldn't have supported her. She heard Tom pour another cup of coffee and she hoped that he was sufficiently involved with his paperwork to ignore her. She needed time to think about what to say, or what not to say, about her suspicions of Francesca's involvement. She also wanted to think about the last words she had read: *in that 24 hours Charlotte was killed*. What did Gareth Jones know?

Claire picked up the paper again. She straightened it out and folded it to the front page. Nothing on the front page, but on the second page, up in the corner next to an article about a schoolboy winning an innovation prize was a small headline: 'She was Suffocated'. Claire swiftly read the bare details of Charlotte's post mortem. In police jargon it said that she had been suffocated soon after she had been abducted. That was all. Nothing more. No elaboration or anything. Had she missed an earlier report – it wasn't unusual for the paper to do two reports on the same story, but surely she would have seen anything that was related to Charlotte. But she hadn't, she was sure. Claire paused - there was just that faint niggle – after all she had missed this report. Could she have missed another? She looked at the front page again before scouring all the other news pages. There was nothing. Perhaps there had been something in last week's paper? It was all very odd. The fact that the funeral had gone ahead before the post mortem results had been made public was unusual. Perhaps it wasn't. She didn't usually take much notice of news items relating to deaths and post mortems if she didn't know the people involved. Who did? Perhaps few details were released. Perhaps it was the norm. The 'perhapses' were coming thick and fast but she was getting nowhere.

Her jumbled thoughts were interrupted by a call from Tom.

'Claire, have you heard the phone recently?'

Claire brought her mind back to the here and now. 'It did ring a few times while we were having supper, I think. Why?'

'Well it seems to have a mass of messages. The answer phone is full.'

'Who are they from? Have you listened to them? Put them on the speaker. I'll come and hear them.'

Tom pressed a series of buttons and a disembodied voice related the message number, the phone number of the caller and the time: 'Mrs Harrison, this is Gareth Jones. I was wondering if you have any comment to make on the article in today's paper. I'll try again later.'

There was a stunned momentary silence before that same mechanical voice repeated the details for 'message number two', and another person was asking for comments on Gareth Jones's article. Tom and Claire looked at each other as further similar messages were relayed, until the tape ran out. The tape ending clunk broke their silence.

'What on earth are they on about? What article are they talking about? What's going on Claire? What...?'

Claire put her hand up to forestall the next question and went back to the sitting room to collect the paper.

She opened it to Jones' article and silently handed it to Tom and told him to read it. She took the chair opposite him and watched him as he read it.

***

Thinking about it later, as she lay beside a sleeping Tom in their bed that night, Claire wondered what she had expected him to say or do at that point. Certainly not what he had done. He had got up from his chair, come round to her side of the table and put his hands out to pull her to her feet, and then hugged her to him. A hug so tight she could hardly breathe. It was only when she had felt his tears on the side of her face join hers that she had gently disengaged herself from his encircling arms.

They had gone into the sitting room, after taking the phone off the hook, and for the next hour or so gone over every aspect of the article, including her suspicions about Gareth Jones' source. Tom had gone very quiet when she had broached the subject, but his arm, which had been resting on her shoulders, had tightened around her before he had said the he now believed that perhaps she was right.

She had told him about her experience in the clinic that day, and he had tried to comfort her for all the pain she had gone through since that fateful day of the sighting. They had made no decisions about what to do, although Tom had wanted to make an announcement about how he was the one at fault. He was the one who had delayed her going to the police, and so he was the one responsible for Charlotte's death, not her. He had been selfish, he said, because he was the one who had insisted they go home. She thought it would just make matters worse if he tried to extricate her from the mess, and that they should just say nothing, but she didn't feel that Tom was going to go along with her suggestion this time. After his initial tears at her hurt he had then been very angry about it. But what could they do? Until the police found out what had happened they were powerless to refute the allegations. And, on what they knew, it now seems that the allegations were facts. The post mortem results testified to that. Charlotte must have died around the time she visited the house, whether they had Charlotte in the house then or not. She must have triggered her death somehow – if she did in fact glimpse Charlotte at Atherstone when she said she did.

That was a pointless road to go down. She did see Charlotte. There was no getting away from it. But in the deepest darkest recesses of her mind, if she was being really truthful with herself, she did have a slight feeling of resentment about Charlotte's death being judged all her fault. She was ashamed of herself for letting that perception take root in her consciousness and tried hard to suppress it, but now it was loose the damage was done. Thoughts like that can't be un-thought.

She briefly let herself imagine a scenario in which Tom did announce it was his fault but she didn't think it would make any difference - most people would believe he was trying to protect her. He had a good reputation in the town, and it was important to her that he kept it. She liked to think that overall she was well thought of too, but if Tom spoke out in her defence she felt sure Francesca would try something. It was difficult to imagine how she could make matters worse than she had already but she guessed she would find a way.

Chapter 10

Claire was just about to leave for work the following morning when the phone rang. When she picked up the receiver a male voice said: 'Sister Harrison?'

'Yes.'

'It's Cyril.'

'Cyril?'

There was a laugh. 'The Man' he said.

'Oh Cyril. I'm sorry. I didn't recognize your voice.' She'd never heard anyone use his Christian name before. He was always known as 'the Man', partly because he was the head porter and perhaps because his surname, Mann, leant itself to the nickname.

'That's OK. I just wanted to warn you that there are reporters after you at the main entrance, and I suspect there are some at the back too. Can I suggest that you drive in the side entrance and park your car in my space – it's marked 'Head Porter', by the Blood Transfusion base, and come in the porters entrance? I'll be waiting to let you in.'

'That's kind of you Cyril. I'm just about to leave, so I'll be with you in about twenty minutes.'

As Claire put the phone down her mind was racing. As she got her car out of the garage she looked round furtively to see if anyone was watching the house. She couldn't see anyone, but who knows? Perhaps they were chatting up her neighbours and watching from their houses. She hadn't asked Cyril any questions so presumably he had seen, or been shown, the article in the paper. He was a good sort. She had always had time for him and respected his position. Perhaps he was returning the compliment. But how did they know her shifts? Who told them? And what did they want? She couldn't tell them anything. What did they expect her to say? 'Yes I was responsible for Charlotte's death,' or something like that. Well she certainly wasn't going to say that. In fact she wasn't going to say anything. But would they invade Out-Patients? What then?

These thoughts continued to whirl round her head as she drove to the hospital. She remembered at the last minute to go the way Cyril had suggested and found his space without any difficulty. He let her in and showed her how to get to Out- Patients from there. She had never had cause to be in that part of the hospital before so was a bit disorientated. He didn't ask her any questions for which Claire was grateful, because her mind was now set on what she would find when she got to her department.

She was usually the first person in Out-Patients. She liked to be there in plenty of time to check that the rooms and cubicles had all been cleaned, before the equipment for each clinic was set out. Although she was overall head of the department, when she was on duty she tended to work in one clinic, and only get called away to another if necessary. She checked the staff rota and noted that they had their full complement. That didn't often happen. A shortage anywhere else in the hospital meant that her staff were poached first; the theory being that a shortfall in her department didn't matter as much as elsewhere. A theory she had absolutely no time for, but she could do nothing about it.

As she went from room to room she heard the receptionists come in and settle down at their computers, and the rest of the staff followed. No sign of any strangers thankfully. She was greeted as she normally was and she felt the tension lift a little. It surprised her that nothing was said about the reporters outside. Perhaps 'The Man' had exaggerated. Perhaps there weren't that many. Perhaps it was just the odd one, and everyone knew that reporters often hung around hospitals trying to find dirt on the great and the good – but that was usually A&E, not the front and back entrances.

By the time the patients started filling the waiting chairs she had exhausted all her suppositions and thought that maybe she was safe until the end of the day.

The first couple of hours of her working day were always the busiest so Claire didn't notice the young man sitting on the back row of her geriatric clinic waiting area. If he had registered she might have thought he had come in with a parent or relative. But he didn't move from his seat, which he certainly would have done if he was in the clinic legitimately, so when he stood up and shouted in a loud voice: 'Claire Harrison. Do you blame yourself for the death of Charlotte Alsopp?' Claire was not the only person to be shocked. He had obviously waited until the department was packed before making his presence felt.

The whole place seemed to go quiet momentarily, but as the young man made his way towards Claire, still shouting the same question at her, the excited buzz of chatter broke out all around her. People were turning in their seats, some standing up to get a better view, while others pointed her out to their neighbours. Initially Claire was frozen to the spot, but then instinct took over and she asked the nearest receptionist to call security, before turning on her heel and walking out of the room, hoping that the cause of the mayhem would follow her. He did - straight into the arms of two of their burliest security men, who had been hovering around outside at the suggestion of The Man, in case they were needed. As he was being taken away, still yelling at her, he managed to toss his card at her, with the audacious request that she call him.

She picked up the card and guessed correctly that the intruder was Gareth Jones.

She gave herself a few moments to compose herself because she knew that she had to go back and face the patients.

Straightening her shoulders she pushed the swing door open, and with her head held high, walked to the desk where the patients notes were laid out. As she was about to pick up a file she heard a quiet voice from Room 5 ask her to go and see him. Professor Andrews had heard the commotion and had seen Claire leave the room as he was saying goodbye to a patient.

'Are you alright Sister? Would you like to sit down/'

'No, I'm fine Prof'.

'Well, you don't look it. Why don't you take an early lunch break. I'm sure the others can cope.'

'No. It's better if I keep going. It will only draw attention to me if I disappear.'

'From the chatter out there I think you'll get a lot of attention if you don't.'

Claire paused before answering him again. He hadn't asked her what it was all about. Did he know? Had he seen the paper? Did he want her out of the department? Was that what he was suggesting?

'Do you think I should leave Professor Andrews?' she said pointedly.

'It's your decision Sister, but I think it may upset the smooth running of the clinic if you don't.'

'Well in that case, if you want me to go, I will.' Turning to go she saw the senior staff nurse hovering by the door. In the short time she had been out of the room obviously plans had been made. She nodded to her deputy and handed her the keys, telling her that she was going home at Professor Andrew's suggestion and so she was now in charge, an assignment she accepted with a scarcely concealed smirk.

The walk to the cloakroom had never been so long. She felt all eyes on her as she left although the noisy chatter in the clinic continued unabated. She was seething with anger, yet hurt and embarrassed. When was the last time Tony Andrews had used her formal title like that? His dismissal of her, his tone of voice, his whole attitude, was so upsetting. She was near to tears but no way was she going to let anyone see her break down.

Remembering not to go to the usual car park, she made her way to Cyril's office, to thank him. She would try and remember to call him Cyril now, since that was the name he had used on the phone to introduce himself, all those hours ago. He was on the phone when she arrived and he beckoned her in, and she realized that he was liaising with the security men who had taken hold of Gareth. Putting the phone down, he apologized for keeping her and then told her that Mr Gareth Jones had been thrown out on his ear.

Claire gave him a watery smile. 'Thank you Cyril for your help this morning, but it has been put to me that I should go home.'

'And whose suggestion was that, may I ask?'

'Professor Andrews'.'

'Oh, him. Well, let me escort you to your car. We must do what he says, mustn't we?' grinned Cyril. He got up from his chair and put a fatherly hand on her arm. 'Don't worry, my dear, it will blow over soon. Just a storm in a teacup.'

'I wish it was Cyril. I really do wish it was, but I don't think so. Somehow I think my time here is at an end. No hospital likes adverse publicity especially in the current climate.'

Nothing more was said until they reached the porters entrance. Cyril told her to stay inside until he had checked that no one was around. Then, holding the door open for her, he told her not to worry, it would all come out in the wash, and with a gentle pat on her back he went back inside.

Leaving the hospital in the middle of the morning felt strange to Claire, and she was beginning to wonder if she should have done. Professor Andrews had no right to dismiss her from the clinic. It should have been the head of Nursing Services, or whatever Miss Patricia O'Sullivan called herself now, not a member of the medical staff. But the thought of going back to argue the rights and wrongs of her dismissal was not appealing. She presumed Prof Andrews would speak to Miss O'Sullivan, or someone in her office, and tell them about the disruption of his clinic. He was bound to complain to someone as he was very much a consultant of the old school; he was the boss and the nurses were there to do his bidding, and he could be very petty if they didn't conform to his old fashioned ideas. Unfortunately Claire didn't see herself as anyone's hand maiden, and if she felt something should be said she said it. She was not a particular favourite of Miss O'Sullivan's either ever since she had spoken up in defence of one of her nurses who she felt had been accused unjustly over some paltry misdemeanour. So she quickly squashed the idea of going back; going home seemed the best thing to do, and if she was bored she could always do the ironing, she reminded herself.

She was having a quiet cup of tea at her kitchen table later, enjoying the luxury of watching Countdown, when she heard something come through the letterbox. She stiffened. Letterbox noises had begun to make her feel uncomfortable, especially ones at the wrong time, but she put her cup down carefully and went to investigate. An expensive looking white envelope was sitting on the doormat and even from quite far away she could see the black bold print on the top left hand side which said: By Hand. She guessed what it was, and she was right. It was a formal letter from Miss O'Sullivan requesting that she attend an interview with her, in her office, the following morning at 10 a.m. However, did it mean she went from her morning clinic to the office, or did she just swan into work two hours late? Was she to be carpeted for having the temerity to upset Professor Andrews, or what?

Looking at her watch she realized that there was time to catch Miss O'Sullivan's secretary, Clare; another Clare but this time without the 'i'. She would know what was going on. Clare answered the phone on the first ring and when Claire announced herself she replied that she had been waiting for her call ever since she had been instructed to get a courier to deliver the letter as soon as she had typed it.

'What have you been doing Mrs Harrison?' she continued, without any preamble. 'Old Prof Andrews was in here earlier giving our Paddy a bollocking about you. I couldn't make out what it was all about.'

'And good afternoon to you too Clare', said Claire with a smile in her voice. The bubbly voice lifted her spirits somewhat. 'How is your mother?'

'She's fine thanks. That walker you got her makes all the difference. How did you persuade the powers that be that she needed the better one?'

'I have friends in high places', she replied, 'happy to do me a favour.'

'Well, I'm very grateful, so is Mum. I'll tell her you asked after her.'

'The reason I'm ringing Clare is to ask if you know any more. Do I go into work first, or do I just go in at ten to see Miss O'Sullivan?'

'I don't know. Nothing was said to me, except type the letter and get it delivered immediately. Shall I ask?'

'Yes please, if she is still there.'

'Oh she's here alright. There's a drinks do in the board room at six and she's getting all tarted up for that. Hang on, I'll go and ask her now.'

Claire heard the phone go down with a clatter, then the chair legs being bashed against the printer table, as Clare got up and knocked on the inner office door. There was a murmur of voices in the background and then she was back, with more clattering as she retrieved the phone from the jumble that seemed to be always on her desk.

'She said you're to come here at ten, and there's no need for you to be in uniform.'

'Thank you, Clare. That's fine. I'll probably see you in the morning. Good bye.'

She put the phone down without letting Clare get another word in. She didn't want any more questions. She wanted to think about the significance of what she had said. 'No need to be in uniform'. That, coupled with the request to be there at ten, she presumed meant she would not be working tomorrow either. Was this the end? If it was, it would mean the end of her nursing career. She couldn't imagine any other hospital employing her if she was sacked. She didn't really think there were grounds to sack her, but who knows? She'd never had cause to think about that sort of thing before.

Putting the laundry away, and preparing dinner, gave her plenty of time to consider her problem from all angles, but it didn't help much. In one way she did regard herself as lucky as Tom earned a very good salary, so there was no financial need for her to work. They wouldn't lose their house, or drown in red bills, like she'd heard others had. She'd just have to find something to fill her day, and that wouldn't be difficult as volunteers were needed all over the place. But, and it was a big but, would anyone take her on once she gave her name.

***

The interview the following morning was every bit as bad as she expected, although she wasn't actually sacked. Someone must have warned Miss O'Sullivan that Claire might have a good case at an 'unfair dismissal' hearing, should she take the hospital authorities to court.

She had arrived at Miss O'Sullivan's office at ten to ten, determined not to be late, having checked with Cyril that the coast was clear before leaving home. He reported that it seemed to be so she had parked in her usual slot. But she needn't have bothered to be punctual as she was kept waiting for twenty minutes or so.

When she was finally summoned into the office Miss O'Sullivan looked up from the paperwork strewn on her desk, shuffled it together and wished Claire a 'good morning.'

She didn't ask her to sit, and it looked like a deliberate snub as the chair that normally faced the desk had been moved away. She leaned across her desk to hand Claire a sheet of paper. As Claire took it she said: 'As you can see that is a formal notice of your suspension, until the furore over your behaviour settles down.'

'What do you mean, 'my behaviour'? Claire spluttered. But her interjection was ignored and Miss O'Sullivan continued, 'but since you have been here a long time it will not be made public that you are suspended. I will announce that you are taking your holiday early. That will be all.'

Claire had never used the phrase 'gob-smacked' but that's exactly the phrase that came to mind to describe her feelings.

'That will *not* be all, Miss O'Sullivan. Explain what you mean by 'my behaviour',' and before anything else was said Claire dragged the chair from the wall to its usual position and sat herself down.

'I had a complaint from Professor Andrews. He said that you had caused havoc in his clinic yesterday. I gather it was something to do with your private life.'

'There was no 'havoc' in yesterday's clinic. A man stood up and shouted at me. That was all.'

'That is not what Professor Andrews said. He was quite distressed about the chaos you caused.'

'*I* caused? There was no chaos, no havoc, no anything, and he certainly wasn't distressed.'

'Reporters shouting accusations at my staff is distressing, and I won't have it, even if the accusations are relevant or not.'

'Do you know what I am accused of?'

'I'm not interested in gossip.'

'I have been accused of failing to report the sighting of a missing child immediately to the police, and as a result I am accused, by some, of being responsible for her death.'

'I'm not interested in what you have been accused off, or even if you are guilty or not. I cannot have disruptions in the working of my hospital. It's unprofessional.'

'I think you, Miss O'Sullivan, are being unprofessional in suspending me.'

'You may think what you like Mrs Harrison. You are fortunate that I am not sacking you. Two occasions of press intrusion relating to you are two too many. I cannot risk a third.

Good day to you.'

A discreet knock on the door followed by the entry of Clare, made Claire realize that Miss O'Sullivan must have pressed some sort of buzzer for her secretary, because she asked Clare 'Miss Williams' to 'please see Mrs Harrison out'

Claire took her time, carefully returning the chair to its place by the wall, before sweeping out of the office without another word. She told Tom later that she had swept out, and it may have looked like that to the onlookers, but in reality she felt like a wet rag. She had walked out of the office suite not daring to say anything to Clare, as she passed her, for fear of saying something she'd regret later.

She was still clutching the suspension letter when she reached the car. She recollected that at the time it was handed to her, that she had been surprised it wasn't in an envelope. Obviously done in a rush, she thought, or perhaps Miss O'Sullivan had wanted her to read it there and then – or perhaps she was just plain mean with official stationary. She looked at the letter now and apart from headings and addresses etc, there were just two lines of text. She was suspended herewith until further notice, and she could count the suspension days as her holiday entitlement. That seemed an odd way of doing things. Either she was suspended or she was on holiday. Which? If she was on holiday she'd be paid, but if she was suspended would she be paid? Something to take up with the finance department, she supposed. But it was all a bit up in the air.

She had promised Tom she would ring after the interview, but as she didn't want Tracey to know what was going on, she sent a brief text to his mobile about seeing him at lunchtime as planned.

Having foreseen the outcome of the interview their lunch was not a particularly downbeat occasion. They ate at a small Italian restaurant they liked, and while eating they discussed the pros and cons of what to do next. Tom was all in favour of getting the law involved, but Claire just wanted to leave things as they were for the time being. She felt that the hospital authorities didn't really have a leg to stand on and that she'd be reinstated in time. She decided that she'd literally take 'gardening leave' and redesign the patch at the bottom of the garden as she had always been meaning to do. So it was with lighter hearts Claire went back home and Tom to work.

Chapter 11

Claire rather enjoyed her 'gardening leave', to begin with, and the garden benefitted too. She heard nothing from the hospital, although Cyril had rung and said that he had heard about her visit to Miss O'Sullivan, and, with a chuckle, wished her a happy holiday. He said he would relay any gossip he heard, to keep her in the picture.

But not everything was something to joke about. The local paper had nearly a page full of letters the week following Gareth Jones' article. Some were conciliatory towards her, but they were in the minority. The majority were for hanging, drawing and quartering her. She didn't recognize any of the names, although some of the letters had 'name and address supplied' at the end of them, so perhaps she might have known them if they had been brave enough to let their names be published. She couldn't understand the mentality of some of the letter writers, and was surprised that one letter in particular was printed; it was so derogatory and nasty. She tried not to take it personally, but it hurt.

She found herself making excuses not to go out, and when she went shopping she went to a huge out of town Tesco's because she knew she wouldn't meet anyone who'd be likely to know her there. Aunt Lou had taken to calling in more frequently, and her lovely elderly neighbour, Dora, was on her doorstep with little queries rather more than was strictly necessary. She loved their visits and made them both very welcome, but she didn't return them. Tom was concerned about her and encouraged her to scan the holiday companies' websites to see where they should go in the summer. He wanted to reinstate their Venice trip but Claire was wary about going away in case the hospital contacted her. They didn't. Holidays were rarely taken more than two weeks at a time, so she had taken to waiting for the mail every day, just in case there were any developments. Towards the end of the second week she found herself dialling the hospital number, but always put the receiver down before the phone was answered. She hated being in such a dithery state, yet she couldn't make the decision to do anything about it.

However, one small matter was resolved.

Claire had continued to scour the local paper each week, as well as the Advertiser, for any reference to Charlotte and the hunt for her killers, and on this occasion it was the small heading 'WPC Charged' that caught her eye. It was a very small item saying:

WPC Alison Mathews, aged 24, of D Division, was last night charged with leaking confidential
    information from the police national computer. She will appear in court on Monday.
    No further details available.

So that was where the information was coming from, thought Claire, just as we suspected. That must be the 'Ally' that Francesca referred to. Gareth Jones' new girlfriend. The one more useful than Francesca.

Without a word Claire handed the paper to Tom and pointed the item out to him. He read it, and then just looked at her for a moment or two.

'That explains it then, doesn't it? We were right about the leak.' Claire nodded.

'And it rather confirms your suspicions about Francesca too.'

She nodded again. She didn't want to say anything because she knew how hard Tom found it to admit that his daughter was the original leaker of information about Claire. Although they had no proof, they were certain she was the one that had talked to Jones. No doubt he had cultivated the relationships with both the young women just to get information. But the good thing about Francesca's leak, if anything about it could be called good, was that she hadn't broken the law, or betrayed a position of responsibility. She wouldn't lose her job or face the prospect of a court appearance, or even the possibility of a prison sentence. But she had betrayed Claire, and degraded herself in her father's eyes - perhaps her worst crime.

***

Tom was very quiet for twenty-four hours after the article appeared in the paper, then he announced that he was going to ask Francesca to come and see them after dinner one evening. He told Claire that he wouldn't tell her why they wanted to see her, although she was bound to ask.

'I'll just say that we haven't seen her for a while', he said.

'I don't suppose she'll believe you for one minute, especially when you specify 'after dinner'. We normally ask her to dinner if we haven't seen her.'

'I thought it would be easier for you. Sitting through a meal, knowing we were going to ask her to explain herself, would ruin a perfectly good dinner.'

'Perhaps we should ask Aunt Lou to come too to act as the referee', she said, by way of a joke. However Tom took her seriously. He thought it a good idea, but Aunt Lou wasn't so sure when Claire phoned her and asked her what she thought about the idea. Surprisingly Aunt Lou didn't ask any questions and when Claire queried this, she said that she had suspected Fran all along as being the source of information.

'Perhaps I should come though' she finally said, 'because Fran will need someone who she thinks will be on her side. She might just clam up and refuse to speak to you.'

'Thanks Aunt Lou. Shall I ask Tom to come and fetch you on his way home from work, and we'll have dinner early?'

But the dinner plans were put on the back burner for a while as the following morning Claire had another formal letter from Miss O'Sullivan telling her that the hospital was offering her early retirement. She phoned Tom, and without checking that Tracey was out of earshot, she told him the contents of the letter. She was surprised at how calmly he took it but, he said, that was what she had been expecting wasn't it? He went on, 'you knew they'd do something like this. You kept telling me they would. Now they have.'

'I know I said it but I didn't really mean it!'

'Well, what explanation are they offering? What's their excuse for getting rid of you?'

'Public opinion apparently.'

'What do you mean?'

'It says, and I quote, 'a petition asking for me to be relieved of my duties in the hospital has been signed by numerous patients', and, 'as a result we feel it is in the best interests of the hospital that you resign'.'

'If I were you I'd ask to see that petition. See if it really is 'signed by numerous patients'.'

'Can I do that?'

'I don't see why not. But before doing that why not ask your new best friend at the hospital and see what he knows' he said with a chuckle.

'I presume you mean Cyril.' She found herself smiling. But he was right. Cyril probably would know something. If he didn't he'd know who to ask.

She had spoken to Cyril a few days ago but he hadn't mentioned a petition. He had said though, that Gareth Jones had been found in the hospital again.

He'd offered a reasonable excuse for being there when challenged - some old friend was a patient, and so they'd had no cause to question what else, if anything, he was doing.

Claire didn't think she was being paranoid but she was beginning to wonder why Gareth Jones had it in for her. He'd obviously got the information he wanted from Francesca and he, presumably, had got the police information from Alison, so why was he still harassing her? What had she ever done to upset him? Why was he continuing to target her when the rest of the world considered the Charlotte story dead and buried? No doubt all aspects of the story would be resurrected when the police found Charlotte's killers, and again when they came to trial, but in the meantime why wasn't he letting it rest? Something or someone was bugging him, and the question was who?

While mulling over these questions in her mind Claire had been doodling over her shopping list, which she had been compiling when the post arrived. Looking at her handiwork she decided that some of the question marks she had drawn were quite stylish, but they weren't getting her anywhere. Tearing a clean sheet of paper off the pad, she wrote down and numbered the questions she would ask Cyril before contacting Miss O'Sullivan's office, but really the only question she wanted a answer to was number one on her list: 'Who was behind the petition?' The other questions would probably be answered once she got the answer to that one.

Unfortunately Cyril didn't know who was behind the petition. He had only heard about it the day before and when he went to investigate he found that there were very few names on it. He saw one in the Geriatric clinic and another in the Diabetic clinic and he said there were only about half a dozen or so names on each, so he thought Miss O'Sullivan was jumping the gun a bit asking her to resign on the strength of a dozen patients. But, Claire noted, those were the two clinics she always worked in. No matter how patchy her staff might be she always made sure she was based in one of those two clinics. And the person who had organized the petition knew that. Was it someone in the hospital, one of the patients perhaps, or was it a snippet of information that Francesca had handed on to Gareth Jones? Perhaps the names on the petition might give her a clue, but when she asked Cyril if he had recognized any of the names he had said no.

Getting nowhere Claire rang Miss O'Sullivan's office and asked Clare to make an appointment for her to see Miss O'Sullivan.

'I suppose it's about that letter I typed the other day.'

'As a matter of fact it is, Clare.'

'Well, let me look in her diary. She's got no gaps tomorrow, but she's free at 2pm on Wednesday, for about fifteen minutes only, or Thursday, she has a longer gap at 11am. Which would you like?'

'I'll take the 2pm on Wednesday slot. I don't suppose what I have to say is likely to take more than fifteen minutes.'

'Alright, Mrs Harrison. I've put you in for Wednesday. See you then.'

'Before you go Clare, please will you make sure Miss O'Sullivan has all the copies of the petition on her desk when I see you?'

'OK, I'll do that.'

***

Over dinner that night Claire and Tom discussed the proposed interview. Tom wanted her to make it as difficult as possible for the hospital authorities and even suggested that she take their lawyer with her.

'After all,' he said, 'if only a dozen people have signed the petition, it's not exactly an overwhelming response, is it? It seems to me that patients aren't that keen for you to go.' But if that dozen really do believe I should go, and they are the sort that are in and out of the clinics all the time, they could make it difficult for me. Supposing they behaved like Gareth Jones' did in Prof Andrews clinic, he'd have me sacked on the spot.'

'Silly old duffer. He should get real. No one behaves like that anymore.'

'*He* does. He still thinks like the old days, when consultants were gods, and no one questioned anything they said or did. However,' she continued thoughtfully, 'there is one thing that really does surprise me about him and this whole fiasco, and that's the business of the petition.'

'What do you mean?'

'It's just that I can't understand how he would allow that sort of petition in *his* clinic. It doesn't go with his old fashioned views. It's just not something he would condone – no matter what he thought about me.'

'Perhaps he doesn't know about it. If he's in one of the consulting rooms all the time he wouldn't be aware of what's going on outside in the waiting room.'

'He usually does. Probably because many of the old ladies like him. They like the way he tells them what to do, and so they witter on about all sorts of things to him. His clinic is inclined to over-run because of all the chattering that goes on, so I'm sure one of them would have told him about it.'

'Well, in this case, it seems they didn't. Seeing as how so few people have signed it, it couldn't have been very obvious, could it?'

'No I suppose not.'

'Anyway, Claire, whatever you decide I'll back you up. If you want to fight them, fine, but if you want to go quietly then that's fine by me too. Now, what's for pudding tonight?'

She laughed. Since she'd been on leave she'd taken to experimenting with different dessert recipes. Some had been successful, but others disastrous. Tonight's concoction looked as if it might be one of her successes.

It was, and while stacking the dishwasher later, she let her mind drift over their earlier conversation. She knew that the hospital didn't really have a case against her but she had decided that she would rather resign quietly, not make a fuss, just go. But she did want to see the petition. She wanted to know who had signed it. While waiting for sleep that night she mentally went down the clinic lists as far as she remembered them. It certainly worked better than counting sheep.

Chapter 12

Claire started her day in a much lighter mood than of late. Now she knew her fate there was no point worrying any more. She phoned Aunt Lou and suggested to her that they went out for lunch to celebrate her decision.

'What decision is that, dear?'

'I'll tell you all about it when I see you. I'll pick you up at twelve, and you can choose the venue.'

'That sounds lovely, dear. I'll be ready.'

Being at home all day, no clinics to worry about, no rotas to readjust, no stroppy patients to soothe, seemed to Claire the ideal way to run her life. Perhaps she'd get more time to read, listen to music, or even enrol on that long put off Open University course. With only Tom to consider, life was going to be good. At least it would be once they had sorted out Francesca. She was the one black cloud on the horizon. She'd talk to Aunt Lou about that at lunch time. They'd decide what day would be best to confront her, although Claire was beginning to have doubts about the wisdom of such a confrontation, as it was likely to sour relations between them for good.

Aunt Lou didn't agree, as they sat over their coffee later. She was of the opinion that it was high time Francesca faced up to the effects her behaviour was having on the rest of the family.

'She's been allowed to behave like a spoilt child long enough', she said, 'and now she has lost you your job. Enough is enough. It's time that young lady took responsibility for her actions.'

'I know you're right Aunt Lou but it's not going to be pleasant. I do feel for Tom. It's going to be a terrible experience for him, isn't it?'

'That's just too bad. Francesca is an adult, and she is no longer his concern. You are. You are the one he loves and cherishes. You are the one that matters.'

Claire felt that Aunt Lou was metaphorically poking her with a finger at every mention of the word 'you' as if to emphasise what she was saying, and the thought of her being so unladylike made her smile.

'So, Aunt Lou, when shall we make this all happen? Are you doing anything tomorrow evening? Or would Thursday be better? We'd better not suggest anytime over the weekend as Francesca is bound to be going out.'

'Actually, I've already spoken to her. I told her that I hadn't seen Tom for a while and I suggested to her that she take me over to see him tomorrow. She took it for granted that I meant at about five. She knows that he usually gets home early on Wednesdays, and that you are usually late, so she took it for granted that it would be just him at home.'

Claire wondered what Francesca's exact words were. Something not very flattering about her she suspected.

'She's going to get a shock when she sees me then, isn't she?'

'I didn't tell her that you would be home, but it does look as if she'll be expecting dinner as usual.'

'That's OK Aunt Lou. I have all the time in the world to cook now. But whether she stays for dinner is another matter.'

'Well, we'll just wait and see, won't we?' With that pithy comment Aunt Lou bent down and picked up her handbag. 'Now dear, I think it's time we did our shopping. Are we going to Sainsbury's, or are you still hiding out at Tesco's?'

'I've decided that I'm not hiding out anywhere anymore Aunt Lou. So it's Sainsbury's. What shall we

have for dinner tomorrow? What do you fancy? I take it
that you will stay even if Francesca doesn't.'

'Of course I will, dear.'

***

Of course she did, but all Claire's careful culinary plans
were wasted as the meal, she thought, tasted like
sawdust.

The day began well. The dinner was organized, the
house was clean and tidy, and Aunt Lou had rung to
wish her good luck with the interview, which rather put
a dampener on her mood as she had been trying to
forget about it. And thinking about it later that was
perhaps when the day began to go downhill because she
knocked her coffee over while reaching for the phone,
ruining her freshly cleaned skirt, which meant a
completely new outfit. So by the time she left for the
hospital she was running late and the traffic was bad,
and her usual parking space was taken. Reaching Miss
O'Sullivan's office dead on two o'clock was not what
she had planned.

She had just asked Clare if the petitions were in the
office when Miss O'Sullivan called her in. The chair
was in its usual place so Claire settled herself down on
it, taking her time to straighten her skirt, and place her
bag neatly on the floor, as if she had all the time in the
world. After a rather frosty greeting Miss O'Sullivan
admitted that the petitions were not in her possession
and suggested that it was not necessary for Claire to see
them.

'When I made the appointment to see you Miss
O'Sullivan, I particularly requested to see the petitions
today.'

'It will only upset you further if you see them. You
might recognize the names.'

'I'm sure I will recognize one or two of the twelve names I gather that are on them. After all I have been here a long time. However I do wish to see them.'

'If you insist.'

This time Claire was aware of Miss O'Sullivan pressing a button to summon Clare, who appeared almost immediately, carrying a couple of sheets of paper.

'Miss Williams, please bring me the petitions that I placed on your desk this morning.'

'I have them here Miss O'Sullivan. Shall I give them to Mrs Harrison?', and without waiting for an answer she handed them to Claire. As she left she gave her a theatrical wink, which momentarily raised Claire's spirits.

There were thirteen names on the petitions, eight on one and five on the other, which obviously meant that not many patients had been keen to sign them, and it was no surprise to see Gerald Pontin's name. It was just the sort of thing he would be happy to support - ruining someone else's life like he was ruining his own. What was a surprise though was to see his signature on the top of both, especially since he didn't attend both clinics. She somehow didn't think he would have had the necessary thought processes to organize the petition, so she wondered who had put him up to it. Another Gareth Jones' ruse perhaps.

She recognized nearly all the other names. That hurt. She had hoped that they may be new patients, being led astray by the likes of Pontin.

She put the papers down on the desk, and looked questioningly at Miss O'Sullivan.

'Have you written your resignation letter Mrs Harrison?' she asked.

'No. I haven't. I'm still thinking about it. But having seen those pathetic excuses for a petition I really don't think you have any cause to ask me to resign.'

'Yes, I do have to agree with you on that point. It is obviously not as popular as I was lead to believe. However I think your position as Sister in Out Patients is untenable now, and there are no other comparable positions currently available.' Having made her position perfectly clear, she sat back in her chair with a chilly smile on her face.

Claire could see the writing on the wall. She was out regardless. She and Tom had discussed this likelihood the previous evening and had come up with a plan to save her face and that of the hospital.

'Miss O'Sullivan, is the rumour true that you are planning to make senior staff redundant to save money?'

'There has been some discussion about it. Why?'

'Staff Nurse Maxwell is perfectly capable of doing my job, as no doubt you have found out already. Therefore I suggest you offer me redundancy and I will accept it. Thus I will have no need to take you to court over your plans to sack me.'

An unsightly flush spread over Miss O'Sullivan's face. She swallowed nervously. 'It would never have come to that I assure you Mrs Harrison. However, your suggestion is worth thinking about. I shall discuss it with the relevant authorities and let you know as soon as possible. But I don't think there will be any objections.'

Claire's 'thank you' was suitably gracious as she got up to leave. This time she really did sweep out, and gave Clare a wide grin as she went passed. That part of the day had gone better than expected but she was not as hopeful about her next encounter.

*****

Francesca's mood had turned aggressive as soon as she arrived and saw Claire. She rounded on Aunt Lou and demanded to know why she hadn't been warned about Claire being home early.

'She is permanently home early, dear. She has lost her job.'

'Huh' was her response. 'And we think you know something about the reason' Tom said, as he came out of the kitchen to meet his guests. He took Aunt Lou's coat and hung it up in the cloakroom, before ushering her into the living room. Francesca had crossed her arms after tugging the lapels of her jacket together, so Tom had not bothered asking her if she wanted to remove her jacket. She followed them into the room and slumped into the armchair that Claire thought of as hers.

'So, what's going on then? What am I on trial about *now*?' she muttered

She was ignored while Claire asked what everyone would like to drink. Small talk was made and when glasses were filled and distributed, and Claire was seated beside Tom, she asked again in a mutinous tone: 'I just asked, what's going on?'

'There have been many times in your life, Francesca, when you have upset me more than words can say about your behaviour towards Claire, but this time you have excelled yourself.' Tom took a sip from his glass before continuing, 'and this time I want a full explanation followed by a sincere apology to Claire.'

There was a moment's silence as Francesca looked first at Tom, then Claire, and finally at Aunt Lou.

'Are you in on this too Gallou?'

'Yes, dear, I am. I'm as shocked as they are about what you appear to have done.'

'And what do I *appear* to have done?' she drawled.

'You know perfectly well.'

'I suppose you mean about that copper.'

Tom and Claire looked at each other questionably, as Aunt Lou frowned and asked Francesca: 'What copper?'

'The one I snitched on.'

Tom put down his glass carefully and cleared his throat.

'We don't know anything about a policeman. We had asked to see you because we want to know why you supplied information to Gareth Jones.'

'Oh, him. He's history.'

'He's not for us Francesca. For us he is very much in the present. Why did you speak to him?'

''Cos he asked, that's why, and he was good fun.'

'Did you ask him what he was planning to do with the information you gave him?''Nah. Why should I? It was all harmless stuff. Nothing to get in a state about?'

'*Nothing to get in a state about*. Let me tell you, young lady, it is very definitely something to get in a state about.' Tom's angry voice was beginning to rise. 'Claire has been vilified by the press, she has lost her reputation and job at the hospital, and even had hate mail sent to her. Is that what you call nothing, eh?'

Claire put a calming hand on Tom's arm as she, Tom and Aunt Lou waited expectantly for a reply from Francesca.

'Well I didn't know she'd lose her job, did I? And that letter was just a joke. How was I to know you'd take it so seriously?' she said offhandedly, and shrugged her shoulders. As she did so splashes of red wine flew from her glass on to her hand and jacket sleeve.

'Oh shit. Looked what you've made me do' was her verbal reaction, as she plonked the glass down on the nearby coffee table, causing a red ring to spread on the beautifully polished surface.

Aunt Lou bent forward and picked up the offending glass and wiped the base with a clean tissue whipped from her bag, almost as quickly as Francesca was in doing the damage. She wiped the table and put the glass on the coaster, left there for just such a purpose, without saying a word. She sat back in her chair, with a weak smile offered to Claire, as they both knew the trouble there would be in trying to remove the wine stain on the wood.

'Joke? You call that vile letter a joke? What on earth got into you?' Tom's voice was rising again, as was his colour. 'What has Claire ever done to you that you want to treat her like this?'

Francesca looked at the three of them in turn. She frowned, took a breath as to speak, then stopped. She looked down at the wine speck on her jacket and rubbed ineffectually at it, and without raising her head announced: 'Well, if you really want to know, I'm fed up with her always treating me like shit.' Up came her head and a triumphal smirk spread across her face.

Silence.

A shocked silence, which Claire finally broke by rising from the sofa, and suggesting she leave the room.

'No, darling, please stay' Tom said. He took her hand and gently pulled her back down to sit beside him again. 'I want you to hear what Francesca has to say before she leaves, permanently.'

'Well, it's true. Ever since I was little she's told stories about me to you' Francesca blustered childishly. 'She's always in the way. I never get you on your own. You're my Dad, but she's not my mother. I hate her' she continued, more like a four year old than her given years. She started feeling unsuccessfully in her pockets for a tissue. Yet again Aunt Lou came to the rescue.

Tom ignored her fake efforts to get his sympathy. 'Claire has always treated you like a daughter, and you have had plenty of time alone with me over the years. She has never come between us. So what you said is ridiculous and well you know it.'

'It isn't ridiculous. She's always telling you things about me that aren't true.'

'Okay. Tell me one thing that Claire has told me about you that isn't true.'

'When I was at school she was always saying things.'

'Well, that's a very long time ago. So what sort of things did she say then?'

'She said I didn't do my homework, when I had, and she told you that I nicked things from Woolworth's when I hadn't.'

'If I remember rightly it was the teachers who told me you weren't doing your homework, and as regards the Woolworth's incident you were caught red-handed. I know you said it was Sadie doing the stealing but you had the goods on you. And again, if my memory serves me correctly, it was Claire's intervention that got you off being charged.'

'Yes, but she told you, and she needn't have done.'

'I'm very glad she did tell me. I needed to know that I couldn't trust my daughter.'

Francesca looked daggers at him. Aunt Lou leaned over and touched her hand but she shook it off. She straightened up from her slouched position, placed her hands on the arms of the chair as if she was going to rise, but instead said in a steely tone, 'what about her letting me down when I was fourteen?'

'Ah. So that's what this is all about. I thought we'd sorted all that out years ago. What was the point of me paying out all that money for counselling when you still blame Claire for your mistake? Anyway, how could you have possibly thought that she could arrange everything without me knowing? I think you owe her a debt of gratitude.'

'Of course I don't. She ruined my life. I lost my friends and everything.'

'You lost a lot more than your so-called friends. If I hadn't been so busy I might have kept a better eye on you. I'm only thankful Claire found out what was going on.'

Tom turned to Claire with a rueful expression on his face. It had been a very difficult time in their lives, causing a great strain on their relationship, but they had come through. Not so Francesca.

The story had gradually come out about how Francesca had got drunk, and possibly drugged, just before her fifteenth birthday, and ended up by being raped by her so-called boyfriend. She had said nothing to anyone about it until Claire had noticed that the shopping list hadn't included the usual tampons. When she had casually asked Francesca why, she had initially lied and said she had bought her own, but as her behaviour had deteriorated so much too Claire had questioned her about what was going on. She was pregnant – which Claire had guessed. Francesca was convinced that Claire could help her get rid of it with her connections at the hospital and that no one need know. Not a plan Claire would condone, and much against Francesca's wishes, she had told Tom.

Tom was all for going to the police but Francesca threatened to commit suicide if he did, and she was in such an emotional state he felt that she might actually mean it. Instead, he had gone to see the young man involved and warned him that if he ever showed his face in the vicinity of his daughter again, he would have him charged with multiple offences. And the last they heard was that the young man in question had been offered a job abroad, which he had accepted.

That was the beginning of the end of the relatively good relationship between step-daughter and step-mother. While going through the abortion, in a clinic far from home, Francesca clung to Claire like her life depended on it. But once she was fit again, with only the mental scars to deal with, she designated Claire the step-mother from hell. Any time it looked as if things were getting easier between them, Francesca would pick away at those scars until they festered again.

Tom's view of his little princess took quite a battering too, and although their relationship survived, Tom's rosy spectacles were irrevocably broken. He had spent a vast amount of money on counselling for her, and for them as a family – all to no avail. And now it looked as if Francesca had found a way to get back at Claire and, indirectly, at him too.

'She was an interfering old cow then, and she still is now,' declared Francesca defiantly, 'and if you are going to carry on picking on me, I'm going home. Are you coming Gallou?' She got up from her chair and swung her handbag onto her shoulder.

'No, dear. We were invited to dinner, so I shall stay. Perhaps Tom, you could take me home later?'

'Of course I will Aunt Lou. However, before you storm off in a huff again Francesca, can you tell us about what you meant when you said you 'snitched' on a policeman.'

Francesca reddened, and sat back down in the chair.

'That Ally was breaking the law, so I reported her. That's all.'

'Who is Ally?' Tom asked innocently, though Claire thought he knew perfectly well who she was.

'She's a copper who gave Gareth information that she shouldn't have done.'

'That was nothing to do with you surely. Why did you 'snitch', as you put it, on her?'

'Gareth ditched me for her. So I reported her.'

'And what was his reaction to that?'

Francesca laughed. 'God, he was livid. Absolutely flaming mad. He lost his source and the paper wouldn't take any more of his other stuff. It was great. I really paid him back.'

'I'm glad you are amused Francesca. However, for us, it isn't funny. Claire's reputation is ruined, and as Claire is my wife it rubs off on me too.'

'I don't give a toss about her reputation. Anyway, who cares? She's only a nurse. No one is going to notice she's gone.'

'You might notice if my reputation is ruined too. Apart from my staff losing their jobs there would be no more handouts from me when you are short at the end of the month. No extra for holidays, etc.'

'That's alright. I get my inheritance soon. That's if you and your wife haven't spent it,' she spat out at him, 'and then you can be shot of me forever.'

Claire cringed at the tone the conversation had sunk to. She got up, shaking off Tom's restraining hand, and went into the kitchen, and shut the door. She leant on the sink and let the tears fall unheeded. She ignored the sound of the door opening but the footsteps warned her it was Aunt Lou, so she quickly pulled off a piece of kitchen roll and scrubbed at her eyes.

'I feel ashamed, Claire. To think it has come to this,' Aunt Lou murmured, as she came and stood beside Claire.

'Well we do know now why Gareth Jones has continued his harassment of me. I supposed he couldn't get at her, so he got at me instead. A bad move on his part. Francesca has obviously not told him what she really thinks of me. It's backfired on him though as she is delighted. I'm just so relieved that he didn't do anything to upset Tom's business. With all that new money coming in from the Chinese he could have really ruined things.'

'No one would believe anything nasty about Tom, dear.'

'No, but they can about me?'

'Oh Claire dear, I didn't mean it to sound like that. That was tactless. I'm sorry, dear.'

'I know you didn't mean it. I'm just feeling a little prickly at the moment. Forget about it.' She wiped away the last of her tears and blew her nose.

The sound of angry voices coming from the sitting room interrupted their conversation, followed by the slam of the front door. They turned expectantly towards the door, waiting for Tom to make an appearance. He didn't. He was still sitting on the sofa, with his head back and his eyes closed, a picture of misery, when Claire went to find him.

She sat down beside him.

'She'll get the money Dad left her on her twenty-fifth birthday, such as it is, and then I will have nothing more to do with her,' Tom said without opening his eyes.

'The way she talked Tom, she obviously thinks she's getting a fortune,' said Aunt Lou, who had followed Claire into the room. Tom opened his eyes and gave them both a bleak smile.

'She knows now she isn't. She'd forgotten that we used a lot of it to buy her the flat, so she wasn't quite so full of bravado when she left.' He took Claire's hand. 'Pull me up' he said. 'It's time to eat I think.'

***

Maybe the dinner tasted like sawdust to Claire but Tom and Aunt Lou appeared to enjoy it, though perhaps there was more left over than usual. By the time Aunt Lou was ready to go home there was some semblance of normality, but as Claire cleared up the kitchen, safe in the knowledge she was on her own, she let the tears of self pity overwhelm her. As she clattered the pots and pans she added her cries and sobs to the noise so was unaware that Tom had returned.

'Darling, what's matter? Why are you crying?'

She swung round in surprise. Her face blotchy and wet with the tears and the mucus from her runny nose. 'Oh Tom, I'm sorry.' She reached for another sheet of kitchen roll, which Tom took from her and gently wiped her face. He got another piece and put it to her nose. 'Blow' he ordered. She tried to smile at this infantile request, but it just made the tears start again.

'What's brought this on, darling? We've had rows with Fran before. Why is this time so much worse?'

'It's just' she hiccupped, 'that I gave up having children because of her, and it's all such a waste,' she wailed. 'We could have had lots, and now we have nothing.' The tears were streaming down her face. The years of her pent up misery, so carefully concealed, over her childlessness, had finally been allowed to come to the surface. She brought her hands up to cover her face and to try and stifle the noise she was making; even in the depths of her misery she was aware of embarrassment over her lack of self control. She brushed past Tom and rushed up the stairs to their bathroom. Tom heard the loo seat drop with a bang, and the sound of the loo roll falling from its holder, again. How many times had he said to himself that he must fix it?

He put the dishwasher on, before doing his nightly patrol to check that all was safe downstairs, before he went up to join Claire. He put the dimmest of their bedside lights on - he didn't think Claire would appreciate having the evidence of her distress too brightly lit, before knocking quietly on the bathroom door.

He heard her sniff before saying: 'The loo roll holder has gone again.'

'I know. I heard it. Can I come in?' He opened the door without waiting for a reply. She was sitting in the dark, but the dim light from the bedroom was enough to illuminate a very dejected Claire hunched on the loo, shivering slightly. Her crying had stopped; just the odd hiccup and pathetic sniff punctuated the silence.

Without turning the light on Tom put the plug in the bath and started running the water. His hand wavered over a collection of bottles on the shelf before he chose his favourite concoction and liberally splashed it into the bath. The lovely familiar smell wafted up from the rapidly filling bath, comforting them both. 'Want some help, or shall I just get out of the way?' Tom asked. She smiled weakly at him and told him she would be okay now.

She undressed quickly and got into the steaming bath and Tom listened as she turned the tap on again. She always did that. She liked the bath deep. She slipped down so that just her head was out of the water, being careful not to create a wave as it would end up sloshing through the overflow pipe. She sighed, and carefully slipped down a little further to briefly submerge her blotchy face. The hot water soothed her body as well as her mind, and she tried to think objectively about her outburst. Why had it all suddenly come out? Over the years they had discussed having children but somehow the decision was always made that it was better for Francesca if she had no competition from step siblings. Why had they thought that? And was it 'they'? Or was it just Tom, or just her? She couldn't remember any real arguments over the matter so they must have agreed. So why now was she making such a fuss? She didn't know. She really didn't know. Was it because her biological clock was running down, quite fast now? Was it because she didn't have a job, perhaps? Was she now more aware that it was just the two of them in the house? It had never bothered her before, so why now? Her thoughts went round and round, going nowhere and the bath was cooling down so she had to get out. Calling to Tom, she asked him to make her some tea while she got dried.

Lying in bed together later she tried to explain to Tom about her outburst, but she couldn't find the right words. Nothing she said seemed right, and as tears were threatening again, he forestalled them by wrapping his arms around her and told her to forget it. Surprisingly she did. All that emotion had obviously worn her out and she slept well.

***

She awoke late, to the sound of tea being poured into a mug. Tom had brought her breakfast in bed. She looked at the clock and then at him.

'Tom, it's time you were at work' she said worriedly as she struggled into a sitting position.

'I'm not going to work today' he said with a broad grin. 'I've taken a sickie.'

'You can't do that.'

'Of course I can. I'm the boss. I gave myself permission to spend the day with my wife. So what would you like to do?'

She picked up her mug and sipped it appreciatively. He sat beside her and passed her a plate of toast and marmalade.

'We'll get crumbs in the bed if we eat that here.'

'Who cares? They'll brush out. Go on be brave' he said as he crunched down on a piece, liberally spraying crumbs in all directions. 'What shall we do then?' he asked, with his mouth full. 'I fancy a walk by the river and lunch in a pub, for starters. What do you think?'

'That sounds good, but you'll have to give me time to clear this mess up first,' she warned, 'and I'll probably have to straighten out my hair since I didn't do anything with it last night.'

'That'll take all of five minutes, but I'll give you fifteen.' He got up from the bed, tipping the toast plate dangerously close to adding more crumbs to the bedding, and made for the door.

'Tom, before you go. Do you think I should ring Aunt Lou? It can't have been pleasant for her yesterday.'

'No. She's fine. We had a long talk on the way home last night. She was the one who put me up to taking a sickie – which is a joke when you consider her views on doing that sort of thing.'

Good for Aunt Lou, thought Claire, as she hastily got herself organized, and rolled up the crumb filled bed linen ready for the wash. Brushing them out was never an option. She looked forward to the unexpectedness of the day as playing hooky was not something they were accustomed to doing. The weather was on their side too as the day was glorious. The sun shone, the river sparkled, and the pub lunch exceeded all expectations.

They called in on Aunt Lou on the way home and had an early supper with her - an arrangement she and Tom had cooked up the evening before. They had a relaxed meal and managed to down a bottle of wine between them, as they casually discussed the new pattern of their lives. Claire had not really put any thought into what she was going to do but she was sure that something would come up. She felt she could be useful somewhere. She would start looking around. Now that everything on the Charlotte front had gone quiet perhaps she wouldn't have to worry about her name being recognized.

When she rang Aunt Lou the following morning to thank her for the meal Claire found that she was a step ahead of her. She had compiled a list of all the local organizations that needed volunteers to help with various activities, and the one at the top of her list she was very excited about.

'Claire dear, remember I told you that Viv and I are going to Cornwall on an Age Concern trip on Sunday. Well, some of the old dears going need lots of help, and the carers can go for free, so I thought you could come with us as a carer because one of the carers has dropped out. What do you think? It's a good idea isn't it?'

Anything less appealing she couldn't think of - but how to put that tactfully to Aunt Lou? What on earth could she say? Then she remembered.

'I'm really sorry Aunt Lou but I couldn't possibly make it this time. The Chinese delegation might be here next week, and if they are Tom is going to bring them home for dinner one night.'

'What a shame. Perhaps next time. I'll see you when I get back then. Mrs D is going to do a bit of shopping for me on Thursday and have everything ready for when I get home again. I told her to ring you or Tom if any disaster happens. I also left her Fran's number in case you two are out. Goodbye dear. See you soon.' The phone went down with a clatter.

Fearful that Aunt Lou would do the unthinkable and phone Tom Claire hastily texted him and asked him to ring her. 'Nothing to worry about though' she added as an afterthought, with every word and piece of punctuation correctly in place. She knew he would laugh at her texting; she could not, or would not, get the hang of text language. Perhaps if she had had children she might have mastered it.

When he did ring her back he took great delight in teasing her about how she would have fitted in so well with all the old folk, as well as promising to remember the supposed Chinese visit should Aunt Lou ring before Sunday. And while he was on the phone he reminded her that he was playing in a golf match with some of his staff on Saturday. She hadn't forgotten. She had been debating with herself whether or not she should go with Tom. She now had no excuse not to go; she didn't have to catch up on housework at weekends anymore, so that excuse wouldn't wash. But she was wary. It must have got around the works that she had lost her job; she was sure Tracey would have made it her business to let them all know.

Her internal debate, however, had been a waste of time she found when Tom came home at the end of the day. He reported that no partners, wives, families, or hangers-on, were going to be allowed to attend the golf match, the team had decided. They needed to concentrate as they felt it was important to beat their rivals once and for all. Nothing must distract them. He told Claire all this in a tone of deadly seriousness, although he found it very difficult to keep a straight face. They were a hopeless set of golfers, he said, and hadn't a hope of winning but the rest of the team didn't seem to be aware of it.

While Tom sorted out his golfing kit she organized dinner. She was aware that an awful lot of activity was going on upstairs. He seemed to be in and out of more than just their bedroom, yet she didn't think it was that difficult to find the golf clothes he usually wore. In the back of her mind there was niggle about what he was doing, but she ignored it and opened the wine. She called him down when everything was ready and asked him if he had found what he was looking for. He smiled a rather enigmatic smile and said 'yes'.

Preparing for bed that night, she followed her usual routine, but she couldn't find her pills. Thinking that perhaps she had run out and forgotten to get a new supply, which was highly unlikely, she went to the bathroom cabinet to get her cap. Maybe she was getting forgetful. All the drama going on in her life had perhaps upset her memory, but the cap was missing too. The box was there but it was empty.

Worried that she was going do-lally, she went into the bedroom holding the empty box, to ask Tom if he had seen it or her pills. He was sitting up in bed, looking very pleased with himself, waiting for her.

'You needn't sit there looking so pleased with yourself. I can't find my pills or my cap,' she grumbled, 'have you any idea what I did with them?'

'I've chucked them out' he announced with a grin.

'You've what?'

'I've got rid of them. You don't need them anymore.'

'What do you mean? I don't need them anymore.'

'I think we should let nature take its course.'

She looked at him in surprise. What on earth was he on about? All these years she had prevented nature taking its course, now he wanted it to.

Tom was grinning from ear to ear. He got up from the bed, turned the bathroom light out, and then led her back to the bed.

'You don't need that on,' he said as he stripped her of her nightie, and pushed her gently down on her side of the bed. He got in on his side and pulled her down beside him, wrapping the duvet cocoon like around them.

'But Tom, you shouldn't have thrown everything away. I'm far too old to risk getting pregnant now. I'll soon be menopausal.' As she said it she realized that she didn't feel menopausal, far from it.

'Rubbish. Of course you're not too old. Anyway it will be fun trying to find out.'

***

Needless to say Tom let the golf team down the next day. He was too tired to play well.

Chapter 13

She folded her section of the paper neatly, added it to the remains of the Observer, and looked across at Tom to see if he was ready for their usual Sunday afternoon walk. He was still wrapped up in the Sports pages so she went into the kitchen to prepare the tea things, though whether they'd manage tea after their larger than usual lunch was debatable.

She had particularly enjoyed cooking the lunch today. It was Tom's favourite, and the Yorkshire pudding had risen perfectly, just as if her light mood had infected it. She blushed slightly at the memory of the rather spectacular baby making practice that had taken place in the bedroom too – it was a very long time since they had been quite so abandoned. Life was going to be good again. Despite all that had happened Tom was there for her.

Glancing out of the window, she thought the weather looked a little threatening, so they wouldn't be out long. After putting the cups and saucers on the tray, she absentmindedly wiped the spotless work tops again and straightened the tea towels, before going into the sitting room for Tom. He didn't look as if he had moved. The paper was sagging a bit. He'd obviously dozed off.

'Tom. Wake up. It's nearly three o'clock. Time to go out.'

The paper sagged a little more. A sleepy Tom peered above it.

'Can't we just forget it for once?'

'No. It's good for us. And we always go out for a walk on a Sunday.'

'Just because we always go doesn't mean that we can't change our minds. After all I walked for miles yesterday.'

'Don't be lazy. You always enjoy it once you're out.'

'I suppose so.'

She took the paper from him and folded it. Adding it to her neat pile she took it out and placed it by the bin, ready for recycling.

'Hey - I haven't finished with it all yet. Just leave it, will you.'

She brought it back and dumped it on his chair before going into the hall for her coat and walking shoes. Tom joined her and sat on the bottom stair to put his shoes on, before pulling a jacket off the rack.

'You can't wear that. It looks just like my coat. We'll look daft dressed in the same outfits.'

'It's not the same. Don't be silly. Anyway who's going to see us?'

'You never know. Anyway I got it for you to wear in the garden, not outside.' Well I'm wearing it now and that's it. Are you ready?' And with that he grumpily opened the front door and waited for her to pass, before slamming it and pocketing the key.

They walked in silence down the drive and without asking Claire which direction she'd like to go Tom strode off left up the lane towards the railway crossing. Since this was the direction they usually took it didn't really matter, but she would have liked to have been asked. They walked one behind the other for a while before Tom dropped back to walk beside her, and with a grin he apologized for his bad temper. He took her hand and gently swung it, smiling to himself. Claire glanced at him and returned his smile, squeezing his hand; she guessed that the memory of last night was still fresh in both their minds.

The lane, with ditches on either side, was just wide enough for one car to pass them so when they heard a car coming they pulled into the side to give it space. It passed at speed with what looked like two young men in it.

'That's odd. Where do they think they're going? They've closed the crossing. Surely they saw the sign.'

'I don't know. Perhaps they're on a joy ride. Or out to dump yet more rubbish in the ditch by the crossing by the look of their outfits', grumbled Claire.

'Well we'll see when we get there and take their number when they pass us on the way back.'

Resuming their walk they pointed out to each other the things they saw in the ditches. Claire was just getting into her stride about the awful habits of the young when they heard the car returning. Tom fished in his pockets for a pencil but of course he hadn't got one in the new jacket, so Claire searched through hers while Tom repositioned himself so that he was the first to see the car when it came back.

***

Meanwhile...

Inside the car Kev and Jason were arguing.

'She's the one in the darker blue jacket. The one that'll be nearest to us when we pass them again.'

'I know stupid. I've got eyes to see too you know.'

'Well, I'm just making sure.

The two young men looked at each other, both very apprehensive. Kev gripped the wheel tightly while Jason made sure his seat belt was secure.

'Ready?'

'Ready.'

Kev put his foot to the floor and revved the car. It careered at high speed back along the lane and as it reached Claire and Tom he swung the wheel and deliberately swerved into the nearest figure but sent both of them flying into the ditch.

'Bloody hell man. You hit them both.'

'I couldn't help it. They were too close.'

'And I think you hit the bloke first. Supposing you've injured the wrong one. What are we going to do?'

'Nothing.'

'What do you mean, nothing? We've got to do something. We just can't leave them.'

'Yes we can. We've done the job. Now let's ditch the car and leg it.'

'But we can't leave them. They could be badly hurt and who'll find them here?'

'It's not our business. We've done the job, so shut it.'

By now the car had reached the roundabout leading into town. Kev took the turning towards an old industrial estate and drove slowly up behind the old buildings looking for a place to hide the car. He stopped.

'Come on, let's go.'

'But we've got to do something.'

'Just fucking well shut up. We've done the job. We get the money. We forget it.'

They got out of the car and removed their caps and overalls and Kev threw them onto the back seat. He went round to the boot and got a can of petrol out which he splashed over the clothes and the seats before throwing in the can as well. He took his gloves off and asked Jason for his, before getting a box of matches out of his pocket.

'I'll deal with this lot. You get going and I'll meet you at the pub later. Okay?'

'I still think we should tell someone.'

'You and your fucking bleeding heart. Just forget it.'

Kev lit a match and watched the fire take hold, before storming off in the direction of the main road. His troubled mate followed at a much slower pace.

Jason's conscience continued to bother him as he slowly made his way home, kicking out at every can and fag packet in his path, muttering to himself. 'Causing a fucking accident to hurt that old cow was dead right, but her bloke had done nothing, and 'sposing we've hurt him too. I'm fucking sure both of them were tipped into the ditch. Kev hit them fucking hard.'

Unintentionally his journey was taking him the long way home, passed the old railway station with an old fashioned red phone box standing by the dilapidated entrance. He walked towards it, then turned back. He stood a moment or two, thinking, before cautiously approaching the vandalized box again. 'Bet it's bust' he mumbled. It wasn't. Shuffling through the change in his pocket he looked for a 20p coin before seeing the notice that said 999 calls were free. He pulled up the hem of his tee-shirt and wrapped his hand in it before picking up the receiver and clumsily dialling 999 with the same hand.

'Which service, please?' said the operator.

Momentarily speechless; he hadn't planned what to say. He slammed the receiver down. Shaken, he hit out at the box and swore loudly as his fist bounced off the broken frame. Glancing around, and fidgeting with the change in his pocket, he considered what he should say. Mumbling again, he reminded himself to be careful. He'd be dead meat if Kev found out.

Picking up the receiver again, he was ready when the operator asked which service he wanted.

'There's two bodies in the ditch by the railway crossing, where the cars can't go...'

'Hang on a minute, caller. What's your name?'

'Two bodies, I saw them. Hit by a car. In the ditch.

***

The squad car cruised slowly along the lane. The caller hadn't been very precise about where he had seen the bodies, but a swift search had shown that only one railway crossing was currently closed to vehicular traffic in the vicinity of the call box the call had come from. They were fully expecting it to be another hoax.

It wasn't. From the comfort of their car they could just see the head of a woman, with her eyes closed, held up by the thicker lower branches of the hedge. Her stillness and pallor suggested a fatality. As the driver rang through the co-ordinates for an ambulance, the second police man got out of the car to assess the situation, and as he reached the ditch he called back, 'There's two here, and it looks bad'.

As the PC stepped down into the ditch the semi-conscious Claire briefly opened her eyes and attempted to speak.

'Don't worry love, we'll sort you out. The ambulance is on its way.'

'It's Tom' she said, 'I think he's hurt. He won't talk to me.' She slipped her fingers through his hair and softly patted his head, and closed her eyes again.

The PC glanced down at Tom - he definitely wasn't asleep. A dumped piece of corrugated iron roofing had all but severed his head. He looked at Claire again and realized that because of the awkward angle she was lying, and the blood dripping down her face from a head injury, she couldn't see what had happened to Tom. However, he could also see right away that her right lower leg was badly fractured, possibly her right arm too. It looked as if the weight of Tom's body resting partially on her thigh had numbed the pain because Claire was not showing any signs of distress. She just continued to stroke Tom's hair.

The wail of an approaching ambulance could be heard. It slewed to a halt behind the squad car. The paramedic jumped out and moved swiftly towards the waiting policemen, while the driver got out and opened up the back of the ambulance and slid a stretcher out. A second ambulance joined the group soon afterwards.

The PC gave what little information he had to the paramedics before two of them got into the ditch to see what they could do. The first one squatted beside Claire and took her hand, feeling for her pulse, while quietly asking her where the pain was, but there was no response. With practiced ease she cut open Claire's jacket sleeve and inserted a drip into her left arm. Meanwhile the second paramedic assessed whether or not they would need the fire service to cut the corrugated iron so that they could lift Tom. The roofing was embedded in the ditch but after looking at the extent of the damage to Tom's neck it soon became obvious that Tom could be lifted free without further help. He called over the second team and in a low voice explained the situation to them. As they got on with the job of lifting Tom the paramedic with Claire gently took her hand from Tom's head and held it, while continuing to talk softly to her.

Within seconds of Tom's body being lifted Claire let out a high pitched, long drawn out scream as the feeling came back into her damaged leg and she flailed around in the blood stained mud. With difficulty the paramedics managed to put a further dose of morphine

155

into the drip, and as they waited for it to take effect Claire continued to scream and desperately call out for Tom.

The first ambulance left with Tom's body, but it was some time before Claire was sufficiently sedated for them to be able to assess what other injuries she had. It was difficult to see as there was so much blood churned into the muddy base of the ditch; all three of them looked as if they had been in a war zone. With the afternoon light going they finally got a silent, comatose Claire onto a stretcher, and with blue lights flashing and the siren wailing they left the police to secure the scene.

The PC had initially noticed what looked like car skid marks but with all the activity following the finding of the accident scene, very little evidence of what might have happened had remained. He also recognized Claire, well enough to tell the paramedics her name. She was the woman, he told them, who was thought to have been the last person to see little Charlotte Alsopp alive. It wasn't until later, after he had written up his report, that he remembered the skid marks; and the team that surveyed the crash site later never did find the scrap of paper with the first part of the car number plate that Tom had written down.

Chapter 14

Claire came back from surgery with her right leg looking like a large metal hedgehog: long spiky pins were sticking out of the swollen, bruised flesh, held there by nuts and bolts. Her heavily bandaged right arm was suspended in a cradle hooked up to a stand by the bed, and she could feel something wrapped around her head, which hurt alarmingly. Various monitors were beeping quietly around her. She guessed she was in the trauma unit. By herself. No Tom. Somehow she knew there was no Tom.

Tears slowly leaked from her closed eyes, down the sides of her face and dampening the neckline of the stiff hospital gown; the gentle warm trickle seemed to ease the thumping in her head, as if the pain was seeping out with them.

She was aware of activity around her but she kept her eyes closed.

'Mrs Harrison?' A pause. 'Claire?' the nurse quietly asked, but Claire said nothing.

'I'm just going to do your obs again, then I'll leave you in peace.'

Claire suspected that the nurse knew she was conscious but wisely ignored the fact. She heard the click of a pen, and the light swishing sound as paper was moved. A nudge at the side of the bed probably meant a drain was being checked, and a slight change of air wafted over her as the nurse moved around to look at the drips which Claire could feel in her left hand and arm. The results were recorded, and the pen clicked again.

Several times later the procedure was repeated and each time Claire pretended to be unaware, but it was becoming progressively more difficult as the pain in her head was threatening to overwhelm her. The tears no longer helped. She finally admitted defeat and asked the nurse for her pain medication to be increased. The relief this brought let her sleep.

It was the sound of staff talking near her that woke her. She opened her eyes and met those of the young man at the foot of her bed.

'Ah. Mrs Harrison. I'm Dr Williams. How are you feeling?'

'Fine', she said.

He looked at her with disbelief. 'How's the pain?' he persisted.

'Under control at the moment.'

'Good. Let your nurse know if it needs to be increased again. I'll be back to see you later', and with a shy smile he moved away.

Without moving her head Claire slowly let her eyes drift around the scene in front of her. She noted her battered right leg; she felt the ache of her right arm in its unnatural position, and she lifted her left arm to see how many drips she had there. Her left leg she presumed was undamaged as she gingerly moved it under the light sheet covering it. Having assessed her injuries she looked to see how many others were in the unit with her. There was one patient opposite but her current field of vision meant she couldn't see any more, but she guessed there would be some. Not Tom though.

This last thought brought the tears back. She closed her eyes again and gave in to her misery. Her mind was perfectly clear. She remembered exactly what had happened. The car approaching, then the sudden swerve into them. There hadn't been a sound from Tom as they were flung into the ditch so deep down she knew he had been killed, despite her garbled words to the paramedic. She couldn't remember how long they were in the ditch, and she suspected that she may have lost consciousness for a while. The trip to the hospital and what happened afterwards was a blur, until she came to in the unit.

She hadn't asked about Tom, and as far as she was aware no one had told her that he was dead. Her injuries looked survivable, though the metalwork in her leg made her think that there might be some problems to face there at some point in the future. The future. Without Tom. Her bulwark gone. She cried softly, and eventually drifted into an uneasy sleep as a new dose of painkillers automatically injected itself into her vein.

***

'Have you told Mrs Harrison yet?' Dr Williams asked her nurse.

'No, but I think she knows.'

'Well she must be told officially. Do you want me to do it?'

'No, I'll do it next time she's awake.'

'What about her family? Have they been in?'

'She hasn't got any family, as far as we know, apart from a stepdaughter; and she refused to see Claire when she was in Casualty. Doesn't get on with her I gather. She made a terrible scene when Claire was brought in – screaming and shouting abuse at her for killing her Dad – but I don't think Claire was conscious at the time.'

'Why does she think that?'

'I expect it is all to do with Claire seeing that child.'

'What child?'

'The one that went missing a while back.'

'What's that got to do with Mrs Harrison?'

The nurse looked at him strangely. 'Don't you know? It was all over the papers and she lost her job here because of it.'

'I'm new', Dr Williams said, 'I only started my rotation at this hospital two weeks ago, so I know nothing about her or a missing child. Was she on the staff then?'

'Yes, she was the sister in Out-Patients, with the reputation of being a bit of a martinet, so she wasn't very popular. I never worked with her so I don't know whether she deserved the reputation or not, but she certainly had Out-Patients running smoothly, so they say.'

'But what's the story about the missing child?'

'Well, a little girl went missing and Claire told the police that she thought she had seen her in a house quite near here. She went to investigate herself instead of telling the police, and it is thought that it was her visit to the house that caused the couple to kill the child. The press think that they didn't mean to kill her; just shut her up in case Claire heard her when she approached the house. Anyway it is thought she was the last person to see the child alive and it was her interfering that caused her death, and the press got onto her – through the stepdaughter, so the press say, and as a result of the furore this caused she was asked to leave. The hospital said she had accepted redundancy, but that's just hogwash, and we all know it.'

'Is her accident anything to do with it?'

'No one is saying, at the moment, but it does seem suspicious, and the police are waiting to talk to her.'

'Oh, so that's why I saw a policeman hanging around. Poor soul. What a mess.'

'If he is still here shall I let him talk to her now?'

'Well, if it were me, I'd rather hear about my husband's death from a nurse, rather than from a copper. Try and break it to her before he gets to see her if you can.'

'OK. I'll see if she is awake when I next do her obs. They are due in', the nurse looked at her watch, 'a few minutes.'

Dr Williams collected up his paperwork and left the unit, while Claire's nurse went over to her bedside again.

Claire's eyes were open and she watched the nurse approach. As the nurse took Claire's left hand in both of hers, Claire forestalled her and said: 'You don't have to tell me. I know. He died, didn't he?'

'Yes.'

'I think he died immediately. He didn't make a sound. I tried to tell myself he was just unconscious, but I really knew he wasn't.' Her words faded to a whisper and her eyes began to leak again. She closed them so that she couldn't see her pain reflected in the eyes of the nurse.

When she opened them again a policeman was sitting by her bed, and the curtains were drawn around it.

'My condolences, Mrs Harrison. I'm sorry to trouble you at this time but we were wondering if you remember anything about your accident?'

'What do you want to know?' she asked him wearily.

'Well, what happened? Where were you, and what were you doing? Did you see who hit you? That's what we need to know.'

'Tom and I were walking along the lane towards the level crossing and a car passed us. We thought it odd because we had seen a sign saying that the crossing was closed to traffic.'

'What sort of car?' the policeman interrupted. 'Do you remember what it looked like? The colour or make?'

'It was small, possibly an Escort, dirty, reddish, with two young men in it.'

The policeman was scribbling in his notebook and said, without looking up, 'What did they look like?'

'We didn't really notice. Both had those peaked hats on - the sort they all wear nowadays, white-ish, and light coloured tops, possibly some sort of overalls.'

'Then what happened?'

'When we heard the car coming back Tom got some paper out and I gave him a pencil and he was going to write their number down because we thought they may have been going to dump stuff near the crossing. There's always a pile of rubbish there.'

Claire stopped. She cleared her throat, and shut her eyes. They were letting her down again, leaking. She swallowed, and after a few seconds, continued. 'They came back along the lane. Driving very fast, and as they reached us they deliberately swerved into us.'

'What makes you think it was deliberate?'

Claire opened her eyes and glared at the policeman. 'I'm not stupid' she said vehemently, 'the lane was straight, no obstructions, and we were standing with our backs to the ditch, so we weren't in their way. They could see us quite easily. The driver deliberately crossed to our side and hit us. They definitely meant to hit me.'

'What makes you think that?' the policeman queried, 'Why would anyone want to hit you?'

'Oh, just go away and read your records. Why do you think anyone would want to hit me? It was me they were after. Instead they got Tom, and he never hurt anyone.' Her angry voice broke with the last few words and Claire turned her head, as much as she was able, away from the policeman, and let her tears drip into the pillow.

The young policeman shuffled his feet, embarrassed by her emotion, and it was a relief when Claire's nurse put her head around the curtain and told him that she thought it was time he left. Mrs Harrison had had enough for one day.

Chapter 15

'Hey, Carol, who's that visiting Claire Harrison?

'I don't know. Why?'

'Well, I haven't seen anyone visit her before.'

'An old lady came in yesterday but she didn't stay as the doctors were with Claire discussing what they were going to do with her leg.'

'Oh, have they made a decision about that yet? Last I heard they were waiting for the swelling to go down.'

'That is still the plan. Then they'll scan it and see how they are going to put it back together again.'

Nurse Fanshawe turned as a buzzer sounded, and looked at which area it came from. 'Oh godfathers! It's that wretched woman again. I wonder what she wants this time. Last time she wanted me to hand her her magazine and if she'd have had bothered to put her hand out she could have got it herself! She must think I am just here to wait on her. I shall be glad when she's gone!' And with that ungracious remark she left Carol to speculate about Claire's visitor.

The visitor was far from comfortable. He had come on business, and he was finding it very difficult to express himself without possibly upsetting Claire. He had introduced himself as James Upton, from Upton and Sons, Funeral Directors, before sitting himself down on the chair by her bed. He took a piece of paper out of his briefcase, cleared his throat nervously, and handed it to Claire saying: 'This statement was presented to my colleague at the office this morning. It's most irregular, so I felt that I, as the senior partner, should come and see you about it.'

Claire took the paper and wondered what else the world had to throw at her. She turned very pale and shivered involuntarily as she read it:

TO WHOM IT MAY CONCERN:

I, the undersigned, request that my husband's daughter Francesca Harrison, organize my husband's, her father's, funeral.
I am too unwell to attend to it myself.

Signed Claire Harrison.

And below her printed name was a fair approximation of her signature.

She stared at the piece of paper, while James Upton squirmed on his chair. He had noted the obvious signs of Claire's injuries, particularly the bandages on her right arm and hand, and there was still a drip site on her left hand. He had already made discreet enquiries and ascertained that Mrs Harrison and her step daughter did not get on. He was also fairly sure that she had not been visited by Francesca. But he had these instructions.

Claire was flabbergasted. She could not believe it. The depths to which Francesca would go. And so quickly. The paper shook slightly in her hand as she continued to stare at it. What to do? If she denied its validity there would be hell to pay from Francesca, yet it was obvious she had not signed it. If she confirmed it she would denying her right to say a formal farewell to Tom.

'Ahem', Mr Upton coughed discreetly. 'We haven't come across a situation like this before. By law we have to take instruction from you, not your step-daughter. But *if* the note is genuine perhaps it can be done, but I shall have to make enquiries.'

Claire barely heard him. Her mind was going round in slow circles, the effects of the hefty painkillers she was still being given were taking their toll. But one thing she was sure of, she had already said goodbye to

Tom. What was left was just a body, a shell. Her Tom was gone. Perhaps Francesca was, involuntarily, doing her a favour by wanting to arrange the formalities. Did she really want to face a congregation of Tom's friends? Probably in a wheelchair, with everyone talking over her head. More whispering, more innuendos. It could all happen while she was still in hospital. A let out for her.

Claire made a decision. She handed the note back to Mr Upton and said: 'I am one of the executors of my husband's will. Greg Foreman, of Foreman Brothers in the High Street, is the other. Can you see him for me? Show him the note and do what he says.'

Mr Upton took the piece of paper and started to ask a question but Claire had closed his eyes and asked Mr Upton to excuse her now as she was very tired. She heard him attempt to say something else, then give up. Picking up his belongings and clumsily scraping the chair on the polished lino he left her bedside. She heard him wish the nurses a good afternoon, before the ward door swung shut behind him.

Claire mentally congratulated herself on not lying, but realized that her relationship with Francesca had reached a new low or, more likely, the end. She took a deep breath and told herself not to cry. She had done crying. Life was going to be difficult. Very difficult.

But this vow was almost broken the next afternoon when she heard a quiet voice say: 'Oh Claire love, what have you been and gone and done to yourself?'

Claire turned and looked into the concerned face of her elderly neighbour, Dora.

'I saw Fran go into the house and I asked her where you were', Dora continued. 'She wasn't best pleased to see me, but I followed her in, so she had to tell me.'

'Hello Dora. So kind of you to visit.' Her eyes filled with tears. It was so kind of her to visit. No one else had.

'I've managed to trace Tom's aunt, and she's coming straight home. She said to tell you she'll be in as soon as she gets home. Mrs Donaldson told me where she was.'

'That's kind of you Dora. I'd forgotten Aunt Lou was in Cornwall.'

'That's not surprising. Fran told me about Tom. I'm so sorry. What an awful thing to happen.'

'What was Francesca doing at the house, Dora? Who let her in? Did you give her the spare key?

'No, I certainly did not. You told me only to give it to you or Tom, so I didn't give it to her. I asked her how she got in and she said she'd used her Dad's key.'

'Tom had a key in his trouser pocket. She must have got it somehow.'

Of course that's where Francesca got the key. She must have been given Tom's things. Claire wondered how she had persuaded the staff to give her Tom's effects. They should have come to her. But it did explain one thing. The letter Mr Upton showed her had been typed on her computer. She could tell by the slight smudge of ink at the edges of the letters - her printer needed new ink. She hadn't got around to getting it. It was just another unimportant little job she hadn't got around to doing. But fancy Francesca planning that. And what else has she been planning?

'How long was Francesca in the house Dora?' she asked. She was worried what else she might have been doing in the house.

'Not long. I stood my ground until she left. But she might have been in before and I didn't see her, or perhaps later. Everything looked fine though.'

If the letter was typed on her computer, and she was pretty sure it had been then it was obvious Francesca had been in before.

'You're a good friend Dora. When did you say Aunt Lou was coming?' she queried again. Her brain wasn't functioning too well. She needed Aunt Lou.

'Just as soon as she gets back, she said. Shouldn't be long, lovey. She'll be here soon. Don't fret now.' She patted Claire's good arm as she noticed the tears.

***

Aunt Lou was given permission to come in after visiting hours that evening on condition she didn't stay too long. This advice was greeted with a cold stare. Aunt Lou was quite good at showing haughty disdain when she felt the need. She had every intention of staying as long as Claire wanted her to stay however distressing it was for the two of them.

'I'm sorry I messed up your holiday, Aunt Lou' whispered Claire as she held tightly to the hand that had been slipped into hers.

'The hotel wasn't special dear. It smelt faintly of wee and stale cabbage. It wasn't my type of place at all, so I was glad to get away.'

'What about Viv? Did she come back too?'

'No. She was happy to stay – she sends her love and condolences, by the way.'

'Thank you. Have you seen Francesca yet?'

'No, not yet. I came straight from the station. Why? What's she done?'

'She took a forged letter to Upton's to say that I had given her permission to arrange the funeral.'

Aunt Lou looked at her open mouthed. Totally bereft of speech. In different circumstances Claire and Tom would have made much of astonishing Aunt Lou to the extent that she was lost for words. It rarely happened. In fact Claire couldn't remember the last time it had happened. But Tom would never know.

'I don't know what to say. I really don't know what to say' mumbled Aunt Lou. Even her familiar speech pattern had disappeared with the shock.

'Can you sort it out for me?' she asked, as an agitated Aunt Lou fidgeted on the hard hospital issue chair.

'Of course, dear. Of course I will.'

'I told Mr Upton to go and see Greg Foreman and go along with anything he said. But now you're here, will you see him?'

'I'll go first thing in the morning. But what do you want, dear?'

'I more or less told him to go ahead without me.'

'Oh Claire. Do you mean that?' Aunt Lou looked at here with tears were rolling down her cheeks, but she seemed unaware of them. The loss of her beloved nephew was taking its toll despite her trying to be brave for Claire. Claire squeezed the hand still in hers. What could she say? Just as Aunt Lou had said nothing. They both knew their loss was beyond words.

Aunt Lou withdrew her hand and searched through her handbag for a tissue.

'There's some on the locker, Aunt Lou' said Claire, indicating the box.

'I can't abide those ones. They are too small and fall apart too easily' announced Aunt Lou, as she found a sensible man-size one from her bag. She sat up straight and blew her nose, and pretended to look business like.

'Now, dear, the first thing to do is for me to see the doctor and find out what is going on with you. Then I shall go home to your house and make sure all is well there. The milk might have gone off and things like that. And, if you don't mind, I shall stay there and keep an eye on things. I'll phone Mrs D in the morning and she can come round and help.'

Aunt Lou ferreted around in her bag again and found her notebook and a pen, before continuing. 'Is there anything I need to know? Should I contact the works, or has that already been done?' She waited, with pen poised, to write down any instructions Claire might give her.

Claire looked at her cherished Aunt by marriage struggling to keep her composure. Here she was comforting her when she probably just wanted to hide away with the pain of her loss. Not a word had been said about the circumstances, no doubt Dora had filled her in, but when would Aunt Lou start to realize that it was her fault that Tom had died? But she somehow knew she wouldn't blame her. It wasn't in her nature to be vindictive.

'I don't know really know what needs to be done Aunt Lou. You'll have to find out what Francesca is doing, and then try and sort things out with her.'

'I guess that's the best thing to do.' She put her notebook and pen back in her bag, and then got up from her chair. 'I'll leave you now dear, and come back tomorrow. I'll see if the doctor is around on my way out. Goodbye Claire, dear. Try and get some rest.' She bent down and kissed Claire, their tears mingling.

Chapter 16

Over the next few days Aunt Lou was in and out bringing in snippets of news about what was going on in the outside world. She was careful about what she said, waiting for Claire to bring up the subject of Tom and his funeral. However Claire was adamant that the funeral should go ahead while Tom's death was fresh in his friends' minds, and she felt that it was fairer to his staff. They would need to know whether their jobs were safe, who was going to be the new boss, and if the works was going to be sold.

Greg Foreman had been to see her about the letter Mr Upton had shown him, and he tried to explain to her how he could get around it. Something to do with enduring power of attorney, she thought he said. As she couldn't sign the official looking bit of paper he'd brought with him she put a wobbly X where her signature should have been, witnessed by two understanding strangers visiting another patient. He also got her to do the same thing on another form, which she thought he said was giving him the power to look after her affairs until she was capable of doing it. His legalese language about trustee power of attorney went over her drugged head, but she knew Tom had trusted him implicitly, so she accepted that what he was doing was right.

In the meantime she was supposed to go to theatre again to have her fractured leg investigated. But after a scan the surgeons decided that there was still too much bruising and swelling. Therefore they couldn't just pin and plate it, as they had hoped, so the hedgehog like set up had to stay for a while longer, which made moving around much more difficult. Her right arm was now in a removable plaster cast and her various drips had come down, so she had full use of her left arm at least. She was moved out of the intensive care unit and put in a side room of a general accident ward, while the debate went on about what to do about getting her home. But they had warned her that if she didn't start eating and drinking they would have to put a drip up again, and then she would not be going home.

Claire desperately wanted to go home although she didn't know how she was going to manage. She would need a wheelchair while the pins were sticking out of her leg, as she wasn't allowed to put any weight on it, and she couldn't use crutches anyway because of her right arm being out of action. She would need help, but who could she get to provide it. She didn't have an army of friends to rally round her, and her only family now was Aunt Lou. She became more and more distressed at her inability to control her life. She tried to put the loss of Tom to the back of her mind while she attempted to find a solution, but it was far from easy.

Aunt Lou told her that the press had been onto the hospital to try and get an interview with her, and there was a big piece, written by a staff reporter, about the 'hit and run' accident, as well as articles about the loss of Tom in his capacity as a local businessman, and of course with the mention of her name the story of Charlotte was resurrected again. The local paper's attitude had not softened towards Claire, but at least there were no more Gareth Jones stories. But no matter how careful Aunt Lou was about not bringing papers into the hospital it was inevitable Claire would see them since a trolley went round each day selling papers, toiletries, sweets, and things like that. And she was not immune to the glances and whispered asides that went on outside her room, as patients and visitors pointed her out to each other.

Cyril made a point of calling to see her most days now that she was out of intensive care and he was generally able to make her smile about some scandalous story or other going the rounds of hospital gossip. She also had a formal visit from Miss O'Sullivan, who used the occasion to bring her the final details of her redundancy package, which, she soon realized, would just about cover the cost of Tom's funeral. Greg Foreman had been in to see her and he and Aunt Lou had liaised with Francesca about it, and he had also discussed what should be done about the works. Tom had left no instructions and his will was very simple; everything he owned was to go to Claire. He had always told Francesca that because her grandfather had left her so much he wasn't making provision for her in his will. However, it was also understood that when Claire died anything left would go to Francesca, and in moments of her deepest depression Claire allowed herself to think the unthinkable, that perhaps Francesca had organized the accident to get rid of both of them. At other times, when she was feeling more charitable, she felt very sorry for Francesca. There was no doubt she had adored her father, but her last encounter with him had been horrendous, for all of them.

On the day of Tom's funeral Aunt Lou came to see her beforehand. She was still unhappy about Claire not being there, but had accepted her decision. She understood the difficulty Claire would encounter, not only because of being in a wheelchair, but with her leg as it was there would have been too much attention focused on her. Also there was the likelihood that the press would show up and start asking questions about Charlotte. She wanted everyone to remember Tom, as he was, not as the accident fatality and her the survivor. The priest taking the service also accepted her decision. He had been in to visit several times and was careful to refer to Aunt Lou as the chief mourner in the absence of Claire. He had obviously not taken to Francesca and he had made it clear that all decisions had to be made by Claire, much to Francesca's chagrin, so Aunt Lou said. Claire wondered how many people had seen the letter Mr Upton had shown her, but no reference was ever made to it again.

A favourite photo of a happy laughing Tom was used on the Order of Service booklet. After the printers had finished with it Aunt Lou had brought it in to sit on Claire's bedside locker. It broke her heart to look at it but she felt it was worth it. In the dark night hours when she couldn't sleep she would hold the photo and talk to Tom. She approved the hymns and the readings that Aunt Lou and Francesca had chosen, but that was all. She left it to others to organize the do in the hotel afterwards. She told Aunt Lou that no expense was to be spared and that an open bar was to be available as long as the last mourner wanted a drink. Aunt Lou tried to dissuade her about that, telling her that there were bound to be some who would take advantage, but Claire was adamant. She didn't want any of Tom's young staff, who had all been given the afternoon off in case they wanted to attend the funeral, to think her mean.

On one particular point Claire insisted that her wishes were carried out, and that was on the matter of flowers. She wanted a spray of white lilies on the coffin, and if the florist could find them, some forget-me-nots tucked in with them, and it was to be clear that they were from her. Aunt Lou brought her the card to write and with her left hand she painstakingly wrote her last message to Tom. With help from Aunt Lou she put it in the tiny envelope and sealed it down, and wrote 'Tom' on it, and signed it with her last kiss. She also asked that her flowers be cremated with his body. As regards flowers from other people, or donations to a charity, Claire left that to Aunt Lou. She guessed that Aunt Lou would favour donations as she had often heard her complaining about how wasteful it was sending flowers to the dead.

In spite of her own distress Claire was aware of the burden she was putting on Aunt Lou, and when she tried to talk to her about it Aunt Lou told her not to worry; she was glad of something to do. Greg Foreman, who visited her the day after the funeral, told her that Aunt Lou had been magnificent, and very stoical, coping with everyone. Francesca too had coped very well, and one or two youngsters from the works had taken her under their wing. Tracey had caused a bit of a stir though, turning up in deepest black, and in a hat with a small veil, as if she was the grieving widow. She rather let herself down later however, Greg told her with a grin, as the free bar caused her to imbibe just that much too much. Greg was also able to tell her that the works were functioning without Tom, as his second in command, John Markham, knew exactly what was to be done. As soon as she was home John wanted to see her and find out what she wanted to do. In the meantime he would carry on with Tom's plans, and so far the Chinese investors were happy.

***

The problem of Claire's homecoming was finally solved by Aunt Lou. She had installed herself in Claire's house, with the connivance of her Mrs D, and, without telling Claire, she had had her dining room converted into a bedroom, putting the collapsed dining table into the spare bedroom, and the chairs had been distributed around the house. The sideboard had been moved so that a single bed could be installed, plus bedside table and lamp, and all the other things Aunt

Lou thought she'd need, all done with the extra help of Mrs D's two hefty sons.

When she and Tom had bought the house they had commented on the wide doors, which the agent put down to the style of the house. But at the time they had wondered if perhaps a previous owner had been confined to a wheelchair. It didn't matter then, but now it was a godsend, and Claire was thrilled with Aunt Lou's illicit plans. She was equally pleased at the thought of having Aunt Lou with her and she felt that between them they could solve any problems that arose.

However, what Aunt Lou hadn't told Claire was that she had installed herself in Claire's house to stop Francesca trashing it. Although Aunt Lou might not have used that word it was definitely what she meant, as she found the house looking as if burglars had been in. She found out from Dora that Francesca had been at the house soon after she knew that her father had died, probably straight from the hospital since she had Tom's key, and still had it. What she had been looking for, Aunt Lou was yet to find out, but she had made considerable mess looking for it. Tom's desk had been ransacked and nearly all the drawers in the house had been tipped out, and every photo that had Claire in it had been wrenched from its frame and her face torn off or defaced. With a very heavy heart Aunt Lou had straightened everything she could, but she was worried about the photos.

She needn't have worried. Claire had her favourite picture, and either didn't notice or refrained from asking about all the others.

**

Claire was delivered home in an ambulance with all the equipment it was thought she would need. It was such a palaver getting the wheelchair into the house that Claire didn't have time to think about Tom not being there. But when she saw the single bed in the dining room she felt her heart painfully contract. Never again would she feel him lying close to her in their lovely big bed. Never again would she feel his warm arms around her or his sleeping breath on the back of her neck. She would even welcome his irritating habit of hogging the duvet if only she could have him back. She allowed the tears to fall silently, giving in to weakness just one last time. She had told herself on leaving the hospital that there were to be no more tears. Tears did no one any good, and they just upset the visitors. She must be strong. But it was so difficult.

With a great deal of ingenuity she managed to manoeuvre the wheelchair out of her room using her left hand and the tips of her fingers on the right. With her right leg stuck out in front of her she needed a wide turning circle so all Aunt Lou's careful furniture arrangements were going to have to be reassessed she decided, as she bumped first into one thing then another. By the time Aunt Lou came to the rescue Claire had recovered from her silent tears, and was able to laugh at her efforts to propel herself from room to room. It was even more difficult when she tried to get near the kitchen table where Aunt Lou had tea ready. Should she ever get back to nursing, she thought, she'd be a lot more aware of what patients go through.

In the end she sat side on to the table that first day home, but eventually they worked out that a tray across the arms of her chair could hold her meal more comfortably.

Looking at each other across the table, it was Aunt Lou who broke the silence.

'Claire, dear, the police want to come and see you again.'

'Why? I've told them all I know. A policeman visited me in hospital to ask about the accident. But I have to admit, I wasn't very polite to him.'

'Well it seems they may have found the car that hit you, so someone is coming tomorrow morning. I thought you'd want to get it over with as soon as possible.'

'Yes, you're right. I'm glad they are doing something. I was beginning to think they thought I'd imagined it again.' She looked around the kitchen slowly, letting her mind briefly touch on events that had happened there, with Tom, and she smiled as she remembered his frantic search for the 'prong things', as he called them, when the poison pen letter came. The smile faded when she remembered who had sent it.

'Aunt Lou, what am I to do about Francesca? She must be suffering as much as the rest of us. Do you think I can heal the rift?'

'I doubt it. At the moment anyway.'

'She behaved alright at the funeral though didn't she? My not being there was probably a help.'

'Yes, she did behave. She was quite dignified in fact. But I have to tell you Claire that when I came here after I got back from Cornwall, she had obviously been looking for something. Tom's desk had been disturbed, and lots of drawers had been looked in.'

'Did you ask her what she was looking for?'

'No, I didn't really get an opportunity. But now you are home perhaps she should be asked.'

Claire sat for a moment, thinking. To ask or not ask, that was the question. Her emotions were still too raw to risk a fight with Francesca, but it would be interesting to know what she was looking for. If she had been ferreting in Tom's desk she must have been looking for some sort of official paperwork. Hers was all there too, such as it was.

'Do you think she was looking for wills and things, Aunt Lou? If she was it was a waste of her time as they are in Greg Foreman's office.'

'I don't think it could be that. Tom had discussed with her what he was putting in his will. She knew that you were going to inherit everything. Perhaps' Aunt Lou paused, 'she was trying to find your will.'

Claire looked at her as a very unpleasant thought occurred to her. 'Do you think it is possible' she said, 'that Francesca thinks I organized the accident to get my hands on Tom's money? Do you think she thinks that badly of me? Does she think I am that much of a witch, Aunt Lou? Does she think that?'

'Of course not, dear. Of course she doesn't think that. No one has ever doubted your love for Tom. Of course she doesn't think that. And you mustn't think like that.'

Claire gave her a bleak smile. 'Sitting in hospital, day after day, my imagination ran riot. I tried to remember the good times, when she was little, when we were all happy.'

Chapter 17

A young policewoman arrived promptly at eleven o'clock the following morning. By then Claire had managed to get herself propped up on the sofa in the sitting room, with the wheelchair out of sight, so she was able to greet her without appearing too much like an invalid. But the effort involved had caused considerable pain. She had hoped that the pain killers would have kicked in by the time the WPC arrived but she was still feeling a bit delicate. As long as she kept still the pain was bearable most of the time, but there were times, even at this late stage, when it was not only the loss of Tom that made her cry. However, she knew the physical pain would lessen, but she was far from sure that the other would.

Having shown the WPC into the sitting room Aunt Lou went off to get some coffee and when she came back Claire asked her to stay so that she could hear what the WPC had to say.

'Miss Harrison' Claire indicated Aunt Lou, 'says you think you have found the car that hit my husband and I. Is that right?'

'We think we may have done. We have found a partially burnt out car. It's small and dark red, which sort of matches the car you described as having hit you.'

'How did you find it?'

'Someone called the fire brigade because they thought some old industrial buildings were on fire, but when they got there they found a car burning. Fortunately the fire had only burnt out the inside leaving the frame intact, and there was evidence that it had been involved in an accident at some time as the front bumper was damaged. We know it is a long shot but I've come to ask what you and your husband were

179

wearing at the time of the accident, to see if we can match up any fibres that might be found.'

Claire turned towards Aunt Lou and asked if she knew what had happened to the clothes they were wearing.

'Francesca might know what happened to Tom's. I know she got his key so I presume she got everything else. But yours Claire, I imagine there were in such a mess I expect they were binned.'

'I thought' said Claire, 'that the police would have taken the clothes. They were at the scene and, I presume, at the hospital. They must have realized it was no accident. Don't they 'bag' clothes or something like that?' She turned to the WPC enquiringly.

'I'm not sure what happened' she said, 'I wasn't there. I was just asked to find out about the clothes.' She turned a little red. She had been warned that Claire Harrison could be difficult.

'From my limited experience of A&E the clothes would have been taken off, or perhaps cut off, the patient and put in a poly bag. If I remember rightly there were special bags for that. But I'm talking about a very long time ago. I don't know what they do now.'

'We asked at the hospital but they didn't know what had happened. It seems that the evening you and your husband were brought in there had been a fight among some local youths, so there was a lot going on. Also Mr Harrison's daughter was very distressed when she arrived. They remember that, but nothing about the clothes.'

'Yes, I heard about that. Understandable I think. If you'd just heard that your father had been killed by a 'hit and run' driver, you'd be mad too, wouldn't you?'

The WPC nodded. Aunt Lou looked at them both, and broke the rising tension by offering more coffee. She moved between them, refilling the cups and asking the WPC if she wanted sugar, or another biscuit. By the time she had stopped fussing Claire had calmed down, and the WPC looked less agitated.

'Would it help' Aunt Lou said, as she sat down again, 'if Claire could remember what she and Tom were wearing? I mean, if they were wearing jeans, for example, that would tell you something wouldn't it?'

'If you knew the particular make it might. I'm not sure. I don't know much about forensics.'

Claire thought she didn't know much about anything. Poor girl. Sent out on a job without any briefing, from the sound of things. She was beginning to feel sorry for her.

'I was wearing indigo coloured Levis – that's the very dark shade of blue, but I imagine they were cut off me looking at the damage to this leg. I think that's where the car hit me. The damage to my arm and head happened when we were thrown into the ditch. Tom, as I expect you know, was almost decapitated by discarded corrugated roofing.' She said this in a very matter-of-fact tone, but inside she was churning. The thought of her beloved Tom injured like that still made her feel sick. The only consolation, if there was any at all, was that he must have been killed instantly. Humans weren't like chickens, thank goodness, able to run around after their heads had been cut off. 'He was wearing' she continued, 'very old dark brown cords, from M&S I expect. Their ones were the only ones that seemed to fit him properly. We both had blue jackets on, but I can't remember, at the moment, where they came from.'

The WPC and Aunt Lou also looked a little sick. The WPC, probably because she was relatively new to the job and hadn't experienced the gorier side of it yet, and for Aunt Lou it was most likely hearing the details.

She had been told at the time how Tom had died but perhaps it hadn't been put quite so baldly.

'I expect that will be a help' said the WPC, as she finished scribbling in her notebook. She snapped the elastic band over the shut notebook and pushed in into her official looking bag along with her pen. 'I'll go back and report what you said. I expect someone will go and see the other Miss Harrison to see if she knows anything about the clothes. I hope we won't have to bother you again.'

The WPC got up to leave, thanking Claire and Aunt Lou for the coffee. Aunt Lou escorted her to the front door, before coming back and collecting up the coffee things.

'I suppose I should be grateful that they believe me this time Aunt Lou, but it all sounds a bit hit and miss to me.'

'Well I don't know anything about these things but I would guess that Levi's and M&S have their own distinctive characteristics, and if they find fibres that match those two then I presume the police will have at least something to go on.'

'I suppose so. But then they have to find the two who were driving the car. She said the inside of the car was burnt out so they won't find any fingerprints, or stuff like that.'

'I expect they have their ways and means. Someone is bound to say something that will get back to them eventually.'

'I do hope so. While I was in hospital I spent a lot of time thinking about why someone would take such extreme action. I know in my heart of hearts that Francesca couldn't be party to that. I know she hates me but she wouldn't risk hurting her Dad. Even after that last visit she wouldn't be capable of doing anything that might hurt him.'

'What about Gareth Jones? His behaviour is very suspect?'

'Somehow I don't think it is him. I think once he got me out of my job his vindictiveness had gone. I presume he was angry at Francesca for reporting his informer to the police, but once they had found Charlotte his story was finished. I expect he has moved on to something else by now.'

'I'm not so sure. Fran must have told him what she thought of you, so pursuing you like that, was really unnecessary if he was just out to get back at her.'

'Perhaps Francesca didn't tell him. Who knows? We'll never find out now anyway. Unless, perhaps, when they find Charlotte's killers. He might surface again then.'

'*If* they find Charlotte's killers. It doesn't sound as if that is very likely.'

'I think they will. I know I haven't been very pro-police up to now, but I do think they will find them. Even if the story has gone cold from the point of view of the press I'm sure there is a team somewhere still working on her case.'

'I hope you're right. But in the meantime, and changing the subject, I must go and organize lunch. Then I shall go and see Mrs D about changing her working venue.'

'Ah, that is something I want to talk to you about Aunt Lou. While Mrs D is here I shall be paying her wages.'

'That's not necessary dear. If she wasn't coming here she'd be going to my place, so I'd be paying her, so I shall continue to pay her as usual.'

'No you won't. When she is working here I pay her. No argument, please Aunt Lou. What would Tom think? I can afford it you know.'

'I'm sure you can dear. Although I don't know how you are going to manage now without Tom's money coming in, and you out of a job. I'm quite worried for you.'

'There's no need, really Aunt Lou. I know the banks have frozen Tom's bank and credit card accounts but once we have sorted all the paperwork things will be fine. Tom had life insurance, and then there's the works. At the moment John Markham is putting money into my account so Greg Foreman told me, so for day to day things there is plenty of money coming in. We don't have to worry about bills or anything, at the moment.'

'That's a relief. When someone dies it takes forever to get things sorted out. When my brother, Tom's Dad, died I thought we'd never get to the end of the paperwork.'

'That was because his affairs were in a mess' said Claire with a smile. 'Don't you remember? He hadn't kept any proper records of what he owned or didn't own, and Tom had a terrible job sorting it all out. In his will he left money to lots of people and to begin with Tom didn't know where it was all going to come from. But eventually he got it all worked out, after finding that his Dad was far wealthier than he originally thought. That's why Tom's affairs are so organized. He vowed that no one was going to have to work as hard as he did.'

'But he hadn't made a decision about the works though, had he?'

'No, that's true. I don't suppose he envisaged his life ending so early. He probably thought he had plenty of time to sort it out.'

'Have you thought about what you are going to do? With the works I mean.'

'No, not really. John is going to come and see me, when I feel up to it. But some decision will have to be made soon. Greg is working on all the things to do with probate. Presumably everything comes to me. But really I don't know. And I don't care. I'd rather have Tom back than any amount of money.'

'Amen to that' said Aunt Lou, as she took the tray to the kitchen.

To a certain extent Claire realized that she was quite lucky. Having those weeks in hospital had given her time to grieve for Tom, without the extra stress of the paperwork involved when someone dies. Now she would have to put her grief aside and get stuck in with the endless forms that needed filling in, the people to tell, the things to cancel. Where was Tom's passport, for example? She guessed most official things were in the desk drawers but she hadn't taken much notice when Tom had tried to involve her in the boring details of things relating to 'if this or that happens'. She hadn't imagined Tom leaving her, or his dying before her. She had taken his presence in her life for granted. So many things had been left unsaid. She lay back on the sofa and tried not to cry.

***

Claire's determination failed her that night.

Aunt Lou had a mobile phone with her at all times so that Claire could call her if she needed help at any time. She had also taken to coming down downstairs a couple of times in the night to make sure Claire was alright, since she knew Claire sometimes found it difficult to get on and off the commode that was left within easy reach of her bed. Claire had been outraged when she had seen the commode: no way was she going to use one of those, she had defiantly told Aunt

Lou. But after the first night of struggling from the bed to the wheelchair while she was bursting to pee, then from the wheelchair to the loo, and then back to bed, she decided that perhaps Aunt Lou was right. The indignity associated with the commode definitely outweighed the alterative.

Claire had gone to bed that night feeling a little queasy. She didn't know if it was the pills she was taking or perhaps something she'd eaten, but something wasn't right. As she sat on the hated commode she realized what it was when she saw the large clot of blood in its base.

The keening cries woke Aunt Lou. She didn't need the mobile to tell her that Claire needed her. Pulling her dressing gown on, she speculated on the reason for the cries, but not in a hundred years would she have guessed. She had not been aware of their plan to let nature take its course so she didn't understand Claire's distress initially. She busied herself looking for the pads she had bought as part of the shopping before Claire came home, as the usual tampons would have been too difficult to deal with, and gave one to Claire. Gradually, however, the reason for Claire's anguish at the sight of menstrual blood sunk in, and the realization hit her like a stone.

'Oh Claire, darling' she began, not knowing how to continue.

Claire's cries had turned to heart rending sobs which she tried to stop as she struggled to get herself back onto the bed. Aunt Lou sat on the bed beside her, having pushed the commode out of the way with her foot, and put her arms around her and gently rocked her. And in that moment they melded together as the mother and child they both missed.

Chapter 18

For the next few days Aunt Lou encouraged Claire to stay in bed to give her heart and mind a little time to heal. She didn't fuss. She left drinks and little tidbits to eat by the bed but didn't comment if nothing was touched. She noticed that the books and magazines were ignored but the picture of Tom was becoming more and more crumpled.

So she was surprised on the fourth day to find a very gaunt pale Claire out of bed and ready to face the day when she came down to prepare their breakfast. She bent and kissed her and then asked what she fancied that morning.

'A cup of coffee would be nice' she said, with a faint smile.

'Something to eat as well, I hope' said Aunt Lou, returning the smile.

'I'll try some toast please, but only a small piece to start with.' As she spoke she reached for the calendar lying open at the end of the table and flicked through the pages.

'We really must make arrangements for John Markham to come and see us, but I think we should see Greg Foreman first to see how he is getting on with the probate issues.' We?' queried Aunt Lou.

'Yes, we' replied Claire. 'I think you should be in on any arrangements or plans. After all, you are Tom's family too. But I do have an ulterior motive for asking you to be present.'

'And what's that then, dear?'

'I've been thinking about Francesca. When I die everything goes to her – apart from any small bequests I want to make. So she gets the house, if I haven't sold it to pay for care, and if the works are still in our possession she will get that too. I also want to make sure you are well provided for as well. So, I thought, if you are present for any discussions you can make sure I'm doing the right thing by Francesca.'

'Is that what Tom wanted?

'He didn't exactly spell it out in words of one syllable, but I'm sure that is what he would have wanted.'

'I'm not sure he would have wanted that. After all, the last time she spoke to him, he was adamant that he wanted no more to do with her.'

'Well, I think that was in the heat of the moment, don't you?' She hesitated for a second or two, before carrying on in a quiet voice, 'we didn't get around to discussing her, but I'm sure Tom wouldn't have maintained that view. In time he would have softened, don't you think?'

'Perhaps' she paused. 'I suppose if I was to think about it, I would probably agree with you. Tom wasn't one to bear a grudge too long.'

They were both silent for a few minutes. Claire watched Aunt Lou making the coffee and while her back was towards her she said 'I think I must have failed Francesca.' She bent her head and with her left hand doodled designs on the table as she continued, 'perhaps we should have given her a brother or sister. Or perhaps we didn't address the subject of her losing her mother properly. I've been thinking about it and wondering what I should have done differently.' She raised her head to see how Aunt Lou was reacting to her comments. She desperately wanted assurance that they had done things right by Francesca even though it was obvious they hadn't.

Aunt Lou put the bread in the toaster and then sat down opposite Claire and put her hand on Claire's.

'Now Claire dear, you and Tom were excellent parents to Fran. She was so young when her mother died she is unlikely to even remember her. After all, Jocelyn was hardly ever at home to care for her anyway, so there is no cause for you to worry about that. Tom and I did most of the care for her, and I've remained a constant in her life ever since. No, her problems started when she was raped, and the fact that you told Tom and he lost his idea of her being perfect. Despite all the help she was given then her mind seems to have stuck in a time warp. But that's not your fault. It's not Tom's either. It's her fault.'

'I still think I must have failed her.'

'Well I don't think you did' said Aunt Lou with an air of finality, which Claire ignored. 'That's why I want you to be present when plans are made about the future.'

'If that's what you want dear, then I'll be there. Now let's concentrate on breakfast, can we?'

Claire smiled. She loved Aunt Lou and forever gave thanks to any God that may be listening for her.

***

The next few days were taken quietly. Greg Foreman made arrangements to visit at the same time as John Markham, which surprised Claire. She wondered what they were going to say. Perhaps there was no money, or the works was in trouble, but definitely something awful. Why else would they both come? She shared these worries with Aunt Lou who pooh-poohed them all. They were just saving time coming together she assured Claire. Of course the works wasn't in trouble, otherwise the Chinese wouldn't have invested and, she had stressed, the Chinese had been told about Tom and they were still involved, so therefore all is well. Claire hoped she was right. Since everything else was wrong she was taking it for granted very pessimistically that the business affairs would be wrong too.

However, her pessimism was misplaced. So much for her thinking Tom hadn't done anything about the works – he had, and sometime ago too. She wasn't sure that she took in all the facts that the two men gave her but the gist of it was that she had no cause to worry about money. She would inherit his shares in Harrison Electronics, from which she'd be able to draw an income, and they told that there was a bank account in her name which had a sizeable amount of money in it. Tom had been depositing money in it for years. When Claire heard about that she put two and two together; Tom had always told her that there was no reason for her to work. He had hinted about there being a special account for her, but he hadn't been explicit and she had never asked. So now she knew. He had told her on many occasions that she didn't have to worry about money, but her childhood penury was buried deep in her subconscious and she did worry. She wondered when Tom had been going to tell her about this account. She remembered the elaborate plans he had had for a world cruise, which she had said, as a matter of course, was much too expensive. He had said it wasn't. Now there was no Tom but just a lot of cold hard cash.

Her musings were interrupted by John telling her that he had shares as well, and if she were agreeable, he would continue to run the works. When Tom had made him manager he had given him the shares then, plus a sizeable increase in salary, and he felt that with the new enthusiastic designer they had recently taken on the business was really going places. So it was decided that there would be no sale, and things should remain as Tom left them. Claire felt that John was very relieved about that decision as she knew that he would have to be the one to explain to the Chinese investors.

Thinking later about what Greg and John had told her she thought they'd said something about dodging inheritance tax. She had doubts about that. She somehow didn't think Tom would dodge tax? Being realistic though she guessed he might, especially that one. No one likes paying inheritance tax. But somewhere in the back of her mind she had a feeling that inheritance tax wasn't paid on stuff willed by a husband or a wife to the other, so what those two had been on about she didn't know. But she'd talk to Aunt Lou about it all to see if her version of what Greg and John had told her was the same. The painkillers she was still taking took their toll on her attention span at times.

***

The practicalities of her life took a turn for the better when she went for a check-up in the fracture clinic. A doctor that she hadn't seen before decided, after reviewing her X-rays and a further scan, that the pins sticking out of her leg could be removed. The swelling and bruising had finally settled and he suggested that she could go to theatre again and have pins and plates put in.

She spent a few days in hospital again and this time it was far easier to get home. Now she had a removable plaster on her leg and as soon as she got home she did her best to remove the forest that had grown up around the spikes. Aunt Lou thought it very funny watching Claire trying to shave her leg around all the new stitching.

'No one is going to see it Claire so why bother?'

'I can see it, and it looks horrible. And instead of laughing at me help me.'

Aunt Lou gingerly lifted Claire's damaged leg while Claire tried to get at the hair on the back.

'Shall I do it for you?' she asked, as she watched Claire's bungling left handed assault on her leg.

'No, I can do it' she insisted through gritted teeth, but after snagging a scab from where a spike had been she gave up, and abandoned her attempts.

'Okay that will do. I give up.'

Aunt Lou laughed at her as she busied herself removing the bowl of water, and the rest of the mess the whole operation had made. She handed Claire a clean towel to dry her leg, and then watched as she velcroed the two sections of light weight plaster back on her leg.

'You might have matched the two plaster casts you've got Claire. That purple doesn't match the pink of your arm one.'

'I tried, but they'd run out of pink and I wasn't going to hang around while they got a new supply of pink. Anyway I quite like it. It's cheerful.'

It wasn't the cheerfulness or otherwise that Claire particularly liked. It was the new freedom the plaster gave her. She still had to use the wheelchair to get about as her arm still wasn't strong enough yet for her to use crutches, but she felt more able to manipulate the chair as her arm improved. An added bonus was that her leg could bend at a better angle, now that no pins were sticking out and getting in the way.

While Aunt Lou was out one day Claire decided to implement a plan that she had been working on ever since she had got home. She knew there were going to be difficulties and repercussions from Aunt Lou when she got back, but she was determined to do what she had in mind.

She manoeuvred the wheelchair to the bottom of the stairs and put on the brake. With her left hand she clutched the banister, and with her left leg planted firmly on the floor, she dragged herself out of the chair onto the first step in an untidy heap, letting out an involuntary screech as she jarred her right leg. She had to wait for the pain to settle before she proceeded to drag herself up the stairs, step by step. At the top she paused to think about the best way to get to the bedroom. That's what she told herself anyway. In reality she was shattered. The effort involved had drained her of what little strength she had. She leant against the wall at the top of the stairs and debated with herself about the next move. She used the wall for support as she inched her way along the landing, finally reaching her goal.

Their room looked just as they had left it on that fateful Sunday afternoon. She didn't know why but she hadn't expected that. Her life had been completely overturned and somehow she thought their room would reflect that. It didn't. It was exactly the same. She dragged her self fully into the room and looked around more carefully. The photos were all gone. Perhaps Aunt Lou had thought it would be easier for her not to see reminders of Tom at every turn. The photos from downstairs had all gone too she realised with a start. How come she hadn't noticed before? She must ask Aunt Lou to put them back.

Keeping her back to the wall she moved further into the room before edging towards the wardrobe. She tried to reach the door handle, but no matter how hard she stretched her left hand she couldn't reach it. She had an overwhelming desire to touch Tom's clothes but her inability to get the wardrobe open was frustrating her so much she was in tears of rage. She kicked out at the door with her good leg but it wouldn't budge. She sat in a broken hearted heap. Her inability to do the simplest of things made her feel a total failure. Needing some support she dragged herself to the bed but no matter how she tried she couldn't get up onto it. She pulled a corner of the duvet, thinking that would make her more comfortable on the floor and as she did so she managed to dislodge Tom's pillow. It fell down and briefly brushed her face. It brushed her face with the warm loving scent of Tom. She hugged it to her and breathed in his old familiar smell, and wept.

And that is where Aunt Lou found her an hour later.

Chapter 19

Aunt Lou became much more wary about going out. She was worried about what Claire would get up to once her back was turned, so she made her promise not to attempt the stairs again while she was not there. Aunt Lou wanted to be around to pick up the pieces should Claire fall or otherwise damage herself.

But as Claire got stronger she did venture up the stairs more often, but under supervision. Her goal was to have a shower as she was totally fed up with just using a bowl of water. She was determined to have her way, and as a worried Aunt Lou trailed up the stairs behind her, she told her what she planned to do. The main thing, she said, was not to get the right leg wet. It didn't matter about the right arm, she told Aunt Lou in her best 'don't argue' nursing sister tone; she was sure that it could cope with a little water now. However, it was all a bit of a performance as she found the only way she could do it was to sit on the floor of the shower, with her damaged leg stuck out the door. Then Aunt Lou had to be on hand to lift the shower head off its base and give it to Claire to hold, and then turn it on. In theory it seemed a good idea but the initial spray of cold water made her let out a surprised yelp, but as it slowly warmed up the luxury of the water cascading over her was worth all the trouble of organizing it, though she wasn't so sure Aunt Lou agreed.

Contemplating the bathroom from her low position she saw things she hadn't noticed before, like the streaks on the underside of the sink and the fluff under the pipes. She was thankful that no one else would be in position to see her shoddy housework, or to see the tears flow when she saw Tom's toothbrush looking lonely in the glass above the sink.

She sat in the puddle of water until she looked like a prune, so much so that Aunt Lou risked her disapproval and turned the shower off. Then the whole performance was reversed with, by now, a chilly Claire edging herself out of the shower tray on to the bathroom floor where Aunt Lou had laid a pile of towels and a clean set of clothes. So she achieved her goal as planned, but she was worn out and very sleepy for the rest of the day.

**

Every so often Aunt Lou went to check on her own home, just like Mrs D did regularly. She did it at irregular times, to fool the burglars she told Claire, and as she was about to leave one day she heard a very tentative knock on the front door. She was surprised. It was rare to get visitors. Nothing had been ordered, and anyway delivery men tended to lean on the doorbell till someone answered.

Aunt Lou didn't recognize the woman clutching a spray of beautiful flowers standing a yard or so away from the front door, looking like a frightened rabbit.

'Good afternoon' she said, in a tone barely above a whisper, 'is Claire Harrison at home?'

Aunt Lou paused before replying. She reckoned that she was a good judge of character and this woman didn't look as if she had come to upset Claire, and besides someone had gone to a lot of trouble with the flowers. You didn't do that if you were up to no good.

'Yes, she is. Who shall I say has come to see her?'

'Anne Alsopp.'

'Oh' was Aunt Lou's rather shocked first comment. But she immediately recovered her composure and asked her to come in. Anne stepped into the hallway, still looking rather hesitant, and Aunt Lou shut the door and indicated that Anne should follow her. As she reached the sitting room door, which was ajar, she called to Claire that she had a visitor. She pushed the door open wide and ushered Anne in.

Claire looked up from positioning her leg on the sofa, and her mouth fell open.

'Anne. How nice to see you, so kind of you to come...' she gabbled, 'please sit down.'

Anne perched herself on the seat of the armchair opposite Claire, looking as if she was going to sprint for the door should the atmosphere turn nasty.

'Aunt Lou, this is Anne Alsopp, Charlotte's mother. Anne this is my aunt Louisa Harrison.' With the niceties over Claire went quiet. Gazing at Anne she wondered what on earth had persuaded her to visit. Claire was so accustomed to being considered the enemy, the bogeyman, the killer, she couldn't think straight. As her mind started to construct fantasies about the death of Charlotte being all a big mistake Aunt Lou brought her back to earth by asking Anne if she would like her to put the flowers in water. Once the flowers were dealt with it was time to ask about coffee, or tea perhaps, or a big brandy to counteract the effects of shock might have been a better suggestion Claire thought.

'I felt I had to come' Anne started, 'to say sorry.'

'Sorry?' Claire managed to get her query in just before Aunt Lou did.

'I should have come before, I know, but I was scared.'

'But why? What have you got to be scared about?'

'I was worried about how you'd react. You've had so much to put up with in the last few weeks...'

'I don't suppose your life has been very easy either' Claire interrupted quietly.

'...what with the accident and the loss of your husband. And then I heard through the hospital grapevine that you'd lost your job too, and all on account of my family.' Anne bowed her head as she finished speaking. She looked like a penitent asking for forgiveness, which upset Claire, as she knew it should have been the other way round. It was her family that had caused Anne's anguish.

Claire reached across to briefly touch Anne's clasped hands. 'Anne' she said, 'May I call you that? I feel I know you because you've given me coffee in the hospital so many times over the years.' There was a nod from Anne. 'It's me that should apologise to you. What has been said in the press is most likely true. I should have gone to the police that first day, when I saw Charlotte. I shouldn't have gone to the house. But I did. Although I was sure I had seen your daughter that day, everyone told me I was imagining things; that I was just another loony who imagined seeing missing children. So perhaps I just wanted to prove to myself I wasn't a loony. I didn't want to look silly. Yet I did go to the police because I just knew I had to regardless of whether I looked a prat or not. The police shows on the television all talk about them having a gut instinct about things, well I had the full works, a gut, heart, soul and mind instinct, but it was all for nothing. Instead of helping her I caused her death.'

'I can see why you might think that, and I hated the way you were vilified in the papers. But we still don't know whether they meant to kill her or not. We never had a ransom note or anything like that. So perhaps it might have happened at any time.' Anne paused for a few seconds to take a sip of her coffee. As she put her cup down she added. 'Your going to the house to try and find her was brave, and I admire you for doing it. I know the end result was a disaster but she was found reasonably quickly. At least then we knew. And it did look as if she was cared for. I only hope that she didn't suffer too much.' Tears were trickling down Anne's face as she finished, matched by those of Claire's.

Aunt Lou quietly left the room, closing the door behind her.

Claire reached out to take Anne's hand and as she did so Anne got up and approached her. Dropping to her knees beside the sofa she gave Claire a fierce hug, and as she held her she muttered 'there's something else. I have to tell you something else.' She sat back on her haunches. Twisting her hands together, she added 'I've come to see you before the police do.'

'Why what's happened? A policewoman came a while back to ask about the accident but there was no mention of Charlotte. Is it about Charlotte?' Claire was curious, but scared too. What else could have happened? What on earth was Anne going to tell her? She lifted her right leg so that it was wedged firmly against the back of the sofa, and patted the space she had made, so that Anne could sit more comfortably.

'I'd better sit back over there' Anne said as she stood up. 'You won't want me near you when you hear what I have to say.'

'I don't think anything you tell me could be worse than what has gone on already. So stop worrying and tell me.'

'It's about the accident. I know what happened, and who caused it. I know who killed your husband.'

Claire's still damp eyes opened wide.

'I wanted to tell you before the police did. It was my husband who did it. Well, not exactly him. He just organized it.'

'Organized it' Claire echoed. She was flabbergasted. People didn't organize things like that. That only happened in films. 'How do you mean 'organized it'?'

Anne sat back in the chair and started twisting her hands again. She swallowed nervously. 'I'll tell you what I know, what I've found out. It's hard, so let me say what I have to say, then you can ask me what you want at the end.'

'Okay.'

'Well, when Charlotte went missing my husband Giles started to drink. To begin with it was just at home. Then he started going to the pub. He was off work on compassionate leave, and didn't like being in the empty house, except for me and the police liaison officer of course. She was lovely. I liked her a lot but Giles didn't. So he went to the pub, and more often than not would come home very drunk. I didn't like the policewoman seeing him like that so I told her I was okay and not to bother coming round anymore. After all we knew by then that Charlotte was dead. And we'd had the funeral. But by then he was following all that stuff in the papers about you. I said it was rubbish because I knew you, but he wouldn't listen, which was funny really because he used to say that anything printed in the paper was made up, and that I shouldn't believe everything I read. Yet here was he believing everything he read, and he blamed you for causing Charlotte's death.' She stopped as she saw the stricken look on Claire's face. 'I'm sorry Claire. I really am, but I must finish.'

'One night he came back from the pub, much drunker than usual, and said something about having fixed things. I didn't know what he was on about, but I found out later. But it was too late to stop him. Apparently, in a drunken state, he had been saying to anyone who'd listen that he'd pay anything to get back at you. Two lads took him up on the offer, and staged the accident.'

'Oh, Anne. How did you find out?'

'The police found the car, then the two boys who they thought had driven it, and one of them admitted what they had done and why. He told the police who had paid them, which Giles flatly denied, but other people in the pub had heard him go on about what he wanted to do to you. Also the £500 he paid was taken out of his account at the time the boy said they were paid. He was also seen handing it over because he had a shouting match with the boys. He was yelling at them that they'd made a mess of the job so he wasn't going to pay, and so drew even more attention to himself.'

'So what's happening now?'

'I've left him.' Anne let that bald statement sink in for a while, before adding, 'actually I threw him out. I'm not sure where he is now. Perhaps the police have him. I know he is to be charged with killing your husband and injuring you, but I don't know the details.'

'How ghastly for you.'

'Not really. For a long time we have only been together because of Charlotte, and now she has gone there is no reason to stay. I couldn't leave him while Charlotte was alive as she was adopted. Did you know that? I couldn't break up the family. It would have been awful for Charlotte if I had. I had always told her that she was special, that we had chosen her specially. If I had walked out it would look as if she was being abandoned again. She might have blamed herself, and I couldn't risk that. Giles was a bully towards me, but only verbally. He never hit me or anything like that, and he did adore Charlotte. We adopted her because we couldn't have children, well he couldn't. His sperm count was too low.'

Anne stopped talking for a moment or two, and then started again in a more reflective tone. 'I was surprised we were ever allowed to adopt Charlotte though. I didn't think we fitted the criteria. I suppose Giles' connections because of his job helped, and we did come from stable backgrounds, but I don't think we came over in the interviews as ideal parents. At least I didn't think we did. To be honest I felt somewhat betrayed by Giles. He didn't let on about not being able to have children before we married, although he knew. He didn't let on that he had been married before either. That was a shock. I just found out by chance, and the first wife knew about his low sperm count. It was Charlotte that kept us together. Now she has gone, there is no reason to stay.'

As Anne's confidences poured out of her Claire wondered if she had ever spoken to anyone about them before. Anne said she had been naïve and trusting when she had married Giles, and she was certainly being very trusting in telling Claire. Thinking about their situations now Claire appreciated the fact that though she had lost Tom she had been so lucky having nearly twenty long loving years with him. Anne had nothing, whilst she had her cherished memories.

'What are you planning to do now?' Claire asked.

Anne smiled. 'I was going to ask you the same thing.'

'Well, for me it is a question of waiting for the fractures to heal. I am lucky that I don't have to work if I don't want to, but I think I will want to. But I don't really know what the future will bring.'

'I don't really know either. I shall have to get a paid job now though if I want to keep the house, and I do. I can't lose all the memories of Charlotte that are there. Giles didn't like the idea of my going out to work. That's why I only did voluntary jobs. He had very strict old fashioned ideas about mothers being at home. He was always rather officious when it came to social services rules and regulations, which didn't go down well with some of his staff. Actually I don't think they liked him much, so I don't suppose they'll miss him if he ends up in prison. He insisted that I had to be at home when Charlotte was, so that made even the voluntary jobs difficult since I had to have the school holidays off. But the people I work with are great and they accommodated all my little foibles.' She laughed as she made her last point. For a second or two she looked as if she hadn't a care in the world.

Chapter 20

As Claire's fractures healed she promoted herself from the wheelchair to a zimmer frame for use around the house. She was now able to put a certain amount of weight onto her right arm but it wasn't yet strong enough to use a crutch, but she was getting there. She told herself that the zimmer was only for using in the house but since she never went anywhere telling herself that was pointless. Also, she knew that using a zimmer frame had connotations with old age and so no way was she going to be seen using one. Aunt Lou came and went and Mrs D was in and out but Claire continued to remain in purdah, through her own choice. She didn't want to face the world outside unless she had to. She attended her appointments at the hospital but she made no effort to see any of her old colleagues when she was there. That life had gone.

She followed all the details in the press about Giles Alsopp, and very quickly became aware that she had not been forgotten, which made her even more reluctant to go out and about. More sympathy was shown to him than to her. All the particulars of Charlotte's death were reprinted, with added embellishments, and the story was twisted to make it sound as if he had a right to take revenge, so much so that Claire wondered if Francesca or Gareth Jones had had a hand in writing it. All the details of the 'accident' were rehashed over and over again, and the general consensus was that she 'had asked for it'. Not Tom though. The press continued to treat him kindly - and so they jolly well should, said Claire to the unresponsive newspaper as she read it. At times she imagined that she was talking to Tom, rather than to herself, and she became quite adept at one sided conversations. As she scoured the papers for police updates on their hunt for Charlotte's abductors, or just found some interesting local news she would tell Tom all about it, and hear his beloved voice in her mind replying.

Anne also came in for criticism, which upset Claire. She was disparaged for having left Giles 'in his hour of need'; how could she be so unfeeling, they said. You don't know the half of it, Claire heard herself shouting at the paper. She was furious and when Aunt Lou came in to find out what all the noise was about she gave her chapter and verse on her thoughts about the great British press. 'Don't read it then' was Aunt Lou's pragmatic answer.

Aunt Lou had begun to spend more time in her own home during the day, at Claire's insistence, and so was not often party to Claire's vocal outbursts. She knew Claire talked to Tom when she was on her own because she had come back from shopping unexpectedly early one day and heard her. It was so poignant that she had to wait for her eyes to stop running before she could announce her return.

Apart from occasional visits from Anne, and her neighbour Dora, Claire had no other visitors. She was always keen to ask Aunt Lou though about whom she had seen and who she had spoken to. This was not just because she wanted to make conversation, she was genuinely interested. Aunt Lou had a wide social network and Claire liked to hear the stories that Aunt Lou brought back with her. She had a great sense of humour and could turn the most banal of encounters into a comic story, and a little bit of cheerfulness did her good. The gloom was beginning to lift week by week until such times something would happen which would cause the grief to surface again.

The grief returned with a vengeance on the day she got a letter from Francesca. She recognized the handwriting and thought that perhaps, at last, Francesca was going to call a truce to her hostile behaviour. Why on earth she thought that, she decided later, since letters written by Francesca in the recent past were far from friendly, she didn't know. This letter was as formal as the funeral one and as deadly as the 'poison pen' one. In it she requested that Claire should vacate the house at her earliest convenience as the house now belonged to her, according to the terms of her father's wishes.

Claire had never fainted in her life. Admittedly she had had episodes of light-headedness, like after a previous missive, but this time she felt as if she was about to. Everything began to go black, just a pinprick of light remained, seemingly very far away. Luckily she had sat herself down on the sofa to read the mail, so as the blackness enveloped her she allowed herself to flop back against the cushions without doing any further damage to herself. She didn't know how long she was there, but it felt like a lifetime before her pulse returned to some semblance of normal. She brushed the cold sweat off her forehead with her sleeve, before picking up the offensive letter again to see if she had imagined its contents.

Where had Francesca got the idea that the house was hers? Yes, it could be hers after she had died too, but not before. In the will Claire had seen Tom write he had made it quite clear that the house was hers in her lifetime, and if she chose to sell it before she died she was perfectly entitled to do so. In fact Tom hadn't insisted at all that she will it to Francesca, but she had said she would if it was still in her possession.

Why was Francesca claiming the house now, and what did she expect her to do? Where was she supposed to live? Claire hadn't heard from her since that fateful evening before the accident. She knew Aunt Lou saw her occasionally but there had been no hint about her planning to take the house. She had a perfectly good flat, so why the house? Perhaps she was planning to get married and wanted more space, but she'd heard nothing like that. Perhaps the Giles Alsopp affair had stirred things up again for her. Seeing articles about her Dad and her wicked stepmother perhaps had unbalanced her.

The front door opening and the cheerful 'I'm back' from Aunt Lou startled Claire out of her reverie. She got up and as she stood she clutched the zimmer while waiting for the slight dizziness to pass, before moving slowly into the kitchen.

'I managed to get those poppy seed biscuits you like, dear. But I didn't like the look of the fish so I got some meat instead. Hope that's...' Aunt Lou looked up from unpacking the shopping and dropped the tin she was holding, '... okay with you.' She finished her sentence very slowly, and faced the whey-faced Claire.

'You look terrible, dear. What's happened? Are you hurt? Come and sit down before you fall down.' Aunt Lou pulled a chair away from the table and took the zimmer as Claire sat down, put her elbows on the table and dropped her head into her hands.

'It's Francesca' she muttered into her hands.

'What about her? What's happened to her? Is she alright?'

'She seems perfectly alright. Look.' She pulled the letter out of her pocket. At first she had intended to hide it from Aunt Lou, but on second thoughts she realized that that was a daft thing to do.

Aunt Lou took the letter, pulled out a chair opposite Claire and sat down. She read the letter, and looked up in disbelief, before looking at it a second time.

'Seems to me we need to see Greg Foreman again, don't you think?'

'I suppose so. But why, Aunt Lou? Why is she doing this? She knows it's my home. What's got into her? Has she said anything to you?'

'No, she hasn't said anything to me. She was fine when I last saw her. I tell her how you are getting on, although I know she doesn't want to hear it, and I tell her what I've been doing. We talk about her job and her friends. We just generally chat about all and sundry. She did say, though, that she'd like to have a go at Giles Alsopp for killing her Dad, but that's all she has said about it all. She never mentions you, so I don't know what's she's thinking about on that score.'

'When did you last see her?'

'Last week sometime. Thursday I think. We had a coffee together in that new place in the High Street, in her lunch break. She seemed fine. In fact she was talking about possible promotion at work, but it would mean moving to Manchester, and she wasn't sure whether she wanted that or not.'

'So why demand the house then? Do you think she is just being cussed? Does she just want to remind me that she's around?'

'I've really no idea.'

'I wonder who's put her up to this? It was that Gareth Jones that egged her on before. Perhaps she has a new boyfriend with ideas of his own.'

'The best thing we can do is get Greg to write her a formal letter, letting her know that there'll be hell to pay if she pursues this.'

'I suppose so. Might as well make an appointment to see him as soon as possible then.'

Claire made the call and Greg suggested calling in that evening on his way home. She read the letter to him over the phone so that he would know what she wanted to see him about. 'What a bummer' was his only comment.

While Aunt Lou retrieved the fallen tin and finished unpacking the shopping Claire asked her if she thought Francesca might have a go at Anne since now she knew it was Giles who had killed her Dad.

'Unlikely, I would have thought. But perhaps we should invite her round for a coffee or something, to see if she has heard from Francesca. If she doesn't mention anything we won't either.'

Chapter 21

Nothing more was heard from Francesca. It was all very strange. Nothing for weeks, then that demand for the house, then nothing again. Even Aunt Lou had no contact with her. Greg had sent a very stern reply to her demand, and that seemed to be it. Aunt Lou and Claire debated the likelihood of her having taken that job in Manchester. There were ways, of course, of finding out, but they didn't bother. Let sleeping dogs lie, they decided.

Claire's right arm was now out of plaster officially. She had been leaving it off for short periods already but she didn't tell the doctor that. She'd also been doing gentle exercises, so she thought she'd have the full use of it again soon. The granny zimmer had been abandoned, and she'd tried to bypass crutches and use two sticks instead – also not known, or authorized, at the hospital, but it hadn't worked. She needed crutches. She was gradually putting a little weight on her right leg but she was being sensible about keeping the plaster on. Busting an arm again she could cope with, but she wasn't going to risk all that work the surgeon had down putting her leg back together again.

She remained very solitary. Aunt Lou, Claire knew, was worried about her, but she was quite happy on her own. She could talk to Tom without breaking down. Just occasionally she'd get a whiff of something that would bring him to mind with so much intensity that she'd be moved to tears, but on the whole she was coping. The worst thing was not finding him there when she wanted to tell him something, or discuss something she'd seen on the television or read in the paper. There was a limit to one-sided conversations.

Aunt Lou spent most of the time in her own home now, but Mrs D continued to come and do her housework. Claire wondered why on earth she had always refused to have a cleaner; it was such a joy. Dora came round and advised Claire about what she should do in the garden, and seeing Claire's total incompetence when it came to gardening she found herself sharing the young man that Dora employed. So she wasn't lonely.

Anne would phone to find out how she was getting on, but rarely visited now. She was working full time, and enjoying it. Her parents had helped her pay off Giles so she was able to hang onto the house. She never mentioned Giles to Claire, and the papers had other matters to write headlines about, so Claire didn't know whether he was on remand or not, or even in prison. She hadn't seen any report about a trial so perhaps it hadn't happened yet. She really didn't want to know. Sometimes she did wonder about the two lads that had actually driven the car. Where were they now? Did they think killing Tom was worth what they were paid? There had been no further information in the paper about them either, and the police hadn't told her about a possible court case. She could ask, she supposed, but she didn't. Her curiosity had gone, like everything else in her life.

It was brought home to her how narrow her life had become when she went to the cinema one evening with Aunt Lou. The noisy multi-aged crowd queuing to get in made her realise that her life revolved around three relatively old ladies and one young man of indeterminate age. She didn't know how old Mrs D was but she was a fair bit older than herself so she was added to Aunt Lou and Dora. Yet two of those four were employees, so that left two old ladies as her sole companions. She'd have to do something, but when she asked Tom what she should do he hadn't any suggestions.

Nights out, even if only to the local cinema, were rare, so she and Aunt Lou were very pleased with themselves when they had managed to get good seats for a concert. It was an all Mozart programme and Claire was a bit concerned about how she would be able to cope with the emotion Mozart's music generated in her, but she felt it was time she unbuttoned a bit. She'd take a pile of tissues with her, just in case.

***

The concert was superb, and yes she did cry a bit, but she wasn't the only one. A surreptitious glance around showed that many a concert-goer had damp eyes. It was that sort of music.

Aunt Lou decided to stay over with Claire that night and as they had a late night drink together they discussed how Claire should expand her horizons. It was high time she got out a bit more, Aunt Lou told her. It was time she made a new life for herself. Aunt Lou's new life was going to start with another Age Concern holiday with her friend Viv, but they were not going to that cabbage smelling place, Aunt Lou was quick to point out. This time they were going to Bournemouth. Claire could see the way the conversation was heading, so to head Aunt Lou off from suggesting she join her and Viv, Claire announced that she was thinking of going on holiday to the hotel she and Tom liked so much on the south coast. She had no real intention of doing any such thing, but it kept at bay the suggestion of going to Bournemouth, and it pleased Aunt Lou no end.

Claire was by now sleeping upstairs in her own bed. Mrs D's sons had been back to dismantle her dining room bedroom and put everything back as it had been. The day that happened was the best day of her life post-accident. She saw herself as finally getting back to normal. She had got into the habit of thinking of things as pre and post-accident. Pre-accident was one life and post-accident was another. Pre-accident was Tom and post-accident it was his ghost.

Gone were the days when Aunt Lou brought her tea in bed, and much as she would have liked to she couldn't reciprocate that kind gesture while she still couldn't hold a tray. She had difficulty moving around with just holding a mug. But she was downstairs first the next morning and had got the breakfast ready for them both. She called Aunt Lou but there was no answering call. The mobile phone communication system they had used before had been discarded, so Claire went to the bottom of the stairs and called again. Still no answer. Strange. She had suspected that Aunt Lou was going a little deaf, but not that deaf.

She had developed a good system for getting up the stairs. She sat herself on the bottom step and moved up the stairs on her bottom one at a time, using her good leg to lever herself to the next step, and her good arm to carry the crutches. This worked well until she reached the top. That's where the idea of it being a good system let her down. At the top there was the difficulty of getting to her feet without putting too much pressure on her right leg. But she had found that if she turned and faced the top she could haul herself up with her left hand. It was undignified but it worked.

She knocked on Aunt Lou's bedroom door but there was no answer even though the light was on. She pushed the door open and saw Aunt Lou leaning against her pillows smiling at something she was reading. It must have been a good book if she hadn't heard me calling her was Claire's immediate thought, but her second thought was more frightening. Aunt Lou was dead. Her pallor and the coldness of her skin as

Claire searched for a pulse told her the dreadful truth. A massive heart attack was confirmed later.

Aunt Lou's doctor came and filled out the death certificate after explaining to Claire that he had expected it to happen sooner rather than later. There would be no need for a post mortem as he had seen her within the preceding three weeks, and had warned her then that her heart was in very bad shape. She had been philosophical about it. She had told him, a friend of long standing, that she had a good life and that her dearest wish, which was to see Claire through her trauma, had been granted. She was ready to go whenever it happened.

To say that Claire was devastated was underestimating the desolation that tore through her. As Aunt Lou's body was taken away she felt as if her heart was being ripped out again. While she spent a final few minutes with the woman that meant more to her than life, the doctor, knowing more about her than she thought he knew, had gone round to Dora's house to tell her the news, and to ask her to come in when Aunt Lou left for the last time. Dora phoned Mrs D and between them they cleared the breakfast table and tidied up Aunt Lou's room while Claire lay as if dead herself on her bed. The doctor had given her a hefty sedative and had told the two distraught older ladies that he'd be back before evening surgery.

The sedative numbed her body but not her mind. She felt as if a big black cloud was suffocating her, and if it wasn't for the fact that Aunt Lou was relying on her to see her put to rest, she'd have let it. She heard Mrs D and Dora talking quietly as they stripped and remade Aunt Lou's bed. They put her overnight things and her clothes in the bag she had brought with her the previous day, and Mrs D was going to take them back to Aunt Lou's home. She heard Mrs D leave. One of her son's had come to collect her and take her home. Dora remained downstairs, and every so often she crept up the stairs to check on Claire. Twice she had been into the room to tuck the duvet round her, and another time she had tenderly patted the uncovered hand, but Claire had feigned sleep each time. She didn't trust herself to even say thank you. No doubt in her long life Dora had experienced grief, but Claire suspected that she probably felt as helpless as anyone else in the face of another's heartbreak, so didn't expect her to speak.

She must have fallen asleep eventually because she woke when the doctor came back as promised. He left some pills for her to take at night, and told her to ring if she needed anything. She got herself up and had a shower, to try and disperse the lingering cloud in her head. But it didn't work. Dora made her some tea and told her that there was a meal in the fridge if she felt a little hungry, and then she left after first telling Claire that she had contacted Francesca. She had come to know Claire well enough to know that telling Francesca was the best thing she could do to help her.

***

The next few days went by in a blur. Again Mr Upton came to call on her, and went through the provisional arrangements for Aunt Lou's funeral with her. She had taken a taxi to Aunt Lou's house the day after her death and in Mrs D's presence she had found the paperwork relating to Aunt Lou's wishes about her funeral. Even in the depths of her despair she knew that she had to have a witness to anything she did in regard to Aunt Lou. The spectre of Francesca's potential wrath hovered over her.

The practical arrangements were relatively straightforward. Everyone who knew Aunt Lou had to be told. Putting a suitable notice in the paper was a priority, in case she didn't reach all of Aunt Lou's friends by phone. Claire had spent a long afternoon going through Aunt Lou's address book and phoning all those she thought ought to know, which meant all of them, except one. This one was an Italian name with an address near Venice. Claire didn't trust her limited ability in spoken Italian so she sent him a letter, hoping that it would reach him in time if he wanted to attend the funeral.

She spoke to the vicar of Aunt Lou's church and he announced her death to his parishioners, which brought in a flood of cards and memories, so much so that Claire increased the number of Order of Service booklets. Mrs D was a great help. Being a rather large lady she was very effective in barring the door to visitors when she thought Claire had had enough, and she had a great instinct for knowing when coffee was necessary. From Francesca they heard nothing. Dora assured them that she had spoken to her when Aunt Lou died and again to ask her if she would like to help in the arrangements for the funeral. She had been very shocked initially and incoherent for much of the first phone call, but she was cold and very negative in the second. Greg Foreman had contacted her too as Aunt Lou had left a letter for her which she was to receive before Aunt Lou's will was read. There was one for Claire as well, but when Greg told her she didn't take it in. Having spent time listening to Aunt Lou's friends telling her what a great lady she was, she was finding it very difficult to keep her emotions in check, and at times found herself working on auto-pilot. She knew Aunt Lou was a great lady and she too could produce a fund of stories about her, detailing acts of kindness, et cetera, all of which Claire could cap with her own experience of knowing Aunt Lou.

The only time she really broke down in the presence of anyone else was when she and Mrs D were preparing Aunt Lou's clothes, the ones she was to be buried in. She had asked Mrs D if she could iron the blouse they had decided on and she did this by propping herself against the worktop in the kitchen so that she could use the ironing board. As she smoothed away the creases her stiff upper lip relaxed a little more at each sweep of the iron. Mrs D, sensing the moment, was on hand to catch the iron as she tumbled to the floor and howled. Later, when she put a picture of Tom, herself and the young Francesca in the coffin before the lid was finally screwed down, she was able to maintain her composure. Although it was hard, very hard, she maintained that composure throughout the day of the funeral

On the morning of the funeral, which was being held in Aunt Lou's parish church, St. Margaret's, it was a grey day. The sky was overcast and the threat of rain meant everyone had coats and umbrellas at the ready, but the church was full and there were flowers and lit candles everywhere. Whoever was responsible had totally ignored Aunt Lou's dictum that flowers at a funeral were a waste, and the lusty singing of cheerful hymns, and the entertaining eulogy made it a joyous celebration of her life. The buffet lunch in the church hall was a splendid success and Claire felt that she had done justice to her greatest friend.

Claire had thought long and hard about her position as regards the funeral. In theory she was not a relation, Francesca was the only blood relative. However, she knew that she had every right to organize things, but the lack of input from Francesca was a constant niggle. But she needn't have worried. On the day Francesca totally ignored her, pointedly ignored her, and held court with a favoured few, much to the distress of some of Aunt Lou's friends. She excused herself from the short service at the crematorium late in the day as she had to catch the train back up to Manchester.

It wasn't until about half way through the buffet lunch that Claire became aware that she had two shadows. Whenever anyone approached her she noticed that Gavin or James Donaldson was hovering nearby. They had been on hand to help her in and out of the limousine; one had followed her into the church, the other had gone ahead, and whenever she moved they moved too. It must be like having close protection officers, she decided. During a lull in the proceedings she caught up with Mrs D and asked her what was going on.

'We were concerned about you. Who knows who might have turned up? We didn't want any trouble. Miss Harrison would have wanted us to protect you, in case there are any loonies still out there.'

'That's so kind of you Mrs Donaldson. I never gave it a thought,' she paused and gazed around the packed hall, 'we've done her proud, don't you think. She'd have enjoyed this wouldn't she?'

Chapter 22

You'd have thought it got easier the second time around, Claire told herself, as she battled with another lot of paperwork following Aunt Lou's death. She was, again, an executor with Greg Foreman. She was very lucky that it was him she had to deal with as she thought Aunt Lou had dealt with another group of solicitors in the town. No, said Greg, she had contacted him years and years ago, around the time Tom was setting up Harrison Electronics, and had moved her business over to him then.

Her affairs were very easy to deal with as she had itemized everything and had left clear instructions about what she wanted done. Whereas her funeral plans had been reasonably flexible, the instructions about her belongings were not. But Claire didn't know this until she had read the letter Aunt Lou had left her. Claire asked Greg if Aunt Lou had left a letter for Tom as well. She hadn't, as she had only written the letters for her and Francesca after Tom had died. Francesca's letter had been given to her before she went back to Manchester. Greg had asked her to call into the office before going to the station, and she had had been given her letter then. She had opened it in front of Greg and read it, and her only comment, Greg said, was 'Okay, that's fine by me.'

Claire took her letter home with her. She still felt too raw to read it in front of Greg. She'd done crying, she kept telling herself, but telling herself what to do was one thing, sticking to it was another. Once home she pottered around getting herself something to eat, anything to put off opening the envelope. She put it beside her plate, which held a piece of toast and Marmite, her staple food since Aunt Lou died, and looked at the writing. Aunt Lou had just written her first name, and under her name she had written 'To be opened before reading my will'. Was she being prepared for the fact that Aunt Lou was leaving everything to a cats home, or something like that? Hardly. Aunt Lou didn't like cats. Or was she going to be asked to do something? Something to do with her ashes perhaps?

She even washed up her plate and tidied the kitchen before she got around to opening the letter. She could put it off no longer. And she had to read it that evening as she was seeing Greg in the morning about the will. Finding a sharp knife she slid it under the flap and sliced open the envelope.

Darling girl, it said in Aunt Lou's familiar hand,

If you are reading this it must mean I am dead. I hope you gave me a good send off! I just wanted to tell you that you were to me the daughter I never had, and I couldn't have asked for a better one. I've loved and admired you from that first day you came home with Tom. You coped with a difficult child magnificently so don't ever think otherwise. I think she must have had more of her mother's blood in her than her father's!

The reason for this letter is to tell you about my will. I know that Tom has left you comfortably off, and I know if I left you money you would use it sensibly, but this is to tell you I haven't left you any. I think you will see from my will that I have left it to good causes and I am depending on you to see that it gets there! I have also told Francesca that she will not be getting money from me either.

There is one other thing I would like you to do. In my jewellery box, wrapped in tissue paper, in a small blue box, is a ring. I was given it by a young man called Pietro Farenesi when I was in Italy many,

many years ago. It belonged to his mother, and his grandmother before her, and he refused to take it back when I decided that I couldn't marry him after all. It is a family piece that I think should go back to the family. Pietro's address is in my address book, and I would like you to take money from my estate to pay for the trip. Please do this one last thing for me Claire. I'm sure you will.

God bless you.

Your loving aunt, Louisa x

Claire sat looking at the letter for a long time after reading it. Aunt Lou hadn't had many occasions to write to her. It was usually just shopping lists and the like. She couldn't remember the last time she had seen that much of her writing in one go. She recognized the Italian name though. It was the same Pietro Farenesi she had written to, to tell him about Aunt Lou's death. There had been a very swift reply, in excellent English, to say that he was sorry but he would not be able to come to the funeral. Perhaps Aunt Lou suspected that, and that was why she wanted her to go to Italy to return the ring. But she also suspected that Aunt Lou saw her request as a way to get her to go on holiday, to have a complete change of scene.

Perhaps she was right; she should think about a change. After all there was nothing to stop her. No family to consider. No pets to look after. Nothing.

When Claire arrived at Greg's office the following morning he told her that he knew that the letters were telling Claire and Francesca that they were not going to inherit any money, because Aunt Lou had told him when she had been to see him about rewriting her will just after Tom's death. But he didn't know about the

221

ring. He was intrigued about the failed romance and asked lots of questions but she knew nothing about it. Aunt Lou had never told her. The only time that Aunt Lou had even hinted about it was when she told her that she had nearly come home with a handsome Italian after being in Italy for some time. They'd been talking about Francesca at the time, so Claire hadn't had the opportunity to ask questions, and then she forgot. She wondered whether Aunt Lou would have told her about this Pietro or not. She had always been very reticent when it came to talking about herself, and she'd usually steer the conversations in other directions. Claire was beginning to think that it might be quite exciting to go and meet this Italian who had fallen for Aunt Lou. But first she had better find the ring.

Greg went through Aunt Lou's will with her, telling her as much as he knew about the people and charities that featured. She wasn't surprised to hear that the house and all its furnishings were to go to Mrs Donaldson, but on her death the house was to be sold and the money given to St Catherine's, the children's hospice. The Donaldson boys were both in good jobs so Aunt Lou had probably decided they didn't need anything from her, via their mother. Various bequests to friends were itemized, and a large chunk of money was going to go to the Trauma Unit at the hospital, 'with many thanks for saving my niece'. St Margaret's got a sizeable legacy too, to help fund the new organ, so Aunt Lou was going to be remembered by lots of grateful people, as well as herself. A small parcel of jewellery was to go to Francesca plus any item from the house that she would like, and Claire had the same. She couldn't decide what she wanted from the house but she knew that Tom had particularly liked a water colour painting that hung in the sitting room, so she thought she might ask for that.

She left Greg to contact all the people mentioned in the will. She wasn't really sure what an executor was supposed to do apart from carry out the wishes of the deceased, but she guessed Greg would contact her if he needed her. On her way home she got the taxi to stop at Aunt Lou's so that she could collect the ring. She was keen to see it, but keener still to hear the story behind it. The story would have to wait awhile yet. She didn't want to travel while still in plaster.

**

In the end Claire decided that she couldn't wait for the plaster to be removed. She had become adept at using the crutches and she felt that her only disability now was that she couldn't drive, but there was nothing to stop her getting on a plane. The trip to Italy felt like unfinished business, and she found that she couldn't settle to anything knowing that she hadn't carried out Aunt Lou's last instructions.

She spent some time trawling through Venice hotel sites and flight schedules on her computer weighing up the pros and cons of different hotels. Although Pietro's family lived just outside Venice she decided she'd rather stay in the town so that she could sightsee on her own without looking conspicuous. She finally settled on a central hotel after shutting her eyes and playing her mouse over the list of hotels she had accumulated on the screen. She had no idea what the hotel's name meant but it sounded wonderful when the receptionist answered the phone initially in Italian, then in flawless English, to assure her that they had a room available for her, for two nights, the following week. She booked a midday flight to make sure she arrived in daylight, and then wrote to Pietro to tell him where she would be staying and why.

When she booked into the hotel with the delightful sounding name she was surprised to be handed a letter by the receptionist. It had arrived yesterday said the young man behind the desk, as he flicked his fingers to summon a porter. She followed the porter to the lift clutching the letter, which she didn't open until the porter had shown her to her room and explained all the facilities. He also waited patiently for her to sit down, put the crutches to one side, and find change in her handbag. It was just as well that she had had the foresight to collect plenty of change as so many helpers had had to be tipped, something she wasn't used to. Tipping was what Tom did.

She delayed opening the letter until she had used the loo in the immaculate bathroom, and had a swift peek at the piazza far below her narrow balcony. Satisfied that the hotel, so far, lived up to its four star reputation, she tore the envelope open and read the letter signed Elvira Farenesi. Elvira, she discovered, was Pietro's sister, and she proposed to call on Claire the next afternoon to collect the ring. Pietro was indisposed, she wrote. She frowned as she read it. It wasn't so much the cold tone but the faint air of dismissal that wafted off the paper. She objected to the suggestion in the wording that she was just a courier.

However, by the time Elvira was shown up to the rooftop garden the next afternoon, Claire had decided that she must have imagined all the negative hints in the letter. The sun was shining, she'd had a lovely lunch, and the big arm chairs arranged in small groups in the garden were extremely comfortable, so much so that she had relaxed sufficiently to allow her eyes to close briefly. The hustle and bustle of the crowded piazza below had become just the faintest of noises in the background as she took her ease. The beautiful elderly woman approaching her, after a waiter had pointed her out, was smiling widely, without any hint of pretence. As Claire struggled to her feet Elvira hurriedly told her not to bother, as she took the chair beside her. Immediately she launched into explanations of why Pietro wasn't there, how she didn't know Claire had a damaged leg, and how did she like Venice?

Claire took to her at once, and after they had debated the pros and cons of tea versus something a little stronger, Elvira called a waiter and asked for a bottle of light sparkling wine that she highly recommended, and make sure it is properly chilled, she called after him, as he went to do her bidding. While Elvira dealt with the waiter Claire lifted the little package out of her bag and put it on the small table the waiter had readied for their wine.

'Is that it?' asked Elvira. Claire nodded. 'I haven't seen it since I was a child. My mother used to wear it until Pietro announced that he was going to ask Louisa to marry him. Then she gave it to Pietro and we never saw it again.' Elvira reached over and picked up the little parcel and almost reverently unwrapped it. She opened the lid of the small box. An 'aaah' was whispered as she gazed at the large solitaire diamond set in platinum, as the sunlight flashed over its surface.

'Did you know Louisa?'

'Oh, yes. She and Pietro were always together. But then something happened and she left. He was heartbroken at the time, but he hoped that she'd change her mind and come back, but she didn't. I suppose he gave up thinking that because about five years later he married Guilia.' She paused for a few moments while she shut the lid and rewrapped the parcel. 'Guilia died just before Louisa, so Pietro is in mourning, doubly so I imagine, that's why he isn't here today.'

'Did Pietro ever tell you why she left?'

'No, but it must have been very important because Louisa was very much in love with him.'

'I don't know either because, by the time I knew Aunt Lou, she was looking after her nephew Tom and his baby daughter Francesca. But I've always suspected Aunt Lou came home because Tom needed her. When Jocelyn died, that's Tom's first wife, there was no one else capable of taking charge. Tom's mother was dead, and his father wasn't really much help. And then when I married Tom, when Francesca was four or so, Aunt Lou went to Canada for a while. I don't know why she went to Canada. She never said, And the first I heard of Pietro was when she died and I was going through her address book. Then, in her will, she left me instructions about bringing the ring back to its rightful owner.'

'And after all those years here it is again. I expect Pietro will give it to his son to give to his fiancée. They are to be married sometime later this year.'

Both women sipped their wine and admired the view through the glass balcony wall in contented silence, before Claire's curiosity got the better of her.

'How come you speak such perfect English? And Pietro too?'

'That's easy. Our father was a diplomat and was based in London for a while so we went to school in England. I was a boarder at a ghastly convent in north London, and Pietro was in a boy's school nearby. Three years I had to stick it before coming back home, and to make sure we remained fluent our parents made us speak in English at home. It has been useful though, as I used to use it doing translation work. How about you? What happened to your leg?'

'There was an accident, and my husband was killed.'

'Oh, Claire. How awful for you. How do you manage?'

Claire smiled as she replied 'I was doing quite well until I came here. I went out into the piazza yesterday thinking that I'd have dinner at one of the restaurants, but by the time the ninetieth person said 'scusi' as my crutches got in the way, I decided to eat in the hotel. Then this morning I thought I'd better look at a canal, because you can't go home from Venice and say you haven't seen a canal, but the world and its wife had the same idea! So I came up here and walked all the way round the garden and I'm sure I've seen more of Venice from up here than the average tourist.'

'How long are you here for?'

'I go home tomorrow.'

'That's far too soon, Claire. I could come and act as a chaperone and make sure you weren't hassled by anyone.'

'No, thank you Elvira. I need to go home. There is so much to do. With Louisa dying so soon after Tom, there is still so much to do.'

As Claire said this she felt a pang of homesickness again. It wasn't so much that she wanted to go home, it was the fact that she was in Venice and Tom wasn't. Eating dinner on her own in the hotel restaurant had turned heads, and her waiter had been overly solicitous. She had meant to take a book, to make it look as if eating on her own was the norm, but she was downstairs before she realized that she had left her book behind. She had managed to get a table against the wall, so her solitariness wasn't quite so obvious, but it wasn't something she relished doing too often. Also, dealing with crutches in a crowded tourist spot wasn't easy, and not something she wanted to prolong. That's what she told herself anyway. If she was really being honest with herself though she'd admit that she was desperate to get home, desperate to touch the things Tom had touched, to clutch his things in his wardrobe,

227

to smell his smell again before it faded away. Her initial excitement at the thought of meeting Aunt Lou's Pietro had begun to dissipate from the moment she got into the taxi to go to the airport, on her own. She enjoyed meeting Elvira, and for the first time in a very long time she had relaxed sufficiently to drift into sleep in the middle of the day, but it was time to go home.

***

The car hired to meet her at the airport was late, the driver was surly when he did arrive, and his audible grumbles about having to lift her suitcase into the boot and out again onto her doorstep made sure he got the very meanest of tips.

She struggled to pull her suitcase through the front door, before thankfully shutting it. She abandoned the case and took herself into the kitchen to find a note from Mrs D and a glorious smell coming from the oven. The kettle still had a slightly warm feel to it which suggested Mrs D hadn't been long gone. In theory Mrs D was no longer anyone's cleaner, but certain habits obviously died hard, and Claire thanked God that there were still people like her in the world. As promised, she phoned Dora to tell her she was back, that it wasn't a burglar turning on the lights, and after picking at the beef casserole thoughtfully left for she took herself to bed and hugged Tom's pillow

Chapter 23

Greg kept Claire busy following her trip to Italy. He was worried about her. She obviously wasn't eating properly at home, so he would hatch plans that involved eating out while he suggested things that needed doing. He tried to get her to deliver the small bequests of Aunt Lou's but invariably these were delivered courtesy of the Royal Mail. In the end he had to admit defeat and let her come to terms with her double bereavement in her own way. He was particularly keen to see Claire recover because he had decided that it was time to retire. He had great plans for his retirement, but he wanted to make sure she was fine before he left in a couple of month's time.

Claire told herself that she was coping admirably, and so what if her clothes no longer fitted. She was getting used to being on her own, and as her leg grew stronger she left the plaster off for gradually longer periods. The hospital advised caution, to do things slowly, but she continued to do her own thing. She surprised herself when she stopped off at Cyril's office on one of her hospital appointment days. He was genuinely pleased to see her, and insisted she stay and have a cup of tea with him. He filled her in with all the gossip. Out Patients had gone to pot, he said, a real mess. Nothing was as organized as in her day, and there were rumours that Pat O'Sullivan was moving on to pastures new. A bigger hospital in the Midlands was the most likely of the stories. He discounted one report that was circulating, that she was getting married, as totally ridiculous.

The interaction with her somewhat improbable colleague cheered her up briefly, and as she negotiated the two buses that got her home she found herself smiling at fellow travellers as they moved to allow her to sit down. One old gentleman insisted she have his seat and as he stood beside her he regaled her with stories of how it was in the old days when you broke your leg; weeks in hospital on traction, or the leg was encased in the old fashioned heavy white plaster of paris. Not like today, he had said, nodding towards her purple splint.

These forays into the world became more frequent, even if it was only to the local shop, and Dora took great delight in seeing her in the garden discussing jobs with the young gardener. After a discussion with the retired Mrs D it was decided that Claire would employ a company that sent in a team of cleaners as often or as infrequently as necessary. With just herself in the house, there was no real need to have a daily cleaner, but just a blitz every so often.

Thus life drifted on until little snippets started to appear in the press about the police finding new evidence in the hunt for Charlotte's killers. There was a suggestion that they'd found out about the doll. It was only in the local paper though so Claire wondered if there was any real progress, or just wishful thinking on the part of a local reporter. Gareth Jones' name was nowhere to be seen so Claire guessed that he had moved on. The Advertiser had continued in its old format – no special supplements on Charlotte or anyone else, so perhaps the Gareth Jones piece was to remain a one-off.

The small article about the dolly said that the police had found the person who had hand knitted the dolly's clothes, but it didn't say who it was. It wouldn't have made any difference if they had given a name since it was unlikely she'd recognize it, thought Claire, but she'd have like to have known who it was anyway. Was it a grandmother? She guessed it probably was. Not many youngsters seemed to knit these days if the dearth of wool shops was anything to go by. Perhaps she could ring the police on the pretex of asking how the case was progressing against the two lads, and then casually ask about the doll. But that idea was squashed very quickly. It was highly unlikely that the police would tell her anything. It was thinking about the dolly that might or might not have come from a charity shop that made Claire start thinking about a job. She remembered some of Anne's stories about working in a charity shop and she wondered if she should consider doing that. She liked Anne. Perhaps she could approach her about what it was like to work in a charity shop. But first she would have to be able to get about without the plaster on her leg. She'd be no use to anyone if she couldn't move around freely.

***

Whereas in the past Claire had scoured the newspapers for information, her first port of call now was the internet. She found little items of news there that didn't appear to be reported in the papers. She spent hours flipping from one site to another, noting times and dates, and could see that within minutes of something happening in the world someone had taken photographs or written an article. It was from the net that she learnt the name of the elusive knitter, Mary Smith. Mary apparently had knitted the clothes for the doll, and then given the doll to her grand-daughter Shannon, but she had no idea how Shannon's doll had got into the arms of Charlotte. I bet, said Claire to herself. What about Shannon's parents? Why weren't they interviewed?

They must know what happened to the doll. I suppose if Shannon had grown out of the doll stage it could have been passed on, Claire mused. Given to a charity shop perhaps? But I would want to interview the parents anyway to find out what happened to the doll, Claire decided in her best Scotland Yard mode.

It was all very well telling herself what she would or would not do, but in theory it was impossible. She had no contacts in any department that might be of use, and sitting at home with no one to bounce ideas off, brought home to her, yet again, what a solitary life she was leading. But she did nothing to change it. She looked at the jobs section in the local paper and ringed possibilities but that was as far as she got. She gave up the idea of asking Anne about the charity shop. She really didn't want to work she decided, she didn't want to have to make small talk with her colleagues, she didn't want to discuss what she had seen on television, or just be sociable full stop. She read, she watched television, listened to the wireless, and took exercise by walking to the local shop, or in her garden. Occasionally she went further afield but, she told herself, she was content as she was. Dora was concerned that she was turning into a hermit.

Dora was her only visitor. She'd bustle in with scones or a cake that she'd just made and needed to share them with someone. They'd discuss what Gary had done in their respective gardens, or perhaps something on the news, but the conversation would eventually peter out and Dora would go home. Claire enjoyed her visits and promised herself that she'd get out more, but she didn't. She just let life drift passed her day after day, as if in a dream until she was jolted back into reality.

One evening, while spreading the Marmite on her toast, which was her usual evening meal as well as her breakfast and lunch, she heard the name Charlotte being mentioned on the local television news. She directed her attention to the screen but the newscaster had moved on to tell the viewers what was coming up later in the programme. Come on, come on Claire grumbled at the screen, get on with it. Eventually the details of the Charlotte story were revealed in minimal detail: a young couple had been arrested and charged with the abduction of Charlotte Alsopp. And that was all. The newscaster moved on to another story. Claire couldn't believe it. The most important story of the year and he said one sentence about it. Where were the details? Who were the couple? On and on went the questions in Claire's head but there was no one to ask.

Swallowing the last of her toast she took her mug of coffee up to the study and pressed the button on her computer. The two minutes it took to warm up were the longest two minutes Claire had had to wait in a very long time. She sat at the desk fidgeting with paper and the pens in the pot, which once had been a mug brought back from one of their holidays before it lost its handle. She impatiently pressed the internet connection button repeatedly so that when she did get connected several screens popped up on top of each other. Finally BBC News appeared and she ran the mouse down the list to see if Charlotte's name appeared. Nothing. Absolutely no mention. She swapped to the local area news, and there it was, Charlotte Alsopp. She leaned closer to the screen, as if getting closer would produce more information, but it didn't. Only the bare details again; a couple had been arrested.

She glared at the screen in frustration, willing it to produce more, but that didn't work. Her will was insufficient. Turning off the news she pressed Google into action, asking it to search for Charlotte Alsopp. Reams of articles appeared, all about the original abduction, so Claire checked that day's date and sure enough several articles had been posted. Who had leaked the details she didn't know and didn't care? She just wanted to know what was going on. The young couple arrested were called Darren and Michelle Smith. Ah, said Claire to the screen, the same name as the knitter. Perhaps they are the parents of the doll owner. She scrolled down looking for more snippets. They were arrested at 5pm and taken to the local police station for questioning. So that would account for the lack of details on the early evening news, Claire decided. They were arrested at a house near an industrial site, so it said, as a result of information received. Received from whom? Who had split on them? Perhaps the granny, the knitter? Would someone split on a member of their own family? Perhaps. Would she? If she knew of a relative suspected of killing a child, she thought she would. Would she say anything if it was someone close to her? No, but she might be tempted if it was someone like Francesca.

Exhausting the current date Claire ran the mouse down the list of old stories and noted that her own name was mentioned more than once. Tom's too, his relationship to her, when he was killed, and about his funeral. She googled his name and read again all the articles about him. She had done it lots of times before, but the heartache it produced usually made her turn the computer off. She then googled Aunt Lou and was surprised to see several references to her, about her death and her connection to Tom and herself, and about her generosity to all those who had benefitted from her will. Good news for a change, Claire was glad to see. She had seen it all before in the local papers, but now the whole world would know what a good person she was, like they all knew that she had seen Charlotte and didn't tell the police in time so Charlotte died. She had become accustomed to that accusation, but it suddenly hit her then that the story was now going to be resurrected again. It was bad enough when the story about Giles Alsopp came out. It was likely to be ten times worse if the arrested couple were guilty. And the news said that they were arrested for the abduction so the police must have plenty of evidence. It didn't say that they had been taken in for questioning. Yes it did, she corrected herself, in one report, but on the BBC News she was sure they had said they had been charged.

That night sleep was more elusive than usual. Her book couldn't hold her interest, she had so many sleep inducing drinks she had to keep getting up to go to the loo, and the old films on the television were not her cup of tea at all. In the end she admitted defeat. Even if she couldn't sleep she'd lie quietly and think of Tom and Aunt Lou. Think about all the good times they had had.

The morning brought some more of the details she had willed the computer to produce the previous evening. The Guardian only had a short article in the home news section, really only reiterating what had been said the previous day. The names were given, their ages, and the area they were from, plus the name of the police station where they had been taken. This paragraph was followed by a few lines filling in the background, about the abduction of Charlotte and the subsequent finding of her body. Is that what it all comes down to? A few lines in the press. Claire found it all so depressing. A young life is snuffed out and it gets, Claire ran her finger down the article, only five lines.

She debated about whether she should ring Anne or not, but she was saved from making a decision as Anne rang her.

'Have you seen the news?' she asked.

'Yes. I saw it last night on the local news, and I've read the paper this morning. Were you warned about it beforehand?'

'Briefly. The liaison policewoman came round and warned me, but she couldn't give me any details. I hope to find out more, but I don't know how much they will tell me.'

'Are you on your own? Do you want some company?'

'That's kind of you Claire. I'm not going into work this morning. I wouldn't be able to cope with the questioning I might get. My mother will be here soon and we are going to hole up here.'

Actually Claire didn't think it was kind of her. If she had thought a bit before making that suggestion she might have realized that she might be the last person Anne would want around. No doubt the press will rehash the whole story again and class her as the bogeyman again. I wonder if Francesca will think about what she did. Will she care that I am more than likely going to be vilified again. Claire doubted it.

Chapter 24

Over the next week the full story began to emerge, through leaks no doubt, as Claire got details from anonymous sources on the net that she thought the police wouldn't have authorized to be released. She did wonder if they might jeopardize any court case that might follow. But all in all she thought it was a sad story.

The gist of it, or so Claire thought as she put the story together, was that Darren and Michelle Smith had been drug addicts in their teens and when Michelle fell pregnant with Shannon they had not been capable of caring for her. Michelle thought they were and had tried to prove to the social services that she was a good mother, and when she was not stoned, it was agreed she was an adequate mother. However, after a period of heavy drinking and drug taking Shannon was found filthy, under-nourished, and not properly clothed, by a social worker who called round unexpectedly. Michelle was so out of it she wasn't aware initially that Shannon was to be taken into care. Instead of cleaning up her act she and Darren went on a thieving spree to fund their addictions, and ended up in prison. The first time they were released they had claimed Shannon back, as they had every right to so the law said. By now she was a happy and healthy child, but after a period back with her parents, she was hospitalized for several non-accidental injuries, and taken back into care again. Darren's mother, Mary Smith, kept in touch with the foster parents to begin with but as other grand children came along her attention shifted to them, and family interest dissipated.

Claire didn't think that bit of the story was right because she thought it was the grandmother who had dropped them in it. She obviously still did care or at least had an interest in what was going on. But who knows? Anyway Darren and Michelle were jailed again, and eventually social services allowed Shannon's foster parents to adopt her. When Claire saw that she began digging around on the net again because that bald statement about social services allowing the adoption didn't ring true. She was almost certain social services didn't have that authority.

What Claire found out was that Darren and Michelle, after a period of violent behaviour in their respective prisons, decided to address their addictions, and sort themselves out, thinking that they would get Shannon back if they were clean. This was a remarkable feat, even Claire had to acknowledge that, considering the only way they were able to communicate with each other was through infrequent letters, and the odd visit from a relative. However the real reason for the whole ghastly affair was that they obviously hadn't taken in the fact that the adoption had gone through. Why? Why? Why? Claire had written on a piece of paper as she was sorting the story out. She scanned several sites before she found any reference to the legality of the adoption but, as far as she knew, things had been done by the book. They had been brought from their respective prisons to a court hearing, and although their lawyer pleaded their case, the judge had decided in favour of Shannon's adoption. It's very odd, thought Claire. How come neither of them realised they had lost Shannon? Surely they must have been told the judge's decision? Why didn't their lawyer see that they understood that? So, the story continued, when they found out they had decided to take revenge on the person they held responsible for them losing Shannon - Giles Alsopp. I wonder why they picked on him rather than the judge. Perhaps the judge didn't have any young children, or perhaps they really did think Giles was responsible. Claire couldn't see the reasoning for that though. Anyway, when they came out of prison they hatched their plan to abduct Giles Alsopp's child so that he would know what it was like to lose a child. But the plan went disastrously wrong because a member of the public, namely herself, spooked them and caused Darren to murder the child.

And that was the way the story was told. Various details changed between the different sources but it always ended up with Claire being the cause of Charlotte's death. The heroic achievement of their coming off the drugs was often highlighted, and Claire agreed, it was a great thing to have done, but what about all the damage they had done to Shannon? Little was said about that. Luckily, though, the whereabouts of Shannon was not reported. Perhaps her name had been changed, or perhaps the press couldn't find her. Claire didn't think they were being altruistic in keeping her out of the lime light; there were too many Gareth Jones' among them to think that.

With Claire's name being touted around again it was inevitable that the story of the hit and run car accident was repeated. So, indirectly, Claire was the cause of another death, the cause of Giles Alsopp's fall from grace, the cause of two young men being charged with manslaughter, and finally, the cause of Darren and Michelle being back in prison on remand.

It was a heavy burden to bear, on her own.

***

The days were very long as once again Claire became the focus of press spitefulness. She didn't dare go out, and if it hadn't being for delivery service from Sainsbury's her diet of toast and Marmite and the occasional egg might have become non-existent. She started to get obscene phone calls and poison pen letters, where, in some cases, there was no effort to hide the identity of the writer. At times she could see young men hanging around in the road outside. They had no reason to be there, and it worried her that her neighbours were being affected by events beyond her control.

Things came to a head one evening. She could hear chanting outside and items being thrown, so she phoned the police and asked if someone could come and move the youngsters on as she was afraid of what they might do. She was told by a peevish civilian that someone would come when they had time, which didn't make her feel any safer. But she dialled 999 again soon afterwards when she realized that the youngsters had made a mistake; the house that was under siege was not hers but Dora's. She heard the sound of breaking glass as more and more things were thrown at the house. She looked out of her bedroom window, being careful not to be seen, and she saw the mob laughing at the damage they were causing. She was desperate to help Dora but she knew that she couldn't get to her without being seen. Anyway Dora wouldn't dare open her door for fear of it being one of her tormenters. Claire prayed that other people had also called the police. They might be believed if they described what was going on.

After what seemed like a lifetime she heard the siren of an approaching police car, and the mob heard it too, so they began to scatter. She got downstairs as fast as she could and opened her door. She couldn't see anyone so she went down her drive and up Dora's and arrived as the police car drew up. She grabbed the policeman as he was getting out of the car and urged him to hurry as they trampled over the stones, bricks and cans left behind. As they got closer to the house they found themselves walking on the broken glass.

The policeman tried to persuade her to leave things to him, to go home, but she ignored him. Dora was an old lady, and a great friend, she had to get to her, she told him.

The big front bay window was a mess. Almost all the glass was shattered but through the gaps Claire was able to call to Dora, and tell her that the police were here, that the mob was gone and she was now safe. A shadow moved slowly and Claire suspected that Dora was hurt. She called to her again, and there was a feeble sound in reply. Knowing that Dora's front door had locks on it to rival Fort Knox she suggested to the policeman that he try and get through the broken window since she didn't think he'd get through the door.

The policeman, who had called for an ambulance when Claire said she thought Dora was hurt, put his gloved hand through the broken glass and unlatched the side window and scrambled through, his bulk and all the bits and pieces hanging off his belt making it quite difficult for him to squeeze through. Claire called to Dora to tell her that it was a policeman coming through the window to help, and she'd be there as soon as he opened the door for her.

Claire heard the policeman say something to Dora. He put the sitting room light on before opening the front door for Claire, and for the ambulance team who could be heard in the distance. The brief glimpse Claire got when the policemen turned on a light frightened her. Dora was on the floor and there seemed to be a lot of blood. She made her way into the house cursing the plaster on her leg for holding her up, and moved towards a semi-conscious Dora. She sank to the floor, in an ungainly heap, and took Dora's hand telling her that she was safe now. She ran an expert eye over her and saw that the blood was mostly from a cut on the back of her head, and another smaller one on her neck. There was plenty of glass around, and from where Dora was lying Claire suspected she had tried to hide herself from the missiles that had come through the window by getting on the floor near the sofa. Why, oh why, Dora didn't you go to the back of the house, she heard herself saying. There was a mumbled reply from Dora as the paramedics arrived. Claire got out of the way so that they could sort out Dora.

She was able to give the paramedics and the policeman all the information that they needed, but suggested that it wouldn't be a good idea for her to accompany Dora to the hospital in case she was recognized. The policeman, who had indeed recognize her, agreed, so Claire phoned a very surprised Mrs D and asked her if she could possibly go to the hospital to be with Dora while they sorted her out. Dora was in a state of shock, which was more worrying than her physical injuries. The cuts were mainly superficial, but the head one would definitely need stitching.

Claire too was in a state of shock. It should have been her lying on the floor surrounded by glass and missiles, not Dora. What had Dora done to deserve this? A kinder, more considerate neighbour she couldn't have wished for. It was all her fault. Dora would not want to see her again. All these thoughts were going through her mind as she tried to clear some of the mess in Dora's sitting room, while the policeman went round the house to find out if there was any more damage. He had already contacted a company to come and secure the damaged windows. He had found the front bedroom bay window was also broken, and the dining window was cracked. Obviously the mob had concentrated their efforts on the sitting room window having, possibly, seen a light there, or the flickering television. The television would flicker no more though as half a house brick was sitting where the picture should have been. That particularly frightened Claire. To hit the television like that meant that someone had deliberately aimed at it. Supposing they had aimed specifically at Dora, thinking it was her. She shuddered.

The policeman persuaded her to go home. He would wait for the window people. She sat at the kitchen table and downed a large brandy, and remembered the last time she had drunk brandy. Tom had been there. She slumped forward and rested her head on her arms and let her eyes leak. She vaguely heard activity next door but the effect of the brandy on an empty stomach meant she was not capable of investigating, and soon she drifted into a restless and uncomfortable sleep. Waking, very stiff, a couple of hours later, she stumbled up the stairs and crawled into bed fully clothed.

Chapter 25

The next few days were a nightmare. Police, and more police wanting statements. Dora was in hospital and likely to be there for some time. The shock had rendered her mute; she wouldn't eat or drink, and there was great concern about her mental state. Her house had wooden boards over the damaged windows and until someone organized her insurance company they would stay like that. Mrs D had been round to see the damage for herself and when she called in on Claire afterwards her body language suggested to Claire that she had a lot to answer for. Her visit was very brief, she had refused coffee, and she ventured no further into the house than the hallway. However she did know of a distant relative of Dora's, and contact had been made, which was some small relief for Claire.

The newspapers and television reports continued to spin the Charlotte story, and to Claire's supersensitive ear she thought her name featured too prominently. Michelle Smith had apparently pleaded guilty to causing Charlotte's death but Darren persisted in his 'not guilty' plea. Both were remanded in custody, and the latest news Claire heard was that Darren had been beaten up in prison as other prisoners don't take kindly to child murderers.

Claire was in despair. She had no one to talk to, no one to confide in. Cyril had kindly rung to ask if she was alright, after the newspaper report of Dora's house being trashed came out. She had said she was but the conversation more or less stalled after the initial query. Later she had a brief call from Greg, but even he wasn't quite as friendly as in the past. She was alone, lonely and depressed. Reviewing her options she thought she might move. Go far away and start again somewhere else where she wasn't known. In the meantime, knowing that she might be needed in a court case, she decided that she would go no further than the south coast hotel that she and Tom had visited before. Once the decision to do that was made she phoned the police to tell them where to find her should they need her. However she forgot to tell them that she would be booking in under an assumed name.

Changing her name was easy enough. She just did it. She kept the initials but changed the names to Catherine and Hall. At the hotel she doubted anyone would recognize her as Claire Harrison because her appearance had changed considerably. She'd never been fat, but now she was skinny to the point of scrawniness, and her hair was thinner and greyer than ever before, and the walking stick that had replaced the crutches, would just add to the deception.

Knowing that she might be away from the house for some time she decided that it had to be left looking clean, yet lived in, but without the help of the cleaning company. The work involved gave her something to do, something to wear her out, so that when she did go to bed she was tired enough to sleep, even if it was for only a short period. She set individual lights on time switches to come on and go off at irregular times, but she knew that if the mob came back to trash her house nothing she did would prevent that. To be on the safe side she collected her most valuable possessions, mostly small pieces of jewellery given to her over the years, and took them to the bank to be put in a safety deposit box. The only possession she really didn't know what to do about was the small box containing Tom's ashes. Aunt Lou's she had buried in her garden as requested, but she still had no idea what to do with Tom's. She debated about taking them with her, but that was silly, she told herself. Who took ashes on holiday? But if the house was trashed the box might get damaged. What to do? In the end she decided to put them somewhere a burglar, or whatever, would be unlikely to find them. She put the box in the kitchen drawer, not the knife drawer, as burglars might fancy taking one of her Sabatier knives, but in the one below. She put a small note on the box saying 'Tom', and wedged it in next to the 'prong' things. He would be safe there until she decided what to do.

Without getting the say so of the hospital, Claire discarded the plaster, and had a trial drive in the car. Luckily it was an automatic, and she found she could cope. Tom had laughed at her for getting an automatic. He had hated driving it, and rarely did, but she had always found gear sticks an ordeal. She had failed her driving test more than once for messing up gear changes. The only problem she had left then was getting her suitcase to the car. If it was full she reckoned she wouldn't be strong enough to get it down the stairs, so in the end she found it easier to slide the empty suitcase down the stairs, and then go up and down the stairs collecting the items to put in the case, and then she was able to wheel it to the car where she manhandled it into the boot. She was ready, and once it was dark she left.

*** *

Claire drove through the night, with frequent rest stops. She wasn't as fit as she thought she was. Her left leg ached badly, and she found that she had to get out of the car to stretch it, otherwise it cramped up. By the time she reached the coast her neck was stiff from the tension and she felt as if she had attempted the marathon. Reaching the hotel was a relief and as it was out of season she was able to book in ahead of the usual time. She was vague about how long she intended to stay, but she told the receptionist that it would be definitely the fortnight she had booked, as she was recuperating from an illness. When she had booked her room via the internet as Catherine Hall she had paid for it in advance using her Visa card in her own name. She hadn't thought any further ahead than that, but she guessed there might be difficulties trying to pay for something later as Catherine Hall, when her card said Claire Harrison. But she'd face that problem when she came to it. In the meantime she'd just have to remember to get plenty of cash out when she found a bank machine.

Her room on the first floor overlooked the bay. A glorious view, and just within sight she could see the start of that terrible cliff path down to the beach. I am not, definitely not, going down that path ever again, she told her faint reflection in the window, and gave a tired smile. She was so tired she could hardly summon up the energy to talk to Tom about the last time they had seen that view. The bed, near the window, looked very inviting so she kicked off her shoes and lay down on top of the soft duvet. As she watched the small white clouds scud across the big blue sky she felt some of the tension drain away, and she drifted into sleep.

Her usual diet of toast and Marmite had left her with little inclination to eat anything else, but when she woke from the best sleep she had had in ages she suspected that the strange feeling in her stomach was perhaps hunger. She got up and inspected the contents of her suitcase for a change of clothes before going down to find the dining room to see what was on the lunch menu.

Only a handful of other guests were in the dining room so she was able to claim a small window table to herself. She acknowledged the guests who greeted her, but kept moving as she didn't want to engage in conversation. She had remembered to bring a book in her bag but the view out of the picture window was far more engaging then her book. A foursome were playing croquet on the lawn beyond the patio and the blatant cheating going on entertained her throughout her simple meal of thick vegetable soup and crusty bread. Feeling decidedly better she went back to her room and collected her fleece jacket and a pair of sensible shoes. She was going to the beach.

The last time she had been to this particular beach she had been very fit and healthy, and with the love of her life to lean on should she have got tired. This time it was considerably more difficult. She hadn't walked very far for weeks and weeks, and until this point she had had support for her left leg. She regretted her bravado in abandoning the plaster cast almost immediately, but she gritted her teeth, and with heavy pressure on her one stick she made it, and settled herself with relief on a bench overlooking the sand. The tide was coming in but she was safe to sit where she was for as long as it suited her. She had her book with her but she didn't bother with it. Instead she conjured up all the memories of the previous visits to this beautiful spot, and not once did her eyes leak.

***

She tried to tell herself that she was enjoying her holiday. Her room was lovely, the staff helpful, and the other guests considerate, but she wasn't. Her fortnight was almost up and she still hadn't made any concrete decisions about her future. She couldn't hide forever. She saw the papers left out each day and the Charlotte case continued to provide column inches. The latest piece of news was that Darren had been so badly beaten up he was unlikely to ever appear in court, let alone plead not guilty. His fellow prisoners had decided his plea for him. Although Claire had just an inkling of sympathy for him, she realized that if Michelle was pleading guilty, and Darren couldn't plead at all, then the chances of her being needed to give evidence was vastly reduced. But it was yet another disaster to lay at her door.

Despite her unhappiness she tried to get out at least once a day, and she made use of the indoor swimming pool daily which she felt improved the strength in her left leg. She gave up the walk to the usual beach however and found herself favouring the big meadow, where she and Tom had ventured on their last holiday. She felt drawn to the spectacular drop that had so worried her when Tom had looked over and seen the dark rocky cove at its base. She walked closer and closer to it and then common sense would take over and she'd move back to the centre of the meadow. But it seemed that she got nearer to the edge every day. Sometimes she would go down to the nearby bay, but more often than not she would sit on the bench that had been placed at a strategic point on the edge of the meadow to get the best view of the sea.

It was on one of these trips to the meadow that she became aware that someone was very close to her as she approached the cliff edge. She was angry. This was her space. But as she moved away, to make for 'her' bench, her shadow came up beside her and said 'hello'. She ignored him and kept walking, determined not to be drawn into conversation. She arrived at the seat and sat down and very pointedly put her bag on the seat beside her. He sat beside the bag, and said nothing. She fumbled in her bag for her book but as she did so she tipped it off the seat and the contents spilt out onto the grass. Immediately, and without a word, they both bent down to pick up the various bits and pieces and their heads clashed. Claire let out an involuntary 'Ouch', whereas he just laughed and rubbed his bruised head. In the face of such magnanimity she found she couldn't keep up the pretence he wasn't there, and smiled at him as she rubbed her head.

'Hello. I'm Frank Grayson. I believe we are staying at the same hotel.'

'Yes, we are. I saw you arrive. I'm …' she paused for a second, '…Catherine Hall.'

'No, you're not. You're Claire Harrison.'

Claire was startled, her face draining of colour. 'How do you know? I haven't told anyone here.'

'Don't worry. I'm not going to say anything. It's only by chance that I know, and then I wasn't too sure. But a sadder looking person would be hard to find, so I guessed.'

'I'm not a sad looking person. I'm perfectly fine' she blustered, as her pale face turned pink.

'No, you're not'

'Don't keep saying that. I'm fine, and if you don't mind I want to finish my book' she said with finality. She opened her book and removed the book mark placed about ten pages in.

With a wide grin he repeated 'No you're not. You'll never finish that book. It's boring you to death. You've been on that same page for ages.'

Claire was flustered. He'd only been there a couple of days, and he was spying on her. Who did he think he was? Who was he? Where had he come from? Was he after her? Questions, questions, questions. She began to panic, her heart rate racing. Clasping her bag, and grabbing her stick she made to move.

'Hey, Claire. Stop worrying.' He put out an arm to try and prevent her leaving. 'I'm totally harmless. Anyway it is my job to notice people in trouble. Come on, sit down.' He took her bag off her, placed it back on the seat, and patted the place where she had been sitting.

He did look harmless, Claire had to concede. He was also quite good looking in a grizzled type of way. She sat down, but hung onto her stick in case she had to use it. On him if necessary.

'What is your job then?' she asked, as an excuse to give her pulse time to recover.

'I'm a priest.' Claire stared at him, open mouthed. 'Don't look at me like that. We don't wear dog collars all the time, you know.'

Claire swallowed before saying quietly, 'I'm sorry. Life hasn't been easy recently.'

'No, I'm sure it hasn't. I'm in a bit of a quandary too. Nothing like what you've suffered though. But I'm also here to think about what I do next. I suspect you are in the same boat.'

Claire looked at him, and allowed herself to relax the grip on her stick. She wondered what sort of problem he had. He didn't look like the sort that interfered with choir boys. He looked sort of nice. Perhaps he'd got a female parishioner into trouble.

'I bet you're wondering what sort of trouble I'm, aren't you?' His likeable smile broadened as he added, 'little boys, perhaps?'

Claire blushed. 'No. No, of course I wasn't thinking that at all.' She turned away from him to hide her burning face and pretended that she had trouble placing her stick in a convenient position.

He laughed. 'I don't believe you. Admit it, you were thinking just that.'

She didn't know what to say, but he saved her further embarrassment, by going on to tell her what his problem was. He was a Catholic priest, and he felt that he had lost his vocation, but it would break his father's heart if he were to tell him. His father was ill, and

251

wasn't expected to live much longer, and he was trying to decide whether he ought to know or not before he died. Instinct told him not to tell him, but his conscience was bothering him.

What did she think he should do?

Claire had no doubt that he shouldn't tell his father, and she told him so quite forcibly, but she was more interested in why he thought he had lost his vocation. He tried to put into words his feelings of hopelessness when dealing with his dwindling congregation and all the other priestly activities he had to deal with. He was confused about what he believed in, and just generally in limbo. She encouraged him to keep talking as she guessed that this was the first time he had actually said out loud what was in his heart. But her encouragement had a selfish aspect to it. She didn't want to have to tell Frank what was in her heart. Her own feelings of hopelessness.

Their one-sided conversation continued throughout a shared dinner, and as they parted to go to their respective rooms they made plans to have a walk the next morning before Claire left to face whatever future she had back home. Frank insisted that they would talk about her problems then, not his, and as he gave her a chaste kiss at her door he thanked her for listening to him. She had been a great help. He hoped that he could do the same for her.

***

After dinner the previous evening Claire had gone to reception and booked out, as the next day was changeover day, and she didn't want to be booking out as others were booking in. She looked better for her holiday and she didn't want to run the risk of being recognized. She had left a tip for the restaurant staff,

252

and had made sure she had enough cash left to leave something for the chambermaid. She didn't want to be remembered as mean.

She didn't see Frank at breakfast, which she thought odd, considering their plans, but it didn't bother her unduly. Perhaps he wasn't a breakfast sort of person, she decided, as she cleared the last of her things from her room and wheeled her suitcase to the desk, to hand in her key. She hung around in the foyer until it was well passed their meeting time. Surely he wasn't going to let her down. He had been so insistent about wanting to help her. She had almost felt, after leaving him that perhaps she did have a future.

Fearing that she was beginning to look conspicuous, she approached the desk again and asked if anyone had left a message for her. The receptionist looked up briefly, from her computer and scanned the rows of small boxes that held the room keys.

'Doesn't look like', she said disinterestedly.

'Could it be on the desk?' she asked, trying to keep the anxiety out of her voice.

The receptionist, gave a cursory look along the length of the desk.

'Nope. Nothing there.'

'Well would you call Room 109 for me, please?'

With a bored look she dialled 109 on the internal phone and as she waited for a reply she swivelled her chair round and ended up facing the boxes again. She put the unanswered phone down with a sigh and swivelled back towards Claire, and pointed out that the key for Room 109 was in its box.

'They must have gone out' she said, 'if the key is there.'

'That's strange. I was supposed to meet Mr Grayson here nearly an hour ago.'

The receptionist, whose name tab announced she was called Astrid, heaved a more theatrical sigh as she typed 'Grayson' into her computer. 'He's gone' she said. 'Booked out before I came on duty. Must have been when the night staff were on.' She looked up at Claire and with a pitying look on her face said 'He must have forgot you. Sorry.' As she clicked off the computer she briefly noted the unusual number of long distance phone calls that had been made to and from his room during the night.

With as much dignity as she could muster Claire thanked Astrid for her help and left the hotel. She was desperately upset. She was sure that Frank was genuine. He had wanted to help, she attempted to convince herself, he had. She wheeled her case up to the long term car park, anything over three days was considered long term she had found, and struggled to put her case in the boot. She would have appreciated some help but long term parkers were almost hidden by trees on the edge of the hotel grounds, so she knew she'd have to do it herself. No one else appeared to be leaving that day.

She slammed the boot lid down, giving vent to her anger with herself for thinking anyone was going to help her. She swung her bag onto her shoulder and used her stick to savagely scuff up the car park gravel, as she left it to walk one more time to the meadow. Her eyes filled with tears. Her last hope had gone. She didn't notice the sunlight dancing on the sea, or the baby rabbits run for cover when she arrived. She trudged across the grass, her head bowed, her tears gathering speed, as her feet took her beyond the point of no return.

As she fell unseen to a certain death on the jagged rocks below she knew that no one would miss her, no one would look for her, and no one would care.

Acknowledgements

I would like to thank two of my fellow MA Creative Writing students, Mary Simpson and Liz Wade for their legal advice; Craig Lambert of Thames Valley Police for his help on what police can and cannot do, and Sandra Homewood, a Funeral Director, for her particular type of expertise.

However any legal or police procedural mistakes, or any mistakes relating to funerals, are entirely mine.

Lightning Source UK Ltd.
Milton Keynes UK
UKOW051524250112

186057UK00002B/3/P